DON

CARRIER

These are the stories of Carrier Battle Group Fourteen—a force including a supercarrier, amphibious unit, guided missile cruiser, and destroyer. And these are the novels that capture the blistering reality of international combat. Exciting. Authentic. Explosive.

CARRIER . . . The smash debut thriller about the ultimate military nightmare: the takeover of a U.S. Intelligence ship.

VIPER STRIKE . . . A renegade Chinese fighter group penetrates Thai airspace—and launches a full-scale invasion.

ARMAGEDDON MODE . . . With India and Pakistan on the verge of nuclear destruction, Carrier Battle Group Fourteen must prevent a final showdown.

FLAME-OUT . . . The Soviet Union is reborn in a military takeover—and their strike force shows no mercy.

MAELSTROM . . . The Soviet occupation of Scandinavia leads Carrier Battle Group Fourteen into conventional weapons combat—and possible all-out war.

COUNTDOWN . . . Carrier Battle Group Fourteen must prevent the deployment of Russian submarines. The problem is: They have nukes.

AFTERBURN . . . Carrier Battle Group Fourteen receives orders to enter the Black Sea—in the middle of a Russian civil war.

ALPHA STRIKE . . . When American and Chinese interests collide in the South China Sea, the superpowers risk waging a third world war.

ARCTIC FIRE . . . A Russian splinter group has occupied the Aleutian Islands off the coast of Alaska—in the ultimate invasion of U.S. soil.

ARSENAL . . . Magruder and his crew are trapped b̶e̶t̶w̶e̶e̶n̶ C̶ revolutionaries . . . and a U.S̶ control.

D0776446

NUKE ZONE . . . When a nuclear missile is launched against the U.S. Sixth Fleet, Magruder must face a frightening question: In an age of computer warfare, how do you tell friends from enemies?

CHAIN OF COMMAND . . . Magruder enters the jungles of Vietnam, looking for answers about his missing father. Little does he know that another bloody war is about to be unleashed—with his fleet caught in the crosshairs.

BRINK OF WAR . . . Friendly wargames with the Russians take a deadly turn, and Carrier Battle Group Fourteen must prevent war from erupting in the skies. Little do they know—that's just what someone wants.

TYPHOON . . . An American yacht is attacked by a Chinese helicopter in international waters, and the Carrier Team is called to the front lines of what may be the start of a war between the superpowers.

ENEMY OF MY ENEMY . . . A Greek pilot unwittingly downs a news chopper, and Magruder must keep the peace between Greece and the breakaway republic of Macedonia. But what no one knows is that it wasn't an accident at all.

JOINT OPERATIONS . . . China launches a surprise attack on Hawaii—and the Carrier Team can't handle it alone. As Tombstone and his fleet take charge of the air, Lieutenant Murdock and his SEALs are called in to work ashore.

THE ART OF WAR . . . When Iranian militants take the first bloody step toward toppling the decadent West, the Carrier group are the only ones who can stop the madmen.

ISLAND WARRIORS . . . China launches a full-scale invasion on its tiny capitalist island neighbor—and Carrier Battle Group Fourteen is the only hope to stop it.

FIRST STRIKE . . . A group of radical Russian military officers are planning a nuclear attack on the United States, but Carrier Battle Group Fourteen has been called in to make sure the Cold War ends without a bang.

HELLFIRE . . . A top-secret missile defense system being tested aboard the USS *Jefferson* accidentally targets Russia, igniting Cold War tensions once more—leaving Carrier Battle Group Fourteen to defend itself without starting World War III.

book twenty-one

CARRIER
Terror at Dawn

KEITH DOUGLASS

JOVE BOOKS, NEW YORK

CARRIER: TERROR AT DAWN

A Jove Book / published by arrangement with
the author

PRINTING HISTORY
Jove edition / April 2003

Copyright © 2003 by Penguin Putnam Inc.
Cover art by Danilo Ducak

ISBN: 0-515-13468-6

A JOVE BOOK®
Jove Books are published by The Berkley Publishing Group,
a division of Penguin Putnam Inc.,
375 Hudson Street, New York, New York 10014.
JOVE and the "J" design
are trademarks belonging to Penguin Putnam Inc.

PRINTED IN THE UNITED STATES OF AMERICA

10 9 8 7 6 5 4 3 2 1

ONE

By the time the aircraft carrier USS *United States* arrived on station in the Persian Gulf, the allure of the United States Navy had long since lost its charm for Airman Gary Williams. He had been promised exciting adventures, the chance to see the world, training to work on highly sophisticated electronics gear, and more intangibly, a sense of meaning to his life.

None of the above had materialized, at least not in a way that he'd expected. The much-anticipated "exciting adventures" had consisted primarily of being yelled at by chief petty officers, first in boot camp and then at his A school. All he'd seen of the world so far was Great Lakes, Illinois, and it had been a cold, inhospitable place filled with people who talked funny to a kid from San Diego. The high-tech training, okay, the Navy had come through on that count, but it wasn't exactly like he'd had a chance to use it. His Data System A school had been six months long, and he'd studied hard to graduate first in his class. He'd been given first choice of the available billets and he'd picked VF-95, an F-14 Tomcat squadron currently deployed to the Persian Gulf on board the USS *United States*.

And the Persian Gulf—now that was another whole disappointment in itself, wasn't it? The war on terrorism had shifted its focus back into the Middle East, as the connection between Osama bin Laden's henchmen and Iraq had become so obvious that even public opinion supported the recent increased presence in the area. With rigorous internal security measures in place within the Continental United States, a growing National Guard involvement in keeping track of foreign visitors, and a few months without overt threats of violence, the President had decided that now was the time to deal with the Middle East once and for all. The USS *United States* was on station in the Persian Gulf, and the USS *Thomas Jefferson* was lurking just outside the Red Sea in the Med, well within weapons range of most targets. Even a casual observer could tell that something was up, that this time the President meant to finish what Desert Storm and Desert Shield had started.

To Williams, that sounded like the place to be for a hotshot young avionics data–systems technician. But daydreams of flying attack missions over hostile territory and astounding his squadron mates with his cold determination and heroism had not survived A school. Somehow, the Navy did not seem to feel that his duties encompassed flying sidekick on combat missions, although he was still convinced he'd heard the recruiter mention something of that nature. Nor did his squadron seem particularly impressed with his potential ability to contribute to the war.

The day Williams checked into his squadron, they'd sent him to the galley for cleaning detail and mess cooking for three months. Since then, he'd been scrubbing decks and peeling potatoes all the way across the Pacific.

Airman Williams was willing to tolerate most of the indignities inflicted on him, except for the failure of the recruiter's last promise to materialize. So far, he wasn't feeling a helluva lot of pride at serving his country. Mostly, he felt tired and lonely.

Like now. His day had started at 0400. Eight hours later, he'd been informed by the mess management specialist senior chief that he was being transferred back to his squadron. He'd been excited, expecting that now he would finally have a chance to show them what he could really do fixing the data systems on an aircraft, but that hadn't materialized either. He'd been assigned to the line division, told to qualify as a plane captain, and then maybe after a year he would be transferred to his rating work center. So much for training and high-tech electronics.

As it happened, the line chief petty officer had had a hole in his night watchbill to fill. Williams showed up just as the petty officer was trying to rearrange too few bodies to cover too many watches, and the young airman had promptly been slotted into the 0200–0400 roving security patrol. Williams spent the rest of the afternoon and evening checking in, and caught three hours of sleep before being roughly awakened by the roving patrol and told to get his ass into the hangar bay. There, another airman had passed over a flashlight, sound-powered phone, walkie-talkie, and a few brief instructions on what he was supposed to do.

It was never really cool this time of year in the Persian Gulf, but the temperature had dropped to an almost bearable ninety degrees. There was a light breeze blowing in through the open hangar bay doors, not enough to really cool him off, but enough so that he could pretend it did. He tried to not remember the fantasies he'd had before reporting to the ship, the ones about walking the streets of exotic cities, hearing the babble of other languages, coolly bargaining down sinister merchants in the local market until an exotic—try as he might, Williams thought that the word *exotic* pretty much summed up everything overseas—an exotic woman approached him, admiring, ever so grateful—although the details of exactly why were always slightly hazy—and willing to express her exoticness in ways that he'd only read about. His current assignment was every bit as hot as his fantasies about exotic women, although in an entirely different and most unpleasant way. For the next two hours, he was expected to walk around the hangar bay checking to make sure that all aircraft were securely tied down, that no fires started, and just generally keeping an eye on the security of the place. His fantasy woman was replaced by the few technicians still working on aircraft, the dim lights of a scented candle replaced by hangar bay lights far overhead.

There were eight aircraft packed into the hangar bay, all in various stages of disassembly. Most minor repairs were taken care of on the flight deck, but major evolutions such as an engine change-out or major component replacement took place below. Aircraft were lowered into the hangar bay on one of six elevators that lined the edge of the flight deck immediately overhead.

It only took about fifteen minutes for Airman Williams to reach his boredom threshold. It was better duty than the galley in some ways. At least he was alone, allowed to roam around at will and take a good hard look at whatever interested him, alone to daydream about how duty in the Persian Gulf was supposed to be. While there might not be any exotic women around—and none of the female sailors he'd met so far came even close to filling that description—at least there was no first-class petty officer standing over him bitching about how many massive pots and pans there were still to clean, no clouds of chemical-laden steam from the dishwashing machine enveloping him. Instead, there was a sharp tang of aviation fuel and grease and the acrid smell of metal.

The carrier was never entirely silent, not even at night. The massive machinery that kept her running vibrated through her steel hull, producing a dull background noise that Williams had long since ceased to hear. Metal clanked on metal as technicians struggled with avionics boxes, slammed panels shut, and shouted for tools.

So what exactly was he supposed to be looking for? It wasn't like this was a shore station, with the threat of civilians wandering onto the base and trying to damage aircraft. Everybody on the ship was Navy except for a cadre of contractor representatives and a few squads of Marines. Sure, he'd heard stories about disgruntled sailors trying to sabotage the birds, but how likely was that? Not very. So what really was the point of this whole watch? At least in the galley, he had a stack of clean pots and pans to show for his hard work.

He paused by one of the open hangar bay doors, a massive opening in the side of the ship. The hangar bay ran two thirds of the length of the ship, and when the hangar bay doors on either side were pulled back, almost the entire area was exposed to the open sea.

With the lights on in the hangar bay, the night outside was a dark, impenetrable black. He could see a few bright stars on the horizon, the lights of the cruiser keeping station to the east, but that was it.

His radio crackled to life, and the brusque voice said, "Hangar Bay, what's your status?"

Carefully remembering his training on proper radio communications, Williams keyed the mike and said, "Watch Supervisor, Hangar Bay. All secure, sir."

"Don't call me sir, asshole. I know who my father is."

"Yes, si—" Williams stopped talking, aware that all he could do was get in more trouble at this point.

"I'm sending down a couple of guys to help secure the hangar bay doors. We've got a report of some small craft in the area."

Williams's heart sank. With the hangar bay doors shut, the entire area would feel like a tomb. "Roger," he acknowledged. "Standing by."

"Yeah, right. Just do what they tell you."

Bridge
USS **United States**
0200 local (GMT +3)

Fireman Apprentice Audrey Smith was no more thrilled with her Navy adventure than Airman Williams was. She had followed a similar track to the ship, the difference being six months of Engineman A school rather than Data System, and she'd done two more months in the galley than he had. Unlike Williams, she was already used to her operational watch station as a lookout. She had been rotated through the various stations, and tonight was on the starboard bridge wing, sound-powered phone clamped over her ears and binoculars making circles around her eyes.

Smith preferred the late-night watches to the daytime ones. There were fewer people around, which meant fewer people to mess with her and fewer witnesses if she screwed up. Standing outside now on the bridge wing, scanning her assigned sector of the horizon, she felt at peace with the world. Behind her, through the open hatch, she could hear the small noises coming from the bridge: the occasional rudder or engine order from the conning officer, a complaint from engineering about the lineup of boilers and reactors and machinery, and the routine reports that kept track of all radar contacts in the area.

With no moon overhead, the horizon and sky blended into nothingness. The blackness was broken only by the running lights of the cruiser and other escorts, and the occasional light configuration from a commercial ship. There were a few small boats out here as well, and the crews on both the bridge and in Combat kept track of them to ensure that the carrier stayed well clear.

Suddenly, she stopped her smooth scan of the water. What was it? Something had caught her attention, although she couldn't exactly see what. She moved her binoculars in a slow, oscillating motion back and forth, trying to see what it was that had distracted her.

There it was again. A small area of darkness against the water, something that looked out of place. Odd. If it was a boat, it should be showing at least one light for safety of navigation. But then again, not all of the fishermen in this area found it necessary to comply with good seamanship practices. She had been warned that there were also smugglers in the area, and they would certainly show no lights.

But this close to the carrier? We're not that hard to miss. The memory of the USS *Cole* came to mind, the gaping hole in the side of the smaller ship the result of a small boat pulling up alongside her and detonating explosives. Even a rowboat could be dangerous.

Smith keyed her sound-powered phone. "Surface Plot, Starboard Lookout. I think I have a contact to the starboard, a small one. Relative bearing 030, showing a slight right-bearing drift. No lights."

"You sure, Starboard? I'm not holding anything there."

Am I sure? No, not really. I can't even see it now.

"Not entirely sure, Surface," she acknowledged. "If it's anything, it's a small boat running without lights."

The voice of the Surface Plot petty officer sighed. "OK, keep an eye on it. I'll take another look in the area and see if there's a possibility. Could be one of the smugglers we were briefed on. Good work."

Behind her on the darkened bridge, Smith heard the operations specialist airman pass her information to the officer of the deck. "Sir, possible unidentified small contact on the starboard bow."

"Range?" asked the OOD, Lieutenant Commander Fred Brisco.

"Close aboard, within two miles, sir. Low-confidence visual contact."

Brisco walked out on the starboard bridge and propped his elbows on the railing next to Smith's companionably. "You getting Surface stirred up over something, Andrea?"

Smith relaxed. Brisco was a good sort, not one of the screamers. He even used her first name sometimes when nobody else could hear him. It made her feel like she was part of the team, even when she screwed up.

"I'm not certain, sir," she allowed. "I thought I saw something, but I can't pick it up now. It was right there." She pointed in the general direction where she'd seen the patch of blackness.

Brisco had his own binoculars up now and was scanning the area carefully. She felt a shiver of relief—she'd reported it, and the officers were taking a look. Now, no matter what it was, it was no longer her sole responsibility. And maybe he could see something that she couldn't.

"I don't see—wait." Brisco abruptly stopped scanning the area and kept the binoculars fixed on one spot. "Yes, I think you're right. A small boat, running without lights. Tell Surface I see it, too." Without dropping his binoculars from his eyes, he raised his voice and said, "Conning Officer, bring us twenty degrees to the left. We've got a small boy up ahead who doesn't seem to realize that tonnage counts."

"Surface Plot, Starboard. OOD says he sees it, too, and we're changing course to avoid," Smith said into her sound-powered phone.

"Roger, keep track of it. We're still not getting anything on the radar."

And that was exactly why they had lookouts, wasn't it? Because very small wooden vessels were difficult to pick up on radar even in the best of conditions. Keeping a visual eye on the ocean as well as an electronic one only made sense.

"Security, close the hangar bay doors," Brisco said suddenly, his voice sharp. "Come on, people—move it!"

"What is it, sir?" she asked, now alarmed.

"Probably nothing," he said. "Just something seems to—hell, I don't know, Andrea. Call it a gut feeling."

Hangar bay
0205 local (GMT +3)

It only took a few minutes for the reinforcements to show up and find Williams. At the same time, the 1MC announcing system boomed, "All hands not actually on watch in the vicinity of the hangar bay report to security team leader to close hangar doors." The technicians working on the E-2 Hawkeye in the forward part of the hangar bay dropped what they were doing and trotted over.

The doors could be opened and closed electronically, but sufficient hands had to be on station in case something went wrong and they had to be closed manually. The hangar bay filled with a hard, grating noise as the massive metal watertight slabs of steel grated along their tracks. The breeze died down as they started to close.

"So what is this all about?" Williams asked.

"Probably just an OOD with a hair up his ass," said one of the petty officers. "Sometimes I think they do this just to see how fast we can move."

That pretty much fit in with what Williams knew so far about the Navy. Every evolution, no matter how trivial, was practiced, timed, and graded ad infinitum. Why should closing the hangar doors be any different?

Suddenly, a star low on the horizon flared into brightness. Williams brought his binoculars up to take a look at it. Beside him, the senior petty officer said, "Oh, shit. Move it!"

Bridge
0206 local (GMT +3)

Brisco leaped from the bridge wing to the bridge and slapped the General Quarters alarm toggle switch, simultaneously picking up the microphone for the whole ship-announcing system. As the insistent gong of the General Quarters alarm started, he said, "All hands, General Quarters. Small boat on the starboard quarter launching Stingers!"

Stingers. Smith's blood ran cold. The small, shoulder-launched missiles had a maximum range of just over two miles, but any explosive warhead could do serious damage to the carrier if you hit it in the right place. It wasn't capable of penetrating the hull, but if you could hit the aircraft on the flight deck, starting a fire, it would prove difficult to control. Or it could—

"The hangar bay," she breathed, her voice full of horror. If a Stinger got inside the hangar bay, it could cause a catastrophe.

White fire seared her retina as a small missile streaked

across black water, destroying her night vision and leaving a trail of light as an afterimage.

"Damage Control, report!" Brisco shouted.

The trail of fire dropped below them as it speared through the half-open hangar bay door.

Hangar bay
0207 local (GMT+3)

The sailors manning the port-side hangar doors were moving faster than those on the starboard. Already more than half of the exposed area was closed off as the massive doors slid along their tracks. The starboard hangar bay doors had barely started to move.

Williams watched, both horrified and terrified at the same time. This wasn't a drill—this was an actual attack. The seconds seem to tick by too slowly as he stared at the white fire racing across the water.

"Get down!" someone shouted, and Williams was smashed to the deck as a petty officer tackled him. They rolled over until they were behind an enclosed part of the hull, out of the open doorway.

"What the hell are you—?" Williams began, his protest cut off as the impact forced the air out of his lungs.

A lightning bolt coursed through the hangar bay, accompanied by a high-pitched screaming sound. The Stinger warhead entered the starboard hatch, flashed across the hangar bay, and slammed into the partially closed port hatch, containing the fire inside. It exploded with a deafening fireball, flames and hot gases engulfing half of the hangar bay, then subsiding into a hard, hot fire engulfing the port side.

"Fire, fire, fire!" the 1MC howled. "Fire in the hangar bay."

No shit, fire!

"Grab the nozzle!" a petty officer said, shoving Williams toward a hose reel mounted on the bulkhead. "I'm activating the AFFF hose reel. You know how to use it, right?" The aqueous film-forming foam was the preferred method of extinguishing a Class B, or fuel, fire.

"Right." Williams grabbed the nozzle head. Another sailor fell in behind him to help manage the hose, and then two more behind him. Everyone moved with an economy of movement born of hours of practical damage-control training.

Everyone except Williams. He stumbled over the hose as he took the nozzleman position, fingers fumbling over the moveable U-shaped handle called the bail. He hadn't spent much time on damage control since a three-day firefighting class in San Diego before deploying but the basics were coming back to him. The AFFF would cover the burning surface and deprive it of oxygen. And in here, with so many fuel lines crisscrossing, lubricants and oils and drums, and the presence of so many aircraft for a possible Class Delta fire, it was the first choice.

The fire was centered against one bulkhead, and had consumed both a toolbox and a stack of supplies left there. It was spreading quickly, reaching out toward a helicopter tied down nearby. If it got the helicopter and started a Class Delta fire, then there would be no chance of extinguishing it. The helicopter would have to be shoved over the side of the ship and into the water.

Bridge
0209 local (GMT +3)

"Where is it?" Brisco shouted, his voice carrying over the babble of damage-control reports now flooding the circuits. "Damn it, I need that contact!"

"We just don't have it, sir," Surface answered, frustration evident in his voice. "Small contact, choppy seas—recommend searchlights, visual targeting, and fifty-cal guns, sir."

"The fifty-cals are already being manned," Brisco said. He turned to Smith and said, "Get on that floodlight. Find them. You and I seem to be the only one with eyes in our heads."

"Aye, aye, sir," she said, already running aft along the catwalk toward the floodlight. She'd only experimented with it once or twice, but she could probably manage it.

She flipped the power switch on, shielding her eyes while she pointed her binoculars in the general direction of where she'd last seen the contact. She flipped the shutters on the floodlight open and aimed them in that general direction. Above her, she could hear the shouts of sailors scrambling to man the fifty-caliber guns.

"There he is!" she shouted, forgetting to depress the button on her sound-powered phone, but her voice carried easily up to the gun crew.

"Roger, we see him," the gun crew chief shouted down at her. Briscoe came running out of the bridge to stand beside her.

"Weapons free," he ordered. "Take it out, Chief."

The hard chatter of the fifty-caliber machine gun drowned out the babble from the bridge. Empty casings rained down on them, bouncing off the steel deck and over the side. Smith concentrated on keeping the searchlights centered on a small craft, nailing it to the water with a spear of light.

The first two seconds of rounds fell short, and then the tracers danced across the small target as the gun crew adjusted their aim. She could see now that it was little more than a rowboat with an outboard motor stuck on it. There were two men standing up in it, their features indistinguishable, but one was yanking frantically on the cord attached to the outboard motor as though it had stalled.

Small waterspouts peppered the water as the fifty-cal rounds stitched a line down the wooden hull, splintering boards into shrapnel. The outboard engine kicked to life, the noise lost in the chatter of the gunfire, but the results evident in the boiling water behind the stern. The boat started to turn away from the carrier, quickly picking up speed. It was listing severely to the starboard side, indicating that at least some of the rounds had found their mark.

"Get them!" Brisco shouted.

The gun crew adjusted their aim, walking the tracer rounds

up the wake to the boat. Almost immediately, the results were evident. A few rounds found the outboard motor and then the fuel can. There was a soft *whoosh* as the gas exploded, the flames immediately obscuring the boat and its occupants. The fire expanded momentarily into a large ball of orange and yellow billowing out black smoke evident even in the dark night. There was a secondary explosion, momentarily doubling the size of the fireball, and then it sank down into a smaller form, eating away at the wooden hull and its contents. The machine gun fell silent. Smith heard one anguished scream, and then nothing more.

She turned to look at Brisco, but he was already gone. The immediate threat eliminated, his priority now was fighting the fire.

Through her feet, Smith could feel the vibrations radiating up from the hull, the odd noises and vibrations induced by water rushing through the fire mains to supply the hose reels and hangar bay. She could see the doors sliding back now as the damage-control crew sought to ventilate the area. A few flames slipped out, licking up the side of the ship. They were one hundred feet below the bridge, but the heat was still palpable.

"Starboard, are you on station?" Surface asked. "Look, there may be more of them. Anything you see, I want to hear about it immediately."

"Roger, Starboard is in position." She hesitated for a moment, aware that she should avoid cluttering the circuit with unnecessary chatter, but not able to avoid asking, "The fire. How bad is it?"

"We don't know. I'll tell you soon as I hear something. In the meantime, keep your eyes on the water."

Smith was cursed with an unusually vivid imagination and it kicked in now, trying to distract her from her watchstanding. She could see how the flames below looked, the liquid way that they raced up bulkheads and ceilings, enveloping fire mains and fuel lines, reaching out with tendrils of heat to seek skin and flesh, growing, engulfing the entire ship. She was so far from the water, so far, the equivalent of an eight-story building from it. If the fire grew out of control, how in the world would she ever get off the bridge? The way down to the lifeboat stations would be blocked, too, and she held no illusions about her ability to survive jumping from the bridge wing into the sea. Even if she avoided hitting the part of the flight deck that jutted out, the fall alone could very well be fatal. She saw her crumpled bleeding body floating facedown in the sea, tendrils of blood streaking the water, and a knife fin cutting through the water toward her.

Stop it. You've got a job to do. By a supreme effort of will, she forced herself to ignore the pictures her mind insisted on creating, and concentrated on the water. But one part of her mind remained focused on the fire below, asking incessantly just how bad it was.

Hangar bay
0210 local (GMT+3)

Fourteen feet away from the fire, Williams came to an abrupt halt. The heat was already painful on his face and hands, although not yet unbearable. The darker parts of his mind responsible for his self-preservation instincts were screaming loud warnings, trying to force him to turn around. The realization that the fire before him was a wild creature, not a chimera under the control of the damage-control-simulator people, came crashing in. For a moment, caught between the instinct for self-preservation and his conscious knowledge of what had to be done, Williams could not move.

"What's wrong?" the man behind him shouted. Williams felt the hose slack starting to accumulate around him. "Go on, go on!"

Williams forced himself to take one step, and then another, his hand steady on the hose and the bail, focusing on the base of the fire. He was too far away now—another ten feet, maybe a little more, and he could unleash the torrential power of his fire hose on the creature before him.

He concentrated on his feet, staring down at the black

safety boots' leather and steel toes, forcing them to move one at a time. The heat grew harder and harder to withstand, but he made himself move. If he didn't, he would not be the only one in danger. The fire had to be contained before it could spread to the aircraft or the rest of the ship.

"Now!" the man behind him shouted. "Go on, sweep the base!"

Williams flipped back the handle of the nozzle, opening it completely. He staggered backwards as the hose tried to squirm out of his hands, a powerful stream of water mixed with foam shooting out the end of it toward the fire. The hose was bucking in his hands like a python, trying to escape. He clung to it grimly, getting the nozzle back under control and sweeping the stream of AFFF across the base of the fire. He was dimly aware of another fire crew approaching from the other side of the fire, doing the same thing.

Williams moved to his left, putting himself and his fire hose between the fire and helicopter closest to it. *Over my dead body*, he thought. As he saw the fire start to respond to the cooling water and the suffocating foam, he felt a wild surge of savage glee. *Take that, you bastard. And that.* Now more confident, he had the nozzle firmly under control, and chose his attack points with more precision.

The effects of the two hoses was starting to be evident. The fire was broken into patches now, fighting against the water and the foam but growing smaller by the minute. Behind it, the bulkheads were charred and blackened, paint peeling off, with twisted lumps of metal that used to be a tool case.

Take that. And that. The fire was almost out now, but Williams felt himself losing control. He longed to run forward and stamp the remaining flames out himself, making it personal. This wasn't just a catastrophe, it was personal. And by God, he was going to make the fire pay for it.

"That's enough," a voice behind him said, and a hard hand clamped down on his shoulder. "Secure the hose. Come on, wild man—that's enough."

Dazed, Williams did not respond. A hand reached forward

and flipped the hose bail forward, cutting off the stream of foam. Two more men crowded up beside him, peeling his hands off the nozzle and taking the hose from him. They stepped away, holding the still-charged hose, a look of awe in their eyes.

"Wild man, that's what you are," the damage-control petty officer said, the gruffness in his voice masking the compliment. "I thought you were going to walk into the middle and start from the inside out." He turned to the two men now holding the hose. "Set the reflash watch. Stay here until I relieve you." He lifted his damage-control radio to his mouth and said, "Central, Team Leader. Fire out. Reflash watch set. Sending the investigator to check for damage in the adjoining compartments now."

"Roger, copy fire out, reflash set. As soon as your investigator confirms no damage to the compartment below, I'll recommend we secure from General Quarters."

Williams was barely aware of the conversation going on around him. Sudden weariness swept over him as the adrenaline left his system. It had been a long day, too long. Now, he was so tired he could barely stay on his feet.

A corpsman appeared at his side, intense green eyes staring at it at him from behind ugly black-framed glasses. "Let me get a look at you. Come over here and sit down." The corpsman took him by the elbow and led him to a stack of pallets. He made Williams sit and crouched down in front of him.

"Do you know where you are?" the corpsman asked.

Williams stared at him. Of course he knew where he was. He was in hell, but hell was disguised as an aircraft carrier. Just then, he became aware of the ugly stench of burnt metal contained in the smoke around him. He ran a hand over his face, surprised to find that it was unburnt.

"What's your name?" the corpsman asked.

"Williams. And yeah, I know where I am. At the fire—geez, man, I'm just tired. That's all."

The corpsman examined his face carefully. "This is going to be uncomfortable, but it's nothing serious. Just first-degree burns. You may have some coughing for a while from the smoke inhalation. Don't you guys know you're supposed to just contain it until the damage-control team in full suits gets there?"

"I had to put it out," Williams said numbly.

The corpsman just shook his head. "Next time, don't get so close."

Next time. There will be a next time. A wave of despair rushed over him.

Bridge
0230 local (GMT+3)

"Secure from General Quarters," the loudspeaker ordered. Smith felt a rush of relief. If the fire was out, then there couldn't be any more danger, could there? No, they would not have secured from General Quarters if there could be.

While the crew was putting out the fire in the hangar bay, the carrier had launched four helicopters from their spots along the side of the flight deck. They were now combing the ocean around the carrier, spotlights illuminating the water below, searching every inch of the sea within a two-mile radius for any other small boats. To the starboard, a small sputtering fire burned, debris from the first boat.

"Smith, put down the binoculars for a minute. I think the helicopters can handle it." Brisco's voice was tart but amused. "Captain wants to talk to you."

Smith let her binoculars dangle from her neck and turned to see the captain of the ship. She had only met him once, during an indoctrination session after she checked on board, and had never actually spoken to him, although she recognized him from his pictures plastered all over the ship.

"Good work, Smith," the captain said, his voice low and gravelly. He clapped one hand on her shoulder. "You got that guy before he could get off more than one shot. It could've been a lot worse if you hadn't seen it."

"Thank you, sir," she said, her voice shaky. Somehow,

having the captain talking to her was almost as nerve-racking as the fire.

"No. Thank *you*. Effective immediately, I'm promoting you from Fireman Apprentice to Fireman. You will be transferred to the engineering department immediately, unless you have some objection."

"No, sir. Thank you. Yes, I'd like very much to work in engineering."

"And the chief engineer will be glad to have you. I expect great things out of you, Smith. Remember that." With that, the captain turned and walked back on the bridge, where he was immediately deluged by damage-control and bridge personnel finalizing their reports on the fire.

Promoted! And transferred into engineering, just like she wanted. For a moment, joy threatened to overwhelm her. But then, hearing a helicopter approach close by, she turned back to the black water surrounding the ship. She might be an engineer, but right now she had a job to do.

TWO

On board the *Jefferson* Admiral William "Coyote" Grant was listening intently to every report that the *United States* made over the classified circuits. Coyote commanded Carrier Battle Group 14, comprised of the aircraft carrier USS *Thomas Jefferson* and her air wing, two Aegis cruisers, three destroyers, and two frigates. They'd been on station in the Med for two weeks now, and had just returned to sea following a three-day port call in Italy.

Fire at sea was every mariner's worst nightmare, and for it to happen to an aircraft carrier was simply unthinkable. That such a massive and powerful ship, the acme of sea power, could be damaged by such a small boat from man's earliest days of going to sea—albeit now with an outboard motor instead of oars—was almost too much to contemplate.

But then again, nobody had believed that terrorists would have—or even *could* have—crashed commercial aircraft into the World Trade Center. Although there'd been some intelligence, some early warnings of terrorist agents and aviation warnings, nobody had really though such a thing could happen. They'd focused on the possibilities of crop dusters and biological weapons, dismissing those dangers by pointing out the difficulties of deploying the proper aerosol and deployment systems. The terrorists, when they'd struck, had relied on a far more primitive and effective method, transforming commercial airliners laden with fuel into suicide bombing runs.

Stingers, though—this scenario was one that aviators had been kicking around for decades. The ubiquitous weapons were the poor nations' answers to almost every problem. Easily transportable, simple to operate, and relatively cheap, they could be brought to bear in almost any scenario.

Recent intelligence reports had done nothing to allay his worries. There were indications that Pakistan had developed a faster, longer-range version of the ubiquitous weapon, which was now making its way into the international arms scene. If that were true, the Middle Eastern nations, with more money to burn than any other region, would have them first. Not even being in the Med instead of the Persian Gulf or the Red Sea made him feel any easier.

If they could reach out and touch the United States, they could get us. It's a little cooler here than in the Gulf, but even staying buttoned up the whole time in the Med ain't gonna be pleasant. But what other choice have we got?

Just as the *United States* reported securing from General Quarters, Coyote's patience with the crowded compartment reached an end. He snapped, "OK, folks. Show's over. Everybody back to work. You know what happened—now figure out how we're going to keep it from happening to us." People shifted uneasily and began moving out of the compartment, heading back to whatever they'd been doing when they'd heard about the fire.

"Admiral?" a low-pitched female voice said at his side. "I'm going to set condition-two antiair in about five minutes."

His gaze still fixed on the large-screen display in front of him, Coyote nodded. "Not antisurface?"

"No, Admiral. I don't think it's going to be the same thing

twice in a row. Besides, after what happened, the full anti-surface team is going to be in Combat whether I set the condition or not."

Coyote gritted his teeth and groaned inside. Captain Jackie Bethlehem, Jefferson's newly appointed commanding officer, was well within her rights to make that decision. He appreciated her informing him of the change before it occurred, and in principle he agreed—but why, oh, why, did every word she speak grate on his nerves?

Bethlehem was a tall woman with dark hair and ice-green eyes. Her hair was short and curly and most days, like today, it had a tousled, just-stepped-out-of-the-shower look. She looked as though she was in her early thirties, but for that to be true she would have had to have been commissioned almost before puberty. Not that Coyote had any indication that she'd ever actually gone through puberty. Her uniforms, while trim and neatly cut, were just generous enough in certain places to hide most of her figure. And her personality—well, Coyote was reasonably certain she probably had one, but her military bearing and command presence were pretty damned near impossible. He'd cracked a couple of jokes during their presail conferences, and even bought her a beer after one meeting, but he was no closer to knowing the woman behind the title than he had been the first day. Maybe she wasn't even human—a robot of some sort, put on his ship—*his* ship—solely to annoy him.

Stop it, he told himself sternly. *This is your problem, not hers.*

When he'd heard Bethlehem had won the highly coveted billet as skipper of his flagship, Coyote had been taken aback. Sure, he knew who she was—everybody in the tight-knit Naval Aviation community did. She'd been first in her class in Basic Flight, first in her Hornet class, first in damn near everything she'd attempted. The word on the flight line was that she wasn't just another bow to political correctness. She was a cold, tough pilot, a superb aviator, and a natural leader. If she'd been born male instead of female, she would have ended up in a command billet eventually.

Eventually. But maybe not so fast. And maybe not as com-mander of the most battle-tested aircraft carrier in the fleet. My carrier, my Jefferson.

Even though she'd managed to resist his considerable per-sonal charm, Coyote had been prepared to give her the ben-efit of the doubt. After all, since he'd commanded *Jefferson* himself, he'd be around to give her a few pointers. He'd succeeded in convincing himself that Captain Bethlehem was going to work out just fine.

And so far, she had. The ship—*her ship*—was in the high-est readiness condition he'd ever seen. Every combat system, every measurement of personnel performance, was breaking records in the fleet. Hell, even the food was better.

So why was it that she was such a thorn in his side? Was he just a tad bit pissed off that her statistics in command of *Jefferson* were higher than his had ever been?

He'd talked it over circumspectly with an old friend, Ad-miral Batman Wayne, not getting right to the heart of it but edging around the issue. Batman, as usual, had nailed the heart of it. "You're a Texan and she's a good-looking woman." Batman had cocked one quizzical eyebrow at him. "You see any reason for this problem you're having?"

"I don't," Coyote had replied stiffly, aware that the back of his neck was itching, as it always did when he strayed from the truth.

"Ah. So it's like that, is it?" Batman smirked.

"No, it's *not*," Coyote snapped. Then belatedly. "Like what?"

Not that he'd had to ask. As soon as he'd seen that snide expression on Batman's face, Coyote had known the truth. Captain Bethlehem, a tall woman with striking blue eyes and blue-black hair, was indeed one of the most attractive women he'd run across in a long time. And not just physically—there was something about her presence, her command pres-ence, that attracted him in a way he didn't understand.

Pushy women weren't his type.

"I've doubled the lookouts as well," Captain Bethlehem

continued, apparently oblivious to the fact that her admiral had yet to turn and look at her.

"Good." Finally, his innate sense of courtesy and good manners shaming him into action, he turned to face her.

Seated, his face was level with hers, although he had a good six inches in height on her when they were both standing. Once again, he was conscious of the fact that they were built along similar lines, both lean and smoothly muscled, both taller than most people around them. On her, however, the overall impression was one of a competitive swimmer, while Coyote had always verged on an awkward lankiness.

"Any new word from *United States*?" she asked. For the first time, Coyote could see the strain in her face, and he felt a moment of shame for his earlier surliness.

"No. Fire's out, reflash set. I imagine we'll hear from them when things settle down. This is bound to change things," he answered.

Coyote was itching to grab the mike and call his counterpart on board *United States* to see how it was going. But he resisted the urge, knowing that the captain and admiral on board the other ship had far more important things to do than talk to him. Eventually, when they got out the required alert messages, treated all the casualties, and made sure that the area around the ship was cleared of potential threats, they'd have time to talk. But not until then.

"We're ready," she said simply, knowing as well as he did what was coming. The *Jefferson* would be ordered into the Red Sea and would take part in any retaliatory strikes. It was only a matter of time.

"I know you are," he said, and was only slightly surprised to realize that he meant it.

The call, when it came, was simple and straight to the point. Admiral Blair Jette, call sign Jetson, sounded tired and unusually candid. "It could've been a lot worse, Coyote. A lot worse. If the fire had spread to the helo, we would've been fighting a Class Delta fire."

Coyote shuddered. "Not a good thing."

"You got that right."

"So. Any damaged operational capabilities I should know about?" Coyote asked.

"Nothing that should affect you. We've had to reroute a few fire lines, but that's about it. Nothing we can't handle with ship's crew. But what worries me is the larger situation here. That small boat—we never held it on radar at all. It was all visual." Jette's voice held a note of wonder, as though he still wasn't able to understand how a small wooden craft had posed such a danger to his carrier.

"That worries me, too," Coyote admitted.

"Listen, the intelligence indications we're getting down here—if I were you, I'd be standing by to inchop the Red Sea. Things look like they're heating up again, and you may want to be in position to strike."

"That bad?"

"Potentially. Nothing we can't handle, of course." The cocky note that Coyote had come to associate with Jette was back, as though he hadn't just fought a fire on board his ship. "Take a look at your intelligence circuits—you'll see what I'm talking about."

Coyote glanced to his right, and Commander "Lab Rat" Busby, *Jefferson*'s intelligence officer, stepped forward. He was a short man, barely topping five feet six inches in height, perhaps 130 pounds soaking wet, and most of that was devoted to brainpower, Coyote believed. Lab Rat's pale blue eyes, light hair, and light eyes had earned him his nickname in his early days of aviation training.

Without keying the mike, Coyote asked, "What's he talking about?"

"Four more violations of the no-fly zone, this time with some fairly serious aggressiveness. There was one strafing run on a group of refugee trucks. Also, we have some human intelligence, not of high confidence, but still, that there are some new developments in Iraq's biological-warfare program."

"What sort of developments?" Coyote asked. The strafing runs, the no-fly zone—normal stuff, even if detestable. But anything having to do with biological weapons really got his attention.

"No one knows for sure, Admiral. The report may have been sanitized pretty heavily before it was sent to us, but if you read between the lines, you can tell what's going on. Whatever it is, the folks back at the CIA are worried about it."

"Ebola? Something like that?"

That diminutive intelligence officer shook his head. "I don't think so, nothing but a few details. If I had to guess—and mind you, it's just a guess—I'd say black plague."

A shudder ran through Coyote. The name alone conjured up apparitions so horrible that he hated to contemplate them.

"Coyote, you still there?" Jette asked.

"Yeah, sure," Coyote answered as he tried to sort out the implications of what Lab Rat had just told him. "Catching up on a few things with my intelligence officer. And I agree with you, it looks like the stage is set for another major play. But under the circumstances, I'm not inclined to move into the Red Sea immediately. The waters are little bit too constrained for my taste."

"Exactly so, but there's no reason to be too concerned about that." The other admiral's voice sounded, if anything, even cockier than before. "This time of year you get a good wind across the deck—no problem launching and recovering."

"Constrained waters," Coyote began again, but Jette cut him off.

"The only reason a carrier needs much water is to launch and recover aircraft, and the prevailing winds are right along the whole length of the Red Sea. So you're a little closer to land—big deal. Nothing that your close-in weapons systems can't deal with."

Like yours just dealt with the Stringer?

Jette should know better. Sure, he was new to his battle group and had spent more time in Washington than on cruises, but that was no excuse. The constrained waters *were* something to worry about, and it had nothing to do with a man's guts or courage. It had to do with good, prudent seamanship.

"Well, we'll stand by for orders," Coyote said finally. "I've been in the Red Sea and know that we can deal with shorter reaction times." *The Silkworm sites—I guess I better brush up on those. There's no telling what else they have in the area now.*

The Silkworm was a powerful, short-range antiship missile that packed a wallop. It could do far more damage than a little Stinger could, penetrating hulls and strakes to detonate deep inside the ship. It didn't have to look for an open hangar bay to kill.

"Just keep your boys and girls on their toes and you won't have any problems," the other admiral advised, oblivious to the reaction he was producing in Coyote's command center area. "And when you get ready to come in where the action is, let me know. We can update you on the situation."

"I'm in the Mediterranean, not San Diego," Coyote snapped. Sure, he was willing to make allowances for Jette's arrogance, given what he'd just been through, but tolerance would go only so far.

"Right, right. Well, catch up on your liberty ports and maybe we'll see you on the front line eventually. *United States* out."

Coyote replaced the microphone in its holder, grinding his teeth in frustration. Why, oh why, did he have to be deployed with that particular admiral on this cruise?

The order came later that night. Unless otherwise directed, the USS *Jefferson* was to inchop the Red Sea and stand by for additional orders. She was to remain in a heightened state of security, particularly in regard to threats from shore-based installations and small boats.

Coyote scanned the orders, then passed his copy to the Chief of Staff. "I'll be in Medical, if anyone needs me."

"Anything wrong, Admiral?" his chief of staff asked.

Coyote shook his head. "Nope. Just antsy about the biochem thing. I'll feel better when I know exactly what we're doing to plan for it, that's all."

He trudged down the ladders and passageways toward Medical. All around him, the crisscrossing lines and pipes were evidence of *Jefferson*'s intricate, self-contained life-support system. Potable and firefighting lines, electrical junction boxes and compressed air lines and steam lines, all meticulously labeled, surrounded him. Not for the first time, he marveled at how self-contained the *Jefferson* was. The nuclear power plant provided virtually unlimited energy, sufficient for the ship to make all the fresh water she needed, run the pumps and filters that cleaned her air, provide power to everything from ovens to power tools, not to mention the lights and the air-conditioning. If threatened by nuclear fall-out or biological and chemical weapons, *Jefferson* could button up and put a positive pressure gradient on her interior spaces, making it virtually impossible for any foreign material to enter the ship.

But every strength had its corresponding weakness. Setting Dog Zebra, the material condition that isolated *Jefferson*'s interior from the outside world, could make her a safe haven in a dangerous environment—or turn her into an incubator. And that little nightmare was just what he wanted to talk to Medical about.

THREE

Kyle Smart had had one particular characteristic in mind when he went hunting for a new dog. Previously he'd been primarily interested in how the dog would get along with the kids, whether it could be trusted around the chickens, and at least the possibility that it might turn into some sort of hunting dog. Black Dog—which is how the last dog had been known—had met those criteria admirably. Though he'd never been much to look at, with his slightly bulging eyes, short shiny black coat, and German Shepherd build, he'd slipped into the family as though he'd been born there.

One night, Kyle had heard the rabid baying of the coyotes. The next morning, Black Dog failed to show up for breakfast.

That was then. This was now. Kyle no longer worried about how good a dog was with kids.

The Internet was responsible for Kyle's change of priorities. The computer hooked up to the phone line had originally been purchased with the idea that the kids needed it for school. It was an older model, running at a modem speed that would be laughable to most other people, but to Kyle it was a gateway to skills and talents he never knew he had. He understood immediately how it worked, and discovered the Internet was a vast storehouse of knowledge. And if there was anything that Kyle needed right now, it was that.

Things hadn't been going all that well at the farm. The two hundred acres that had been in his family for generations were still struggling valiantly to produce crops, but time and overfarming had taken their toll. More and more, Kyle had to rely on man-made chemicals that he couldn't really afford to bolster production. And without the added production, he couldn't afford the chemicals. The vicious circle went on.

It wasn't just the land, either. It was the way the whole world seemed to be going, as though not much made sense anymore. Sure, he knew about the '60s and hippies and everything like that, although he been too young to participate. And there was no denying that some things had changed in some ways for the better over the last several decades. But what bothered him most was the way the government seemed to be working.

Or, more precisely, not working. Increasingly, the measures that came floating out of Washington to the remote areas of Idaho seems aimed personally at him. Farm subsidies were down. Added taxes sent the cost of fuel and fertilizer skyrocketing. The bombing in Oklahoma had even made purchasing fertilizer more difficult, and every day it seemed that taxes went up just a little bit more.

He knew he wasn't the only one feeling the changes. Last Sunday afternoon, while the children screamed around the church playground and the women gathered in corners to talk about God knows what, Kyle and the other men had tried to figure things out. If only they could see a reason for it all. Like if all the government shit was necessary to protect them from the Soviet Union. Or nuclear war, or depression. But no matter how they turned the issue around, upside down, and inside out, it didn't seem to make any sense.

Finally, Gus Armstrong, who owned a stretch of land two farms to the north of the Smart spread, put it this way. "It's not our government anymore. Boys, we just have to face the facts. America's not what she used to be. And if we don't do something about it, it's all going to be gone for good."

There was a general murmur of agreement, some of the voices angrier than others. "Next election," Kyle began, but was cut off by a snort of disgust from Gus.

"I'm not talking about elections. There's nobody left to vote for, anyway. Ever since Nixon, it's been downhill— except maybe for Ronald Reagan."

"They're making the ordinary citizen out to be a criminal, and electing the real criminals to office," put in another. "It's just not right."

No, it wasn't right. Kyle could feel it in his bones, with an even deeper conviction than any he'd ever felt inside the church behind them. Standing there, with his neighbors and his parents, their grandparents and his grandparents buried nearby, he felt a small surge of hope, or something like it. At least he wasn't alone. They knew what he was talking about, and it affected all of them.

Gus stood a little straighter, his hands on his hips, pelvis tilted forward slightly. A bank walker, that's what Gus was, Kyle thought. He had been ever since he was a kid. Strutting around naked on the bank of the pond after the rest of them had jumped in, trying to show off what he had. Not that it was all that much. But it didn't matter to a real bank walker.

"I, for one, am not letting them take everything I've worked for. That my family's worked for. If they come after me like they came at Ruby Ridge, they'd better be prepared to die."

One part of Kyle's mind stepped back at that point, marveling at just how odd the world was getting. From a general discussion of the economy, the price of gas, and the difficulty of getting fertilizer, all at once they were back on Ruby Ridge. And what was even more worrisome was that no one else found it odd.

"Maybe we ought to be ready for something like that," one of them said hesitantly. They all, even Kyle, turned to Gus expectantly. The silence settled over them.

"It wouldn't hurt any," Gus allowed. "There are people out there that think like we do. It wouldn't hurt to talk to them. It would just be talking, that's all."

People out there. Kyle knew what Gus was talking about. While he tried to keep up with the newspapers and magazines, the Internet was now his main source of information. He'd read about the groups that organized around the country, read through their various manifestos and articles and declarations. Most of them were tax protesters. He'd also read the IRS rebuttal to the claims that income tax was unlawful, and he knew what happened to most of the ones that refused to pay taxes. They went to jail on a federal beef.

No, those homegrown militia tax protesters didn't have anything going for them. And even if they did, they didn't have a chance against the federal government.

But despite Kyle's intellectual conclusions, there was something in his gut that howled in warm recognition of the sentiments expressed on some of the Web sites. It was something he didn't like about himself, particularly when it came to the racist stuff. And yet, underlying all the distasteful stuff, there was something that appealed to him. Something that echoed what he was feeling right now about his country, the one he'd served in the Army, the one he'd been taught to love. Whatever else they had wrong, they had one thing right. The country was going down the tubes.

"I'll ask around," Gus said, making eye contact with each one of them in turn. "I'll just ask. You understand this isn't anything we ought to be talking about with other folks. Just us, here. No outsiders."

Kyle felt the small shiver of eagerness and excitement that ran through the group. They were all feeling that compelling need to do something, anything. But what?

As the group broke up, the men making their way back to their women, who were herding the children back toward cars, Kyle felt that same surge of hope.

Maybe there was something they could do. At the very least, they could be ready for anything that came.

When they got home, Kyle's new dog, a Rottweiler-

Doberman cross, greeted them enthusiastically. He was an impressive animal, with the build of the Doberman except for the head. He had large jaws, the joints massive and distinct under his skin, the jaws powerful. Kyle had already seen him deal with one coyote, and he knew that if the dog got his jaws on something, it wasn't going anywhere.

The dog approached them slowly, waiting to be invited closer, and then leaned against him as Kyle proffered his hand for a scratch. Betsy herded the kids inside, and then turned to him. "Just what was that all about?" she asked.

"What was *what* about?"

"Back at the church. The five of you looked so serious." She paused to stroke the dog affectionately. "We all noticed it."

"Nothing in particular. Just, you know—talking. About the way things are." Kyle looked away, refusing to meet her eyes.

"What does that mean?"

Kyle saw the look of uneasiness on her face, and reached out to draw her close. He would give a lot to spare her any worry, but if Gus was right, there was no way around it. "It's probably nothing, honey," he said. "But just in case there's a problem, any kind of problem, I think we ought to have an emergency plan. You know, just some general guidelines about what we do if trouble starts."

"What kind of trouble?" she asked, trying to pull away from him. "Kyle, you're starting to scare me."

"Any kind of trouble. It's not just for us—it's for the kids." He tried to smile. "Honey, it's just something we need to talk over."

Later that night, after supper, after the kids were out, they talked for a long time. Kyle discovered that Betsy was just as worried as he was about the way the country was going. And when they finally got through the initial fear and anger, they were in complete agreement about what they would do. If it ever came to that.

FOUR

Lance Corporal Barry Griffin, USMC, was on his first deployment as a member of a recon team. His first assignment after boot camp had been as a member of the security force on board USS *United States,* and he found while he had a natural aptitude for the military lifestyle, he chafed at seeing other, more senior Marines load up in the helicopter and head for land on special missions while he guarded the door to the admiral's cabin.

Oh, sure, he understood that the new kid had to pay his dues, and he wasn't the only one on security duty. Still, as the cruise stretched on, he found himself determined to find a more active, a more—well, Marine—job within the United States Marine Corps. At his first opportunity, he applied for reconnaissance training.

The year of schooling had been alternately boring and everything he'd dreamed of. Over a twelve-month period, he'd earned dive, jump, and reconnaissance sniper certifications. The practical classroom sessions he found useful only so far as they would support the actual practice of his new skills, but he quickly discovered that knowledge was power. Jumping out of airplanes or drawing a bead on a bad guy's head, he found himself in his element. During the simulated graduation exercises from reconnaissance and Ranger training, he knew he was in his element.

His orders to the USS *United States* had come as a pleasant surprise. God knows he'd spent enough time learning his way around the ship on his first cruise that he didn't mind skipping that part of the transfer. He already knew the damage-control stations, the galley hours, where the best bunks were, and that the gym was better equipped than most shore stations. It was with a good deal of pleasure that he reported back on board, and soon found himself heading for the gym attired in minimal workout clothes while other jarheads took up his former duty of guarding doors. Life in recon, at least on board the ship, consisted mostly of eating, working out, weapons training and cleaning, and staying ready.

His first mission to shore had sounded like a piece of cake. He and a first sergeant went in by rubber raft to a remote part of the Iraqi coast. Evading the military patrols, both friendly and enemy, as well as a host of smaller fishing vessels and massive commercial tankers, they went ashore in the dead of night. From there, a quick overland hike to check out the suspected terrorist training camp. They snooped around the perimeter, scurrying for cover in the barren land, and found little more than abandoned tents and bunkers.

Inside one of the bunkers was where the real surprises were. From a seemingly innocuous Quonset-type construction, the bunker spread down two levels. In the lower levels, they found caches of weapons, rations, and one other surprise—an Iraqi soldier, dead, desiccated, awkwardly sprawled on the concrete deck. They checked out the weapons first, including an abundance of medium-range ground-to-ground attack projectiles and a number of sets of MOPP gear.

As Griffin searched what appeared to be the barracks, he was surprised to find that whoever had occupied that area had left behind a good deal of personal gear. Not just clothes and uniforms, but also the pictures of families, toiletries, books—most of them appeared to be the Koran, but he couldn't be certain of that. The sort of stuff you expected a man to take with him even if he was in a hurry.

"Maybe they bugged out," he suggested to the first sergeant, who hadn't spoken a word since they'd started searching the barracks. "Those bastards didn't even give them time to get the pictures."

"Maybe." The first sergeant's voice held a note of doubt. "Come on. Let's get the hell out of here."

"But we're not done yet."

"Yes, we are. Move, asshole." Griffin followed the first sergeant up two levels and out of the bunker, blinking as he emerged. The sun was just starting to come up, and already he could feel the temperature soaring.

"Over here." To Griffin's surprise, the first sergeant was standing under what appeared to be an outside shower and was stripping off his gear. The sergeant turned the handle, and water gushed out. Stripping down, the sergeant stepped under the water, shut his eyes, and washed down, rubbing hard at his skin. He motioned to Griffin to follow suit.

What was this, some sort of initiation ritual? So far, the first sergeant had offered not one word of explanation.

Seeing his hesitation, the first sergeant unfroze slightly. "Wash down," he said. "I don't know what that guy died of, but we sure as hell don't want to carry it back to the ship."

Even under the hot sun, Griffin felt his blood run cold as he considered the implications. It hadn't occurred to him immediately, but it had to the first sergeant. The man left dead on the deck, the hastily abandoned barracks—the weapons. They'd been briefed on the possibility of biological and chemical weapons in the Iraqi arsenal, but all the reports said that any weapons, if they did exist, were stored far inland. Nobody had said anything about biochem at this site, nobody. But the first sergeant was acting as if . . .

"You think that's what it was?" Griffin asked, his voice quiet as though to avoid alerting any deadly virus that happened to be around. He started stripping down, following the first sergeant's lead, figuring he knew what he was doing. The water, when it hit him, was cool, and for a moment he luxuriated in the sensation, forgetting how dangerous the situation might be.

"Maybe. Maybe not," the first sergeant said, his voice under tight control. "No point in taking chances. Soon as we get back, we go to Medical to get checked out."

Griffin felt a rush of nausea. "I think I'm feeling—I'm not feeling so good." He imagined he could feel the first signs of a disease creeping into his body, invading his lungs and worming its way into his blood through his skin.

"Bullshit," the first sergeant said, in a not unkindly voice. "If it was chem, we'd already be dead. If it's bio, we won't know for a while. Best place for us is back on the ship."

The no-nonsense tone of the first sergeant voice reassured Griffin, if only slightly. Still, he was relieved when they finally headed back across the sand, the sun now hammering at their backs and casting long shadows in front of them.

Yeah, back on the ship. That's where they needed to be. He tried not to remember the spate of inhalation anthrax cases that had followed the September 11th attacks, tried not to imagine that he could feel disease racing through his veins.

Get back to the ship—just get back to the ship. Everything is OK.

But somehow, deep down in his gut, Griffith knew it was not.

USS **Jefferson**
0600 local (GMT+3)

Dirty brown water moved sluggishly past the hull, leaving a thin sheet of oil behind it as it lapped against the steel. The Suez Canal was not much more than a large ditch dredged out between the Mediterranean and the Red Sea.

Coyote stared out at the water from the Admiral's Bridge, fighting off the feeling of claustrophobia. All aircraft on deck with none airborne, the constrained waters, his escorts strung out before and after the carrier in a sitting-duck formation—every war-fighting instinct in his body was screaming warnings. But this was an international waterway, and there were conventions to be observed. All nations were supposed recognize the rights of transit for the canal and forgo exercising attacks. At least that was the theory among civilized nations, and Coyote wasn't so sure that particular description applied to any of the countries with a thousand miles of them.

They'd entered the canal just after dawn, in a queue of ships waiting for daylight. Several miles ahead of them, two supertankers trudged their way toward the oil refineries, empty now and riding high in the water. All around them, fishing boats and other smaller craft seemed determined to commit suicide under the bow of the massive aircraft carrier.

The attack on the USS *United States* had made everyone edgy, and the possibility that biological weapons were involved even more so. *Jefferson* was buttoned up tight. While Coyote felt immense sympathy for the sailors working belowdecks and in the hangar bay, there was no way he was transiting with the hangar bay doors open, no matter what the international rules of the sea said.

At the end of the transit, the Red Sea beckoned. More constrained waters, although not nearly on the order of the canal. What Coyote really wanted was one thousand miles of blue water in every direction. He thought longingly of previous cruises to the western Pacific, of the patrols off the coasts of Taiwan and Japan. At least there they'd had blue water to run to if they had to. Not that the *Jefferson* ran—not ever.

It was, he reflected, more a question of presence than anything else. The long-range land-attack Tomahawk weapons carried by the destroyers and cruisers could reach every target they needed to hit from the safety of the Indian Ocean. Launching air wing strikes would be no more difficult, just a matter of putting more gas in the air and asking the aircrews to suffer through a couple of more tankings. Coyote knew that they all would've gladly traded the extra tanking in exchange for the security of blue water.

Patrolling the Red Sea, sometimes within view of the coast, was intended to send a message to the littoral nations. A line from Hollywood echoed through his mind: "You want to send a message, use Western Union."

No, the problem wasn't that the aircraft carrier couldn't fight from these waters—it was a question of defense. So close to land, their reaction time to a shore-launched missile or incoming raid was calculated in seconds rather than minutes. At sea, a broad, relatively flat ocean increased their radar-detection envelope tenfold, and they had more of that most precious commodity: time. Time to launch aircraft, time to deploy countermeasures, time to retaliate before the first shot even hit.

Had all the rules changed? The attack on the *United States* had proved that even a small, wooden vessel could launch a potentially serious attack on an aircraft carrier. Would it have been any easier for the *United States* to see it coming if they been in blue water instead of near land? Maybe. Maybe not.

The entire bridge crew was edgy over the small boats around them. Not that he could blame them. Added to the additional hazards of navigation with small boats in the area, there was the undercurrent of concern that any one of them might be preparing to launch a Stinger. If even one missile hit the flight deck, assuming they could make it given the steep angle up the side of the carrier, the results could be devastating.

Admiral," a voice said quietly. "I think you want to see this."

Coyote turned with a sigh. Captain Jason Coggins, commander of the air wing, stood at the entrance to the bridge, waiting for permission to approach. With him was Commander Bird Dog Robinson and a chief petty officer that Coyote recognized as chief of the avionics division.

Coyote started to ask whether it could wait so that he could devote his full attention to the transit. But he choked the question off, knowing Coggins would not have tracked him

down unless it had been urgent. And besides, Captain Bethlehem was on the bridge one deck below, personally overseeing the transit. How would *he* have felt when he was a
skipper of the *Jefferson* if Batman had been riding his ass at
a time like this?

*He did. It took a long time for him to turn you loose and
trust your judgment, didn't it? I thought I wasn't going to
repeat his mistakes.*

Coyote motioned them forward. Without speaking, the
chief stepped forward and held out a bundle of wires, the
ends encased in electrical connections, the other ends cut
jaggedly. Coyote recognized it for what it was, a wire bundle
from an avionics box from a Tomcat. He took the wire bundle and examined the cut ends. They were snipped raggedly,
the insulation stripped off in spots.

"They found it on the preflight of 101," Coggins said so-
berly.

"In the aircraft?" Coyote asked. "Not in the work center?"

Bird Dog shook his head. "No, Admiral. One-zero-one
was on the flight schedule this morning for surface surveillance after we complete the canal transit. The plane captain
went out to check it early—he's a new kid, pretty compul-
sive—and found it. We checked with avionics. No one was
supposed to be working on this bird."

"That's not how they would do it, even if they were," the
maintenance chief put in. "A mess like this—no way. And
even if they had cut the wires while the gear was still installed, the whole aircraft would have been tagged out. And
nobody in avionics knows anything about it."

Coyote studied the wire bundle, trying to avoid the con-
clusion that was staring him in the face. "Any chance somebody made a mistake and was just too stupid to admit it?"

All three of the other men shook their heads in the nega-
tive. Coyote sighed.

"Somebody cut this deliberately," the chief said, speaking
slowly, as though to give the officers time to catch up with
him. "This was no maintenance action."

Coyote turned bright, hard eyes on Bird Dog. "Sabotage. That's what you're telling me."

Bird Dog's face was cold and hard, and he looked older than Coyote had ever seen. There was no trace of the young lieutenant who had reported on board *Jefferson* so many years ago for his first cruise, a happy-go-lucky pilot who had since then seen more than his fair share of combat. No, there was a new expression of maturity and command in Bird Dog's face. Coyote felt relieved to see it, and at the same time a bit sad. *That's what we do, turn youngsters into men. Takes longer with some than others.*

"I've ordered an investigation," Bird Dog said, his voice tight. It was clear that he took this personally. "And I want to get the master-at-arms involved in fingerprinting the bird right away, just on the off chance that something turns up."

"There are a lot of people whose fingerprints ought to be on the bird," CAG commented. "Be tough eliminating them."

"I know. But it's a step we have to take."

"But why?" the chief said, angry. "Oh, sure, we have a few troublemakers, but those kids all know that something like this would risk the pilot's life. None of them would go this far—or at least I would have sworn they wouldn't. I guess I don't know them as well as I thought." A new note of bitterness was in his voice.

Coyote held up one hand. "Let's not jump to conclusions. Like Bird Dog said, we'll print it. Everybody's prints are on file. Maybe it will turn out to be a mess cook or a yeoman. But how they would know where to cut, what would do the most damage—hell, I would've bet a lot of them couldn't even find the flight deck. It's not necessarily somebody in your squadron, Chief," he said, including Bird Dog in his comments with a glance. "But you're right, this is surely and truly fucked. We will find whoever did it, and I'll make the bastard wish he'd never been born."

The deck shifted slightly under his feet. The *Jefferson* was incapable of making the hard, tight turns of a destroyer or frigate, but she was fairly nimble, given her size. The movement was noticeable, and Coyote darted to the bridge wing to look out.

Far below, a ragged fishing boat was chugging up the starboard side, apparently oblivious to the tons of steel blocking its way. The vessel came astern, and moved so close that it disappeared in the shadow cast by the flight deck.

"General Quarters," a strong female voice announced on the 1MC. As she spoke, the ship's horn blasted out five short blasts, the international signal for immediate danger. The fishing boat appeared to take no notice.

Coyote swore violently and grabbed a bullhorn mounted along the bulkhead. "Fishing vessel on my starboard quarter, this is the captain of the USS *Jefferson*. Be advised you are standing into danger. Come right immediately to open distance and decrease your speed to fall astern of us."

His words seemed to have some effect where the ship's whistle had not. Coyote saw darkly tanned faces turn up toward him, a look of surly anger on the face of what appeared to be the vessel's master. A few of the deckhands extended a middle finger at Coyote, then turned their backs to him. One sauntered to the edge of the deck, unbuttoned his fly, and took a leak over the side, aiming in Coyote's direction.

For moment, Coyote was seized with the overpowering desire to either grab his .45 and let them know just how serious he was on a one-to-one basis, or jump over the side, swim over to the boat, and personally throttle its master.

A large hand descended heavily on his shoulder, and he turned to face CAG, who had a grim expression on his face. No words were necessary. Coyote let out his breath, tried to drain the tension out.

"You're not the captain of *Jefferson*, Admiral," CAG said quietly, his voice reaching only Coyote. "Bethlehem's got it under control."

FIVE

USS United States
Forward crew galley
1200 local (GMT+3)

Griffin was not particularly hungry, but in four hours he was supposed to meet his squad in the weight room, and it was better to carb out now rather than try to choke down food after a workout. Still, as he contemplated the chili mac and overcooked vegetables, he wasn't convinced that he really wanted to eat. The Jell-O and the ice cream down at the far end of the food line looked far more inviting.

The mess cook dumped a large ladle of chili mac on his plate and shoved it at him. Griffin eyed it suspiciously. "A little small, isn't it?"

"You want more, you can come back," the mess cook said. "We got plenty."

"Then give me some more now and save me a trip," Griffin said, one part of his mind wondering why he was even bothering. He wasn't so sure he was hungry. Still, it was the point of the thing. The mess cooks knew they were supposed to give the Marines bigger portions, knew that they'd work it off during the day. Every Marine knew that and so did this mess cook. So why bother with this bullshit about coming back?

"That's the portion size," the mess cook said, his voice taking on a whining note. "Or, like I said, you want more, come back."

"Chill, Barry," the Marine behind him said. It was Gonzo, his team partner. "Not worth the hassle." Griffin knew what he meant—brawling in the mess hall would bring the captain's anger down on them, and it would be even worse when the top sergeant got ahold of them. Still, this squid was trying to shortchange him, wasn't he? Griffin had just started to open his mouth to take the next verbal shot, intending to follow up with physical action within the next twenty seconds or so, when the nausea hit.

It was all-encompassing, consuming. It started like an atom bomb in his gut and worked its way both up and down simultaneously. He doubled over, moaning as a wave of cramps convulsed through his gut, the pain intensifying each moment. It seemed as if somebody had skewered his intestines and was slowly extracting them through his navel. The mess hall around him was tilting, whirling about him, his entire world suddenly unsteady. He got a glimpse of Gonzo's face looming over him before the pain forced his eyes shut. He heard someone moaning, crying and praying, and vaguely realized it was his own voice. Around him, the Marines backed away in horror.

Hospital Corpsman Second Class David Evans shoved his way through the crowd to Griffin's side. The Navy corpsman was their medic and an integral part of the squad. Evans ran his hands over Griffin, checking to make sure he was breathing and his heart was still beating. "Get Medical down here," he snapped, turning to Gonzo. He kept his fingertips on Griffin's neck, feeling the thready pulse under his fingers. "No, not you—you," he said, motioning with his chin to a Marine farther back in the crowd that had gathered. "Get to the phone, tell Medical to get down here—full decontamination gear."

"Oh, shit," one Marine muttered. "Don't tell me—"

"The rest of you," the corpsman continued, pointing at Gonzo, "get over against a wall, anyone who was within five—no, ten feet of him. Anybody else, move to the other side of the compartment. Now move." The corpsman was only a petty officer second class, but the note of command in his voice kicked in the reflexes of every Marine and sailor present. They did as they were directed, the senior man in each group taking charge of his cadre, holding them in position as the corpsman tended to Griffin. A few moments later, the order blared over the loudspeaker. "Medical to forward crew's galley. Man down. Contamination gear required. Now set MOPP Level Three throughout the ship." The few Marines who had not figured out what the corpsman was doing now tumbled to the danger. There were more protests, but the larger group at the back of the compartment moved as far away as possible from the group that had been near Griffin. Forty seconds later, the first ship's corpsman arrived, hastily donning a gauze mask and rubber gloves. He stopped ten feet away from Griffin.

"What happened?" he asked.

"He went down—cramps, nausea—oh, shit," Evans said as Griffin's body started to buck under his hands. He moved to Griffin's head and placed a hand on either side of his face, trying to prevent the Marine from slamming his head against the deck. "Convulsions! Hold on, buddy, hold on."

"Why the contam gear?"

"They were on a mission to the beach today, to the interior. They saw something that look like it could be biochem warheads. Those guys were around him," he said, nodding toward the group that had been nearest to Griffin. "The others, ten feet away. The cooks, I haven't done anything about them."

More medical people were arriving on the scene, including a young doctor who darted forward. The first-class corpsman clamped his hand on his upper arm and jerked him back. "Hey! Let me go!" The doctor struggled and tried to pull away. "There's a man down!"

"You don't have your gear on," the senior corpsman said,

not relaxing his grip. Briefly, he sketched in the details. While the doctor stood stock still in stunned silence, the corpsman took charge.

"Full contamination gear," he said to a second group of men and women arriving. "Get a stretcher. Call Medical, tell them to set up an isolation chamber. Until we know what's going on with him, we're not going to take any chances." He glanced over at the doctor, who had regained control of himself and was nodding agreement. Then he looked at the corpsman by Griffin's side. "Plus an isolation ward," he said. "One room and one ward. You want to hold these guys— how long ago was he in country?"

"About six hours ago."

"Right." The senior corpsman turned back to the doctor. "You want to hold them for at least seventy-two hours in isolation. Right, sir?"

"Right," the doctor said, staring unbelievably at Griffin and Evans.

Things moved with surprising efficiency after that. The medical teams had practiced exactly this scenario time and time again, but never, ever, had any of them thought they'd really have to do it for real.

Finally, after Griffin was loaded onto an isolation stretcher and prepared for transport, and the passageways and ladders between the galley and Medical were cleared of all personnel, the senior corpsman turned to Evans. "Full decontamination procedures for you. We've got Griffin from here— follow along, and I want you in the decontam shower the second we get there. Got it?"

The strain were starting to show in Evans's face. "Got it," he said, pleased that his voice was steady. As he started to head off, following Griffin, the senior corpsman, now completely gowned and gloved, stopped him. "Good going."

Evans shook his head. "Maybe."

"No maybe about it. Now go get showered," the senior corpsman said, his voice unexpectedly gentle. "We got it in time—you'll be okay."

"Yeah. I'll be okay." But as Evans watched another convulsion wrack Griffin's body, as he saw them insert an IV needle in his arm, he wasn't so sure.

USS Jefferson
1230 local (GMT + 3)

Coyote took a deep breath before he picked up the handset to call Admiral Jette. He could not let his personal feelings get in the way of duty. Like it or not, they were going to be working together, and that meant they needed to coordinate their resources and plans. Gone with the days of autonomous operations. There were too few people and too little equipment.

"Your people got the plans we sent over, I take it?" Coyote said after a few preliminary remarks. "Any feedback?"

"Yeah, as a matter of fact. My people are wondering why there aren't more specifics. Seems like a lot of TBAs," Jette answered.

There it was again, that faintly supercilious, superior tone of voice that had been driving Coyote crazy for the last few months. How could a man rise to one-star rank and still have no clue as to how things were actually done in a combat flight schedule?

"To Be Arranged gives us more flexibility. My experience has been," Coyote began carefully, striving for self-control and patience, "that a target list changes radically from day to day. The shelf life of intelligence is pretty short, often measured in hours rather than days. If I start assigning flights to specific targets now, people start planning around those. Then, when we have to make changes, they're caught short. That's why I leave a lot of the details TBA so people will continue to think outside the box."

"But we know where their bases and major facilities are. So what if you have to fine-tune a few details?"

"The devil is in the details," Coyote answered, aware that his voice was getting sharper. "It's a specific Silkworm site that will kill you, not the general knowledge that there's a missile somewhere within a five-mile area. Unless," he said, trying unsuccessfully to control his temper, "you really want to send a Tomcat driver out with orders just to find something that looks dangerous and kill it?"

"I put a lot of faith in the guy in the cockpit."

"Like I don't? Listen, buddy, I've been there, been back, and got the Air Medal. And I'm telling you, this has nothing to do with dissing the judgment of an individual pilot. It has to do with how old your intelligence is, how good it is, and what the hell is going on in the rest of the world. Not whether your flight schedule has all the blanks filled in days or weeks before the actual event."

"Flight schedules can change."

"They can. But they don't. You put the details in, it's like setting it in stone. People figure you know what you're doing and they start their planning based on your flight schedule. Tankers, the logistics and weapons people, even national authority."

"Yes, master. Grasshopper understand."

"Knock it off."

"You going to make me?"

I don't believe this. What are we, back on the playground? Is he going to helo over here and try to beat the shit out of me? "Listen, you've got my flight plan. Now get me yours and we'll see what kind of plans we can come up with."

"What if I don't?"

Coyote smiled. It was not a pretty sight. "Hasn't it occurred to you," he said, his voice soft and level, "that I'm a year senior to you? When it comes down to coordinating our operations, who do think it's going to be in overall command? You? Nope. So, Admiral—yes, I am going to make you knock it off. I will expect your proposed flight plan on my desk tomorrow morning, submitted for *my approval*, and I will let you know what further tasking we have for you. *Jefferson* out."

USS **Lincoln**
Off the coast of Korea
1900 local (GMT+9)

Had the admiral on board *Lincoln* been privy to the pissing contest between Coyote and his nemesis, he would have undoubtedly agreed with Coyote. As it was, he was far more interested in the conflicting intelligence reports he was getting from Korea to worry about what was going on in the Middle East.

For perhaps the fourth time in the last hour, he read the latest intelligence summary. According to what the spooks termed "sources of questionable reliability," North Korean troops were poised to move south. Already, the source claimed, cadres of guerrilla fighters had been filtering into areas along the Demilitarized Zone. The bulk of the troops, never more than a day or so's travel from the DMZ, were in a heightened state of readiness and could be deployed at any time.

Or maybe not. The problem lay in the fact that there was no supporting source of information. The satellite spooks had not yet turned up any evidence of increased troop movements, nor had any of the international news agencies that followed the area. The only one crying wolf was one lone intelligence source on the ground, a foreign national at that.

It didn't make a whole lot of difference, though, did it? What would you do differently if you were certain that trouble was starting in Korea?

Get some more assets in the area, for starters. One cruiser isn't enough. And a higher priority on repairs, intelligence—everything.

And that, he concluded, was the real issue—priority. Most of America's focus was centered on its problems at home and in the Middle East. Let gasoline prices go up two cents at the pump and everybody would be howling about Middle East stability. Problems with Korea were low on the national priority list.

And they shouldn't be. Not with China involved.

China had far more power to affect the world than the Middle East even dreamed about, and her first forays into the international arena had taken place here, in Korea, where China knew the ground, the terrain, and the people. Some people remembered that, most notably the veterans of the Korean War, but they were aging and dying off and their voices seldom were heard.

I think it's happening. And I think it's happening now. China is not going to miss the fact that we are preoccupied with the Middle East and domestic problems. It's a situation tailor-made for them. We don't have the resources to handle the Middle East and Korea at the same time and they know it.

He picked up his desk phone and dialed the chief of staff. "Round up the intelligence officer, will you? And Strike. I think we need to take a serious look at this latest intel."

This time, he was going with his gut. And his gut was screaming that he'd better be ready.

Pyongyang, North Korea
0900 local (GMT+9)

Chan Su Lee would have taken some comfort from it if he'd known of Coyote's worries, and there were few comforts to be found in North Korea for the senior officer from the People's Republic of China. Never in all his military career, not even under the worst field conditions, had being in North Korea seemed such a hardship. The most miserable part of this tour of duty was the smell. The stench of rotting fish and kimchi assailed Chan the moment he woke up. It clung to his clothes and his hair, permeating everything he owned, promising to follow him home to China. Everything he owned and had brought to North Korea would have to be burned downwind from any of his family or friends.

Even after two months in North Korea, the Chinese had not yet fully acclimated. Every day, some misunderstanding or problem arose from the differences in their cultures. In particular, he found the Koreans far too prickly about their national pride and prestige. It struck him as ludicrous that such an insignificant peninsula could matter at all to the rest of the world. The area known as Korea was part of the greater Chinese Empire, and everyone know it. If the rest of the world would stop interfering in what was purely a territorial matter, the matter would resolve itself simply and quietly.

Chan rolled out of his bed. His feet hit the old wooden floor last polished perhaps ten years ago. The deprivations in the North were felt at all levels of the society, and senior visiting dignitaries, even military ones, were not exempt. At home, his accommodations would have been more in keeping with his status. Here, however, he had to cope with damp and cold quarters. No matter that this was the best available. That did not prevent them from being truly miserable accommodations.

His aides and personal servants were already hard at work, organizing the rest of his day. There were a number of political and social obligations, but in truth, nothing much mattered after his morning conference. Oh, yes, there were alliances to be made, and other work to be done. But the man he was meeting this morning was really the only one he needed to talk to.

An hour later, there was a soft tap on his door, which was answered by his aide. He heard a few murmured words, and then his aide was at his office door, announcing the visitor. Chan stood as the man entered the room.

"Thank you for coming this morning," Chan said politely. "You are well?"

"I am well." The North Korean officer studied him, his entire body giving the impression of a coiled spring. There was an energy about him that Chan found deeply disturbing, something that went beyond the normal coarse spirit one would expect after years of combat. No, there was something deeply wrong about this man, the commander of the southern forces. A dark, brutal streak of wrongness, something that made him glory in and take personal pleasure in the pain he caused his enemies. It went beyond simple pride in his unit and in his performance, beyond that of the warriors. It was darkness.

Chan offered both food and drink, and settled into the polite inquiries that were the normal preliminaries, even with the military, to serious discussions. The Korean refused both, responded to Chan's first few questions abruptly, and then suddenly stood. "We don't have time for this. I understand that you consider me a barbarian, a man completely without manners. I also know that you have dealt with us long enough to understand that here I am not considered so." He bowed ever so slightly, softening the harsh words. "There is not much time. When can we expect our shipments to arrive?"

Chan kept his face impassive. There was an art to telling lies, and no one was better at it than he was. "That will depend on your own progress. You will also pardon my bluntness, but I do not see that your forces are yet ready for them."

The Korean general started to protest, and Chan cut him off. "With my own eyes I have seen the problems. Until they are corrected, I cannot authorize further assistance."

"We are in the positions you ordered."

"*Suggested.* I do not order your troops."

The Korean waved away the distinction. "We are at our staging areas, ready to move forward. Everything, as you well know, is predicated on your country providing the weapons as agreed. And it was you, if I recall, who insisted that there would be no problems, that we could trust you and your people." The Korean lifted one eyebrow, a sardonic expression on his face. "So far, your words mean nothing."

The arrogance. The sheer unthinking arrogance. He has been to China. He knows that compared to this squabbling little strip of land, China is so far advanced. And yet he presumes to talk to me as an equal, to demand—demand— answers of me.

Chan let the silence stretch out, waiting for the other man to become uncomfortable. He wouldn't, though—he never did. He operated on a different plane from anyone Chan had ever dealt with, one grounded in the concrete rather than in the abstract. Political promises meant nothing to him, nor did solemn oaths of assistance and friendship. In the Korean's mind, a friend was someone who showed up with ammunition or weapons. When Chan followed through on his part of the bargain, the Chinese would become a very, very special friend—but not until then.

"Two weeks," Chan said, reaching a decision. "Fourteen days to improve your security forces, to make arrangements for the secure transport of these weapons. And for those components that you yourself are to supply to be here, waiting."

"The components are ready."

"Since when?"

"Since now. I received a call this morning before leaving my quarters."

Yes. Two weeks. That had been the right decision. The security, the transport, none of that really mattered. What mattered was that the delicate assemblies that China was providing had to be housed in casings uniquely identifiable as Korean.

"And the submarines?" the Korean continued. "The repairs you promised would be completed have not been done. Under the circumstances, I will not authorize any more of your forces to enter our country. Not until all of our submarines are seaworthy."

"Had the problems been dealt with early on," Chan responded mildly, "your own technicians could have dealt with them."

The Korean waved aside the objection. "Events have not permitted our forces to linger in port. Nor have your requirements."

Time for this to end. "Two weeks, then," Chan said, standing to indicate that the meeting was over. "I assure you that—"

The Korean reached across a desk and grabbed him by the

throat before Chan realized what was happening. Black eyes, so black they were almost blue, stared into Chan's dark brown ones. The Korean did not speak.

My God, he's growling. It can't be—but he is.

Chan considered struggling or trying to call on his mediocre martial arts skills, but quickly dismissed the idea. There was no dignity in trying. The Korean was a warrior, one of the physical types. Chan's spirit was no less warlike, but his skills were in different areas. He dealt in strategy, the intricate maneuvering of people behind the scenes, the positioning of forces to create maximum dismay, the careful intrigues that preceded and accompanied bloodshed between nations.

Chan stood still, unflinching, never taking his gaze from the other. He let his eyes speak for him. *Not today, my friend. Perhaps not tomorrow. But know, know with complete certainty, that you'll pay for this. In time. My time.*

Some part of his message must have gotten through. The Korean did not quail, but Chan saw a grudging respect in his eyes. Abruptly, he released the Chinese strategist. Chan caught himself before he staggered, maintaining his balance on the balls of his feet.

The Korean turned and stalked out of the room.

Once he was alone, Chan slid back into his chair, willing his muscles to relax, waiting while the adrenaline seeped out of his system. The Korean would pay for this. He would pay.

SIX

The two doctors stood before Admiral Jette and Captain Arnot, waiting for a reaction. Both the captain and the admiral seemed frozen, as though to react to the news was to make it even more real that it might be. Finally, the captain cleared his throat and leaned forward. "Just how sure are you that this is what you think it is?" He avoided saying the names that ran like a litany of doom through his mind: black plague, Ebola, hemorrhagic fever.

Dr. Evan Bender, a captain and the senior medical officer on board *United States,* pursed his lips. "We're not certain of anything at this point, Captain. The lab reports are inconclusive, not surprising with what we have to work with on board. It will take a full culture in level-four containment facilities to make sure." He glanced over at the younger doctor to his side, Dr. Marcia Henning, and said, "And that could take a few days, couldn't it?"

Dr. Henning was one of the more junior doctors aboard, but she had completed a one-semester work project with the Center for Disease Control in Atlanta, and was the closest thing the ship had to an infectious disease specialist. "Maybe just forty-eight hours," she said, "although it could be longer, depending on what they think they're looking for. And if it's a new strain that hasn't been identified yet and this is the first time it's popped up, some mutated organism of some sort—well, it could be longer. They'll try to sequence the DNA and see if they can find out what family of diseases it belongs to first."

"Until then," Dr. Bender put in, "the first course of action for us is full isolation procedures. It could be that our young Marine is just suffering from a nasty case of the flu. But until we know more . . ." He spread his hands in front of him, palms up, and a look of helplessness spread across his face. "I can't recommend we take any chances with this, sir. The potential for disaster . . ." Again, he left the sentence unfinished.

The captain, although he appeared to be looking at the doctors, was in reality mentally replaying a seminar from the Naval War College. The seminar had been part of an intelligence briefing, highly classified, restricted on a need-to-know basis. Every man and woman in the room had been headed for command. The intelligence officer from the CIA had seemed peculiarly uneasy, and with an unerring instinct born of years of command, the captain and everyone else in the room had known that he was holding something back. The CIA, they understood, had been extremely reluctant to provide any information on the topic of biochemical warfare, at least not at a level of specificity that would do anyone any good. Sure, there were plenty of unclassified briefings around, tons of material to study. But getting someone to put their ass on the line and say yes, this is something every one of you is going to face within the next few months—well, that was something else entirely.

The CIA officer had declined to give his name, introducing himself as Jim. He had sharply cut features, darkly tanned with a slight sunburn on his nose, eyes that had seen too much that he could never tell. Still, once Jim had gotten started, the captain had appreciated his no-nonsense manner.

"There is a good possibility," he had begun, "that one of

you will face the possibility that a biochemical weapon has been used against you. Better than a possibility—I would go so far as to say an eighty-percent chance." He paused to let that sink in.

Around him, the captain had heard the sharp intakes of breath. Putting a number to the threat made it real.

Eighty percent. For some reason, it had floated through his mind that presidential elections often reflected a voter turnout about a third of that.

Jim punched a button on his remote control, and the computer threw up a map of the world, some areas shaded in red. "These are the areas in which biochemical weapons are being developed—particularly biological agents. Some of them are quite primitive, and in our estimation the countries or groups involved are incapable of actually deploying the weapons. That doesn't mean they can't sell the warheads to a third party or make them available on the international arms market."

Our new friend Jim has the look of someone who ought to be out in the field. Wonder how he got tapped to do this presentation. Maybe an injury—maybe he screwed up somehow and got yanked back to a desk?

The slides went on and on, describing what particular forms of death were being developed in each region, the availability of delivery systems, political estimates of which groups were intending to actually use the weapons. Only occasionally were Jim's comments modified by, "We believe," or, "We estimate." More often, the data was accompanied by hard numbers, specific statistics, and projections even more frightening for their banality. Finally, when Jim opened the floor to questions, the captain asked, "So what do we do?"

Jim studied him for a moment, his gaze flat. "Arnot—deployed in four months to the Middle East." It was not a question, but the captain nodded in response anyway. "There will be a precruise briefing that will answer most of your questions, Captain. In general, you must be prepared to react immediately to any unexplained outbreak of illness, particularly if it comes aboard following a shore deployment in one of these areas. Absent hard laboratory evidence to the contrary, you must—I repeat, must—assume that the patient has been infected with a contagious biological weapon." Jim's eyes bored into Arnot's, seeking confirmation that the captain understood what he was saying. "Prior to deployment, your medical staff will be briefed as well. You'll have some additional equipment aboard that will help them refine their analysis and diagnosis, as well as extra supplies of antibiotics, other supplies necessary to provide symptomatic treatment and life support."

"Guess we all better get our flu shots," someone in the back of the room muttered uneasily.

"You'll be getting more than that," Jim said, his gaze still fixed on Captain Arnot. "There are a number of vaccines in development now. Whether enough will be available prior to deployment is still questionable."

"FDA-approved?" a medical officer headed for command of Balboa Naval Hospital asked.

"In some cases," Jim said, and waited for the inevitable reaction of groans and complaints to subside. "Yes, we all know what happened with the anthrax vaccine. The court cases when sailors refused to take it, claiming it was dangerous. The problems in the manufacture, complaints about the series of shots. That will not be an issue."

Jim stopped suddenly, as though he had said more than he intended to.

"Why?" the medical officer asked.

"We think the legal precedents have been set at this point," Jim continued, his voice unconvincing. "And our studies showed that most sailors will prefer the protection of the vaccine to any unsubstantiated and undocumented potential side effects. There are the procedures in place to deal with that possibility, too."

They're not going to tell them. The thought shot through Arnot like a comet. *They'll tell them it's a flu vaccine, some sort of booster—or just include whatever they're testing out and not tell anybody.* A wave of anger, then a shameful surge of relief. Yes, it was terribly wrong—but he wouldn't know about it, would he? Even the captain of the ship would not be told, if that was what they were planning. And if he didn't know, he wouldn't have to deal with the possible protests.

Now, as he stared at the two medical officers standing tall in front of his desk, the captain's doubts resurfaced. Had they been vaccinated against some form of biochem weapon in the last routine flu shot? If so, against what? And was there any way to find out—hell, could he even ask questions about the possibility?—without violating the nondisclosure agreement he'd signed prior to the CIA briefing?

He glanced over at the admiral, wondering if he had attended a similar CIA briefing. He'd try to find out later, if he could.

The admiral was still silent, although his face had gone pale. He stared at the two medical officers wide-eyed, and the captain was surprised to see a tiny tremor in his right hand. And that color—even as he watched, the admiral seemed to go a shade paler.

"Admiral?" he asked. "Do you have any guidance on this?"

The admiral turned to stare at him as though he didn't recognize Arnot. Then, in a rush, color came flooding back to his face. "I suggest we arrange for evacuation of those men involved to shore. They're better equipped to deal with this than we are. There are—how many, forty-eight?—potential victims and we don't even know what we're dealing with. The ship doesn't have the resources to run a full isolation ward. It will interfere with our mission."

"Losing those men and women if this turns out to be just the flu will interfere, too," Arnot said.

"Damn it all, Arnot, are you paying attention?" The admiral pointed at the senior doctor, and now Arnot could clearly see the quiver in the admiral's finger. "Do you know how many people the black plague wiped out in Europe? Do know how contagious this ship is? I'm not having it on my ship—I'm not having it." The admiral's voice was slightly higher, his words tumbling over each other. "What about the air wing? We start losing pilots right and left, what good are we?"

Arnot and the doctors stared at him, consternation on their faces for a moment before they all settled back into professional Naval officer expressions. "Planning evacuation is premature," the senior doctor said shortly. "Once we have some preliminary lab results back, then we might consider—"

"No. I'm not taking the risk. I want an evacuation plan on my desk in twenty minutes." The admiral shot up from his seat and rose to his full height. "Now move." The admiral turned and stomped out of the room, his back stiff.

When he was gone, Arnot turned back to the doctors, and let out an involuntary sigh. "I'll talk to him. How soon do you think you'll know something else?"

"Twelve hours, Captain," the younger doctor said. "I started cultures as best I can—but I can't do any DNA sequencing here. We're running a couple of tests to determine if it's a normal variant of some sort of flu. But even if it is, we can't be absolutely certain that it hasn't been genetically altered in some way. Mostly we're going to have to monitor the kid, treat his symptoms, and provide life-function support. If he's got something truly nasty, he's going to get worse fast, given how fast it came on initially after the possible exposure."

"What about evacuation?" the captain asked. "The plans I saw said we could do it."

"Yes, we do have contingency plans," the senior medical officer said. "But in the case of a possible biological-warfare outbreak, we have to get permission from Fifth Fleet and from JCS. There's some question in my mind whether they're going to want anyone off the ship at all. They may prefer to fly in additional experts and treatment equipment."

"Quarantine us," the captain said. The doctor nodded. "You think that's what they'll do?"

"I do." This time, it was the younger medical officer who answered. "The first priority with any epidemic is to contain the spread."

Epidemic. Quarantine. Dear God.

"I'll talk to the admiral, make sure he understands the procedural requirements for evacuation. In the meantime, I'll let you get back to your patient. I don't need to tell you that I want to be informed of any change in his condition and any preliminary lab results." Both officers nodded.

Alone in the conference room, the captain relaxed for a moment, and let a wave of despair sweep through him. He allowed himself approximately fifteen seconds to feel the crushing burden of command, then resolutely put it aside in that compartment of his mind dedicated to dealing with such fears. He scribbled a few notes on a notepad, then took a deep breath and went to see the admiral.

Fifteen minutes later, he left the admiral's cabin in a foul mood. As he'd suspected, Admiral Jette had changed his mind when he'd learned evacuation would require requesting permission from Fifth Fleet. Arnot had pointed out that evacuation might be devastating to the morale of the medical department, since they'd had extensive training and additional resources supplied to deal with such a contingency. Without coming right out and saying it, he'd led the admiral to conclude that an immediate request for an evacuation might reflect on the admiral's ability to rely on his own resources. Admiral Jette had not needed any prompting to remember when the promotion board to two stars met.

He cares more about his own career than he does that kid, not to mention the rest of the crew. By God, if I thought I was endangering anyone on the ship, I'd be howling for that evacuation right now.

Easy to make snap judgments, though. Arnot grimaced. After this cruise, he'd be up for promotion to one-star himself, and someday might be sitting in the seat Jette occupied now.

And would I want my captain thinking about me the things I'm thinking about Jette?

No. He'd give the admiral the benefit of the doubt, Arnot decided.

Or give him enough rope to hang himself.

Aft crew galley
1400 local (GMT +3)

With the forward galley secured since Griffin had fallen ill, the aft galley was far more crowded than normal. Williams entered the galley, and saw that the line stretched around the compartment before arriving at the stack of trays and the food line. Those going on watch had front-of-the-line privileges, and he started to walk around the line and invoke them when he noticed a woman standing at the end of the line. Short dark hair framed translucent skin, the mouth broad and generous, the eyes dark blue. She had the look of someone who was about to laugh at any moment. Where had he seen her before?

Oh, right. In the galley. She had just finished her tour of mess cranking when he reported in.

He headed for the end of the line to stand directly behind her. She didn't turn around. Williams cleared his throat, scuffed his foot on the floor, and finally said, "Hey."

She glanced behind at him, and a look of recognition crossed her face. "Hey." She nodded a pleasant if not altogether friendly acknowledgment.

"Hey," he said again, a bit at a loss for words. "You were in the galley, weren't you?" He could see the look of disdain on her face—of course she had been in the galley—all sailors spent a tour there. Probably every guy in the world tried to come on to her, so she was playing it cool. Well, he would just have to show her he was different. "You got off right after I got here," he continued doggedly, wondering if he was making any sense at all. "I just got off last week. Three months total."

"How very nice for you," she said politely, then turned to face forward. He noticed the insignia on her sleeve.

"Engineman, huh? How do you like it down there? I'm in aviation data systems. VF-95." He saw her start to lose interest at the mention of aviation, and said, "It's really pretty interesting. And dangerous. I was down in the hanger bay when the fire broke out." There was a small flicker of interest in her eyes. He debated telling her how the petty officer had called him a wild man, but had the good sense to quit while he was ahead.

"I was on the bridge when it happened," she said finally. "I saw the boat just before it fired."

"Really? What did it look like?"

She shrugged. "Small, wooden. An outboard motor. I almost missed it. Not that it would have made any difference if I had, I guess. We still got hit."

"It could have been a lot worse," he said. "We had enough time to get the hanger bay doors at least partially shut and there was only one missile fired."

"Yeah. I guess. But if I'd seen it a minute earlier, maybe even thirty seconds before . . ." Her voice broke off and she looked over his head as if staring at something only she could see.

"A minute—we could have gotten the doors closed all the way if we'd had that long," he said unthinkingly. She recoiled as though he'd slapped her. "But there wasn't any way to, was there? I mean, it wasn't showing up on radar or anything, I heard."

"No. That's why we have lookouts. But still—it was there. Like I said, if I'd seen it earlier, things might have been different."

"Yeah, and if we were off the coast of Florida, it wouldn't be so damn hot," he said.

Her head snapped up, eyes suspicious, as though she suspected he might be making fun of her. He continued, hurrying. "From what I hear, most people wouldn't have seen it all. The first we would have known about it was taking a missile in the gut. But the way it did go down, we had the fire crew on scene and we were able to contain it before it spread to any of the aircraft. The warning we did get made the difference between being out of commission for a long time and taking a little hit. That's what I meant."

Her face was still hard, but he thought he saw a slight softening around her eyes. "I keep wondering what would have happened if I paid more attention," she said quietly.

"Could you have?" he asked, aware of the tremendous risk he was taking.

She shut her eyes, squeezing them shut as though reliving the incident. "Maybe."

"No. I don't think so. And if you keep thinking like that, you're just going to screw everything up. You'll be thinking about that, and you will miss the next one. You weren't slacking off—and you know it." He made his voice as hard as her expression.

She opened her eyes the slightest bit. "You seem to think you know a lot about me."

He nodded, the feeling of certainty settling on him. "Yeah, I think I do. You don't look like the type to screw around while you're on watch. Did anyone tell you that you should've done a better job, seen it earlier?"

"No. Actually . . ." She hesitated for moment, a blush coloring her cheeks. "The captain told me I did a good job. He transferred me to engineering just like I wanted."

"Well, there you go. The captain, he's been in the Navy how long? Twenty-four, maybe twenty-five years? And he told you you did a good job and you don't want to believe it? Well, I know who I believe."

She considered him for moment, then stuck out her hand. "Andrea Smith."

He took her hand in his, feeling the small, delicate bones, the silky skin over them. "Gary Williams. Nice to meet you again."

"Williams?" Then her expression did relax. She laughed, even. "I heard about you and the fire. Somebody said—"

A new voice broke in. "Hey, you two lovebirds want to move ahead?" Williams looked up and saw that the line had already reached the stacks of trays. They'd been edging forward as they'd talked, but a gap was developing between them and the people in front of them.

"Oh, boy," she said, taking a tray and handing him one. "It either looks better than usual or I'm starving."

Williams followed her through the line, barely paying attention to what was put on his tray. It might be galley food, but he had a feeling this was going to the best meal he'd had in a long time.

SEVEN

Hank Greenfield was hungry, tired, and a damned sight colder than the weather warranted. He was wearing a lightly insulated jacket, as were the other FBI agents clustered around him. But the chill in his bones came from inside, a cold, clear warning signal he'd learned long ago not to ignore. There was something very wrong about this mission, and his body was reacting to it as though it was a threat to self-preservation.

Greenfield had joined the FBI fifteen years ago, following two tours in the Army. Despite his military experience, he'd come out with a strong belief in his country in general and law enforcement in particular. With his college degree in military justice and his test scores, he'd been accepted on his first application. He began his career with several tours in field offices, working on every type of case from breaking up drug rings to organized crime and kidnapping. It was on his last case as a junior agent, the kidnapping of the three-year-old daughter of a wealthy oil tycoon, that he began to experience the first glimmers of doubt about the FBI way of life.

The kidnappers had been clear—and to Greenfield's mind, entirely serious. The money was to be delivered or the girl would die.

He'd watched dumbfounded at the political maneuverings that had taken place over what to do. The father, who had insisted on calling in the FBI over the mother's protest, supported the FBI plan to nab the kidnappers at the pickup. If the girl wasn't with them, they would force whoever they got to lead them back to her. Everything would be, the agents assured the father, all right. They had used this tactic countless times.

What the father had not asked, but the mother had, was how many times it had worked. Greenfield had watched the senior agent dodge the question, offering soothing remarks about the mother's state of mind, the horrible tragedy of it all, and advising her to leave it all in their hands. Reluctantly, and only at the insistence of the father, she had acquiesced.

What they had not reckoned on were the kidnappers' political leanings. One was a former employee at the father's business, mentally unstable at best, psychotic at worst. The FBI had nabbed the pickup man, who led them back to the house where they were holding the girl. But by the time they'd arrived, both the girl and her other captor were dead. The small crumpled body with its throat covered with hard black bruises was never far from Greenfield's thoughts.

Why think about that now? He tried to shake the memory off, to concentrate on the operation at hand, but her face kept intruding on his thoughts. Maybe it was the house—yes, that was it. The house where they'd finally tracked her down bore an uncanny resemblance to Smarts' home. Both were isolated, small white buildings with mountains in the background. The only difference was that Kyle Smart's home looked a good deal better kept than the other one had.

It wasn't that he disagreed with mounting a raid on the Smart residence. At least, not in principle. The militia groups rising up around the United States were almost as much a

threat to national security as the possibility of a foreign terrorist act. Drug dealers, child pornography peddlers, and domestic terrorists, they were all the same to him.

But however much he might agree in principle, as a law-
enforcement action, this mission was something entirely different from any he'd ever been involved with. Operating
under the direction of the new Homeland Security policy,
and given what was probably domestic terrorism in post-
September 11th America, the HSD had decided to take preemptive action. Greenfield knew that the power struggle
going on in Washington right now was driving part of the
decision to act. The Homeland Security folks were growing
increasingly insistent that all domestic law-enforcement
agencies should be under their command, including the FBI.
The FBI, for its part, was adamantly opposed to being drawn
in under the broad HSD umbrella. Having outsiders peering
into their private files and their carefully developed informants and sources, changing procedures and practices that had
served them so well for decades, was anathema. The FBI
needed to be what it thought it was—a lean, mean crime-
fighting machine. No matter that layers of bureaucracy and
political battling had always been part of its culture, being
supervised by Homeland Security was far worse than anything the FBI had ever dreamed up itself.

"Everybody straight on the plan?" Greenfield asked, surveying the faces around him. They were in camouflage, with
masks of paint and fabric, and each was armed with an automatic weapon.

One by one, they nodded their readiness. Greenfield cast
around for some reason to delay the inevitable, but there was
no help for it.

Intel supporting this operation was far too skimpy for his
tastes. Greenfield had a hard-won law degree, earned at night
at the University of Columbia. Many agents did, but he had
the feeling that he took his a good deal more seriously than
others. Evidence, probable cause—for most agents, these
were artificial barriers to doing the right thing. To Greenfield,

the successful preparation of the case was far more important.

He ran through the evidence—if you could dignify the meager collection of facts with that name. A few confidential informants, one whose information had proved to be reliable in the past. Some intercepted e-mails, Kyle Smart's visits to subversive Web sites, and what sounded like a few hastily spoken political opinions. Hardly sufficient, in Greenfield's mind, to justify what they were planning.

But the decision wasn't yours, was it? You do what you're told, just like a good little soldier.

But I'm not a good little soldier. Regardless of what they think, this isn't the military. And okay, maybe I take my membership more seriously than most of them do.

Above your pay grade. Get on with it.

"All right. Positions, everyone. Wait for the go signal." More nods of agreement. Greenfield had no doubts about his team. Most of them were experienced field agents, and the ones who weren't were paired with senior agents. It was the people who had sent them here that worried him.

Five minutes later, a series of clicks on his headset indicated that everyone was in place. Drawing in a deep breath, fighting down his doubts, Greenfield whispered, "Now."

Bull Run, Idaho
0315 local (GMT −7)

Kyle heard the dog bark once, a sharp, warning sound, followed by a low growl. The flap covering the dog door made a small scratching noise, and then the dog padded quietly into the bedroom.

Kyle reached for the rifle. He put his hand on Betsy's mouth to wake her and whispered, "Get the kids."

Betsy's eyes went wide with alarm, but she nodded. She slid out from under the covers, pulled a .45 pistol from under the mattress, and moved quietly down the hall to the kids' rooms.

Now that he was fully awake, Kyle could hear the noises that had alerted the dog. Small sounds like an inexperienced man trying to move silently, an almost inaudible clink of metal on metal. For just an instant, he wondered what unit would tolerate such sloppiness.

He slipped on his shoes, crouching down to avoid being outlined in the window. The dog followed. In the hall, the door that led down to the basement was just closing behind Betsy and the kids. Better that they remain below, out of the line of fire.

What the hell is happening? I can't believe it—no, this isn't real. I'm dreaming.

The Rottweiler muttered a low warning growl. Not a dream. All too real.

I'll just walk out and deal with them. There's obviously some sort of misunderstanding—something we can clear up right away. Hell, it's probably the boys playing a trick on me, anyway. For just a moment, Kyle considered that possibility.

The Rottweiler growled again. He waited.

To Kyle's right, a front window shattered. Something hit the floor, then rolled, followed by a hissing noise.

Tear gas! Dear God, it's real!

Kyle ran to the kitchen and grabbed a dish towel. He wet it down and held it against his nose and mouth. The Rottweiler's growl turned to a whimper as the tear gas enveloped the room.

Another canister, the metallic gleam noticeable even in the faint moonlight leaking through the curtains. Kyle coughed, the wet towel helping some but not enough.

"FBI with a search warrant!" a loudspeaker blared out. "Open the door slowly, and come out with your hands up!"

Kyle tried to answer, but every time he opened his mouth the gas forced its way into his lungs. His eyes were watering so badly he could barely see. Beside him, the Rottweiler was moaning, writhing in its skin.

"You've got until I count to five," the voice said. "One."

Kyle stumbled through the living room, headed for the

front door. He heard the short, distinctive noise of a round being chambered in a shotgun. If he set foot outside the door, they would kill him. Coughing hard now, he waited.

"Two."

The back door burst open at the same time the front one did. Men looking like bugs clad in gas masks swarmed into the room, black silhouettes with fluorescent yellow FBI letters on the backs.

"Drop the gun!" one shouted, his voice distorted by the gas mask. "Put it down. Now!"

Kyle stumbled and fell forward, keeping his hold on his rifle. He hit the ground, his finger inside the trigger guard, and the gun discharged.

"Three, four, five."

Kyle had just a split second to realize how fatal his error was before the man opened fire.

"Hold fire!" the voice shouted, commanding. "Fall back, regroup." The men pulled back, and the man who'd shouted advanced to check Kyle's body. "Get some windows open and get this area cleared out." He turned to other men. "The computer—don't touch it. The rest of the team is on its way in."

Suddenly, the lace curtains framing the front window burst into flames. The man swore, and another darted over to put it out. But the flames consumed the thin fabric and, fanned by the breeze from the open windows, jumped to the couch, then the carpet and the rest of the furniture. Before they could even begin to control it, the room was an inferno.

"Pull back!"

They retreated, swearing, not entirely sure who'd given the order, but recognizing the futility of trying to fight the fire. There was no chance that the local rural fire department could deal with this, not as quickly as it was spreading.

Greenfield was the last man out of the building. He staggered, coughing up the last of the tear gas as he crouched on the ground. In his brief glimpse of the interior of the house, Greenfield had seen nothing to confirm the reports that this man was a renegade leader. Nothing at all.

I told them not to do it this way, not to plan a commando-type strike, not the kind that had gone wrong so often enough in the past. But no—somebody at the top had decided that this was going to be a demonstration, that this would be the one arrest that made the rest of them sit up and take notice.

The noise increased as the flames consumed the structure. But even over the roar of the fire, Greenfield could hear the thin screams start from the basement.

Four hundred yards away, Special Agent A. J. Bratton watched the fire race out of control through the small house. He was too far away to hear the screams himself, but his directional microphone aimed at the scene picked up the shouts of the agents trying to brave the flames and the anguish in Greenfield's voice in the intercepted phone calls demanding local firefighting assistance. Bratton stayed in position until he was certain he understood what had happened, then moved silently through the trees and brush to clear the area. Five minutes later, there was no trace of his extended surveillance on the Smart house.

There couldn't be. After all, the CIA had no jurisdiction inside the United States. There was no reason for Bratton or the CIA to even be involved.

Yet.

EIGHT

The President kept his handwritten scribbles jotted down on election night in the top left-hand drawer of his desk. Although they were barely legible, the increasing disorganization reflecting his state of mind that night, he could still recite every number by heart. Looking at each stroke of the pencil, he relived his feelings of the moment when that state's electoral votes were tallied.

His mood swings were reflected in the scribbles: the broad, bold, and exuberant tally of California's electoral votes, the dejected abbreviations trailing off as North Dakota and Idaho went to his opponent. And then, the state that had sent him over the edge to victory—Texas—written in almost incomprehensible scrawls of large letters suitable to the size of the state. Over and over again he had written the name, waiting for the number, and finally putting a big circle around it at the very moment Dan Rather announced the projected results.

It had all been over then. Sure, the projected results could have been wrong, but they weren't usually. Ever since the Bush Gore debacle, the networks had been exceedingly cautious about announcing any information that might keep last-minute voters away from the polls.

Texas. Who would have thought? They were joking that TX was just my shorthand for tax, and I guess that's not going to be far from the truth.

The cost of increased domestic security was mounting daily. Even his Homeland Defense Secretary, confident though he might be in public, was worried. Maintaining security in an open society was virtually impossible, and over the last few years they had begun to realize the full extent of the problem. Sure, there had been a decent start made on the problem, but he could not escape the feeling it was more for show than effect.

Every day, he glanced at the scribbles, letting them remind him of those moments when he had been certain he would not be reelected, of the odd, unsettling feeling that in just a few hours he might become a lame-duck President, and just months after that an ordinary, mortal civilian, deprived of all the trappings of power and perks that came with this office.

But that fate had been averted, and here he was, a better President than he'd been last term. He felt an increased freedom in his choices, free from the constraints of considering what effect his actions might have on public opinion, free to do what he thought best for the country regardless of public opinion and considerations of reelection.

There had been a time not so many months ago when he'd fallen into that trap, of contemplating the political fallout from his decisions. That he'd let himself be caught up in that chafed even now.

"Mr. President?" His Chief of Staff stood at the door, holding another scrap of paper. Were all great decisions made in this way, all important news scribbled notes on the backs of envelopes or on memo pads?

"Yes, Jim?"

"There's been an incident, sir. The FBI, conducting a takedown at Bull Run in Idaho. Four fatalities, Mr. President. A man, his wife, and two children."

"They shot children?" A chill swept through him. The worst scenario possible—dead children, shot by federal agents.

But looking at his Chief of Staff's face, he knew he was wrong. Knew he was wrong and that the truth would be even worse.

"No, sir. The tear-gas canisters—there was a fire, sir. The woman and the children were hiding in the basement and were trapped. They—it will take some time to identify the bodies, but we're pretty certain who they are. There's not much left."

A groan escaped his lips involuntarily. Children, burning. "How old?"

"Eight and four."

The President slumped back in his chair. The sheer insanity and tragedy of it overwhelmed him. Children, dead in a fire. A fire caused by his agents.

"There's more, sir," his Chief of Staff continued doggedly. "The agents weren't in the house long, just long enough to seize his computer and a few other items before the fire broke out. But from what they've been able to determine so far, sir, he wasn't the man they were looking for."

"What!" The President slammed his hands down on his desk, now outraged. "We killed children and it's not even the right man?"

The Chief of Staff stood silent. One of his roles in the Administration was to absorb any initial flack, calming the President down so that he could decide what his public move would be. He knew that none of what would follow was directed at him.

"Get Bratton over here," the President shouted. "I want to see that son of a bitch standing tall in front of my desk within the next ten minutes. Ten minutes, do you hear? Ten minutes or I'll have his head!"

"Ten minutes, sir." The Chief of Staff left and closed the door quietly behind him.

He would give it five minutes, he decided, before he went back into the Oval Office. A few moments for the President to collect his thoughts and decide what his next move would be. Bratton was still on his way back from Idaho, but the

President wouldn't want to hear that. Best to wait until he calmed down just a bit.

In the Oval Office, the President buried his face in his hands. He had three children of his own, and the thought of anything happening to them, particularly such an inconceivable horror, was simply beyond contemplation. And it had happened because of something his people did—no, he couldn't face it. Not right this second.

Eventually he would. He had not survived the last four years, nor would he survive the coming term, by succumbing to raw emotion, no matter how painful. The simple fact was that when he made decisions, people died. Sometimes the enemy, sometimes his own troops.

And now his own civilian citizens.

Terrorism had to be stopped. With all the resources this nation had, there was no excuse for not being able to execute a mission without such tragic results. Something had gone badly wrong, and he intended to find out what it was. He pulled open the upper-right drawer and looked at the slip of paper again. The letters TX stared back at him, and for some reason that led him to think of a certain retired Naval officer—an admiral at that—who had a reputation for being able to get things done: Tombstone Magruder, on the pointy end of the spear in so many conflicts overseas. Now that he was a civilian, how would he feel about operating inside his own country?

But why the Magruders? Why any civilians at all? He didn't know why it seemed so important that they be involved, but he had long since learned to trust such strong intuitions.

Four minutes had elapsed since he had sent his Chief of Staff out of the office, and he was beginning to calm himself, dividing the problem into the compartments inside his mind that he could examine at will. He stretched, stood, and walked to the door. He opened it and called out, "Jim?"

The Chief of Staff was standing nearby, and immediately came over. The President felt an entirely inappropriate flash of amusement. *Am I so predictable?*

"Sir, Mr. Bratton is on his way back from Idaho right now. It will be a few more hours until he lands."

The President said, "Track down the two Magruders, wherever they are. Work it out so that the Magruders are here before Bratton. Any questions?"

"No, Mr. President."

"Sir, Senator Hamlin is calling," one of the secretaries said, directing her announcement at the Chief of Staff. In addition to screening the staff from his boss's raw emotions, the Chief of Staff also served to screen the President from those who felt they had a claim on his time.

The President groaned. "The last thing I need." Ben Hamlin, the Senior Senator from Idaho, had been one of the President's most vocal opponents during the election.

"I'll take it," the Chief of Staff said, heading for his own office.

"No," the President said wearily. "I'll have to talk to him sooner or later. Better sooner, so he doesn't have a chance to go spouting off that I'm stonewalling him."

The Chief of Staff hesitated. "Are you sure, Mr. President? Perhaps we should take a few minutes to work out a statement."

The President shook his head. "No. I know what I'm going to say to him. It's his state, Jim. He's got a right to talk to me right now."

The President went back into his office and stared at the phone for a moment before touching the flashing number-one button and picking up the receiver. "Hello, Senator. What can I do for you?"

The flat mountain tones were clearly audible, and sometimes the President suspected that the Senator intentionally deepened his accent. "I'm calling about this outrage, Mr. President. I just heard the most horrendous story from my staff, and I—"

"Come over and see me, Senator," the President said quietly. "Off the record—no announcements. No photo opportunities, no noise. Just get over here so we can figure out what happened. I'll give you full access to everything we know."

There was a moment of silence on the line; then the Senator said, "All right. I'll be there, sir. And I hope you have better answers than the ones I'm getting right now."

The phone went dead. The president felt a flash of rage. *So he thinks he can just hang up on me, does he?* For a moment, he was tempted to let the Senator cool his heels in the outer office once he arrived to show him where the power was around the White House. He dismissed the thought as quickly as it occurred to him.

His Chief of Staff came back and said, "Sir, I found the Magruders at their office. They're on their way over right now."

"Stall them," the President said. He smiled a brief, wintry smile, aware of the incongruity of demanding that they dance attendance on him and then putting them in a holding pattern. But this was the White House—what was considered common courtesy in other parts of Washington was not an issue. They would understand. "Apologize to the Magruders for me and stash them somewhere that Hamlin won't see them. Once I pour some oil on the water, I'll let them ignite it."

Pamela Drake's home
0921 local (GMT −5)

Pamela Drake was suffering from a severe case of jet lag. As a result, when the call came in, she was still at home, staring bleakly at her second cup of coffee and seriously contemplating calling in sick. It was an option, sure. Most of the reporters did it routinely the day after they returned from an assignment halfway around the world. But Pamela had built a reputation around being the toughest of them all, and had never taken advantage of that. Maybe it was time to start.

The call came in on her cell phone, on the number she gave out only to certain people. It was the one she answered before all others, the ring at which she broke off whatever she was doing in order to take the call.

Adrenaline surged through her as she grabbed the phone and touched the top button. Drake," she announced.

"Idaho," said the voice. "It's going to make Ruby Ridge looked like a picnic. Bull Run, way up on the Canadian border. You better get there."

"What happened?" she asked, grabbing a pencil and a piece of paper.

"The FBI had the bright idea that they were taking down a master criminal. Only it turns out he was a nobody. In the process, the guy gets shot and his wife and kids trapped in a burning house. There's some speculation that the fire was set to cover up the lack of evidence. A. J. Bratton was there."

Bratton! Holy shit. Why was the CIA involved in a domestic operation? "Were you there?" she asked, her fingers moving automatically to jot down notes.

There was a long silence. She tried again. "Come on, now—that's not a tough question."

Still no answer.

"We're off the record, you know. As far off as we can go," she reassured her caller.

"We're talking about Idaho," the voice said finally. "That's inside the United States."

"I know that," she said. "And I also know—"

"No," the voice said, cutting her off. "Not on this line."

"OK, then. What else?"

"Nothing. You'll have to get the rest of it somewhere else. I'm just paying back a favor." The line went dead.

Drake swore quietly as she touched the top button and slipped the phone back in its battery charger. Sure, she understood his reluctance to say anything on an open line. Cell phone frequencies were easy to monitor, and there were too many new government programs that searched for key words and phrases in every conversation that floated across the atmosphere.

Without her informant admitting that he was there, the report was suspect. But if there were anything to it, it would be breaking soon. Drake had no illusions about how much of a head start she had.

She stared at the phone for a moment, her gut telling her that this was something big. Regardless of how intra-agency cooperation was touted as a good thing, there was no way that any Congressional oversight committee would ever countenance the CIA conducting operations inside the continental U.S.

So it had to be an FBI operation. Mentally, she ran through her list of contacts there, selected one, and dialed the number from memory.

Five minutes later, Drake had all the confirmation she needed. Her two best sources at the FBI weren't talking. Indeed, they weren't even taking her calls. Even the prearranged code name she'd used, the one that signaled that it really was in their best interest to get on the telephone and talk to her to prevent the release of certain sordid details she knew about their past, even that had not worked.

Something big is going down. I can feel it—I know it.

She punched in the number of her boss at ACN, tapping impatiently on her breakfast room table as she waited. The last vestige of jet lag had been gone for several minutes now, and she felt like her old self. The nuclear furnace was burning in the pit of her stomach again, every newshound instinct screaming at her to move, get off her ass, and beat the competition.

When her boss finally answered, she said, "I'm going to Idaho. Fly the camera crew to the capital, whatever the hell it is." She tried to remember. She could name the capital of every obscure nation in the world, but it had been so long since she'd reported a domestic story that she found herself groping to even localize Idaho on a map.

"Butte," Harbaugh said. "What have you got?"

"I've got a confirmed report that an FBI action in Bull Run, Idaho, went down and went down hard. Four civilians, including two kids, are dead, and my sources tell me that the Feebies got the wrong people. Have a camera crew and tech support meet me at Dulles with my tickets. I'll call you when I know something."

She clicked off, knowing that every rudeness or lack of manners would be forgiven in the chase for the story. And regardless of how much he might dislike her high-handed manner, her boss would feel the same way. There would be a camera crew waiting for her, and probably an entire backup team from the local affiliate as well. And somewhere along the way, there would be a low-level eager national reporter to stand by her side and feed her trivial details. Starting with what the hell the capital of the state really was.

NINE

As Abraham Carter listened to the voice on the other end of the phone call, he felt his blood pressure start to go up. Gus Anderson, a farmer in Bull Run who'd contacted him the week before about Free American Now, was claiming there'd been an abortion of an FBI raid on a neighbor's farm. No one had seen the family since then, and smoke still stained the air from the vicinity of the Smart homestead. All the roads leading to or near the Smart farm were blockaded by civilians—if that's what they really were. A neighbor in the National Guard had been ordered to report to the armory with gear packed for a two-week "exercise," but according to Anderson, there'd been none of the normal pre-exercise preparation there.

"Jackson," Abraham shouted. "Get your ass in here and pick up the extension. Now Gus, you were right to call me. I want you to start over again from the beginning."

His son, Jackson, ambled into the room from the kitchen and flopped down on a couch. Without comment, he picked up the other phone and listened to Anderson retell the story. His face remained impassive, even when Anderson's voice choked as he described the Smarts' children. After Anderson hung up, reassured by the senior Carter that they'd get to the bottom of it, Jackson rolled into a sitting position.

"Feds killing people again," his father muttered, his gaze staring off in the distance. "I told you, boy. It's coming to a head real soon."

"And about time," Jackson said, his voice soft and deadly.

As outraged as he was, Abraham was disturbed by something in Jackson's tone. He glanced over at his son, wondering again what combination of genes between him and Nellie had produced such an enigma.

Physically, Jackson resembled his father more than his mother. He was tall, almost an inch taller than his father at six feet two inches, and built along the same lanky, rambling lines. His beard and hair were a shade darker than his father's, picking up an almost blue-black sheen that he'd inherited from his mother. His eyes were all Nellie, though. Ice-green, flat, and unreadable, unlike his father's own dark brown ones that burned with passion.

But even if you could trace out the source of his son's physical characteristics that wasn't what bothered Abraham. It was the boy's mind. Not that he was dumb—far from it. If anything, he had more sheer raw mental ability than either his father or his mother, and Abraham was no slouch in the brains department himself. Formerly employed as a chemical engineer for a large household products company, Abraham had excelled at analytical chemistry and synthesis. He was particularly keen on coming up with new ways to combine existing products to create another one that did pretty much the same stuff but could be relabeled as a new product.

Abraham had survived for ten years in the corporate world, and had had a fairly good career for a Ph.D. He had been headed for a slot as manager of his own product line, and he and Nellie had been living the good life. Jackson had been just a little tyke, no more than six or seven years old, when Abraham's world collapsed.

Nellie got sick, and nobody could figure out what was wrong with her. What started abruptly transitioned into a long, lingering illness during which she gradually went downhill as one by one her bodily functions shut down. Finally, she was little more than a husk of flesh, barely aware of where she was or anybody around her. Abraham had been frantic for a diagnosis, anything. If they knew what it was, he had the feeling he could bring his analytical chemistry abilities to bear on the problem and single-handedly save her.

But the best the doctors could come up with was environmental poisoning. For some reason, her liver had stopped processing out the toxins she absorbed from food, water, and even the air she breathed. They accumulated, gradually destroying tissue in all her major organs. Finally, as her kidneys began shutting down, it was simply too much for her body.

When she died, Abraham was devastated, Jackson only slightly less so. Nellie had been the center of both of their worlds, and when she was gone they found they had little in common. Abraham began to suspect that part of the problem had been chemicals of the products that he himself was responsible for. How could he have been so blind, to look away from the consequences of what he was doing? Sure, he'd read the warning labels—even helped to write them. But he never, ever allowed himself to contemplate what the cumulative effect of all his chemicals on a susceptible body might be.

When the realization finally came, Abraham left his position at the company, cashed in his 401(k) plan, and headed for the mountains. He bought a stretch of land with a small cabin on it and began raising his own crops and animals. He hunted year-round, providing a steady stream of meat for the table, and he stored vegetables from the growing season in a root cellar. He lost himself in the mindless hard work required to keep his small spread going.

Jackson, at first, had had a harder time of it. Plucked from an upper-middle-class existence in the suburbs and transplanted into an alien world, he'd lashed out at his father. His mother was gone and nothing in his life made sense anymore. And, in his anger, he began looking for answers. Abraham struggled to keep the boy under control, but there were increasingly frequent incidents of vandalism, failing grades, and the beginnings of drug use.

It was Abraham's quest for a program that could help him deal with Jackson that had led him to the Free America Now militia. At first, he thought they were primarily a social service agency with a good healthy dose of discipline and structure. Later on, as he found that their more privately held views reflected his own disillusionment with corporate American culture, he knew he'd found a home.

Jackson, too. He hooked up with boys tougher and stronger than he was who showed him the ropes. At first, Abraham was a bit uneasy about their influence on them, but when the destructive impulses and rages at first dwindled and then ceased, he could only be relieved.

In the last year, though, he'd come to understand that his reprieve from worrying about his son had been only temporary. Abraham was active in the organization—Jackson was a fanatic. His son embraced all of the values, and then extended his political opinions into what smacked of racism.

Over the years, Abraham had come to be a district commander for Free America Now. Jackson had risen to a leadership position as well, commanding a small company. They were everything that Kyle and Betsy Smart were not.

Jackson seemed frozen in place, his gaze locked on the TV. The flat, cold eyes betrayed nothing of his feelings. Finally, when the news anchor broke for a commercial, he turned to his father. "We don't have much choice, do we?"

"No, we don't," his father answered heavily. "Not this time."

"Where?"

"I don't know. The council will have to decide."

"I have a list of targets. And contingency plans. All worked out, Dad. Just waiting for the word."

And if anything, that was only the tip of the iceberg of things that disturbed Abraham about Jackson. His son was a violent man, seeming to take pleasure in the physical confrontations involved. But he was a thoughtful violent man, if such a thing existed. He sought out opportunities for violence and planned methodically and carefully for larger-scale operations. The one characteristic in all of his plans was that they were calculated to wreak maximum devastation among a civilian population.

Jackson's cold eyes stayed locked on his father. "You know we can—I can—get away with it." *This time* was the unspoken addition to the statement.

Abraham forced a commanding note into his voice. "You wait for orders. That clear?"

Jackson nodded. But as his enigmatic son turned his gaze back to the television, Abraham knew a moment of despair.

TEN

Smith, Williams discovered, was a woman of meticulous habits. Indeed, everything about her was meticulous—her uniform, her hair, and even the way she ate. He felt like a big, bumbling oaf next to her, his own massive hands clumsy as he watched her delicate ones pick a few remaining grapes out of her fruit salad. Even her daily routine on board the ship was orderly. When he'd found out that she always ate lunch late, he made a point of being there just a few minutes before her whenever he could. At first, he tried to tell himself that she would just think he was as well organized as she was, but he soon realized that she was on to him.

Not that she seemed to mind. The experience they had in common of being on different ends of the fire had formed a bond between them. More and more, he found himself admiring her for how she'd reacted, what she had done, and the determination she brought to her new duties inside the engineering department. Not that he understood everything she talked about. A lot of the mechanical stuff was over his head. Still, she seemed to enjoy explaining the intricacies of pumps and engines to him, and never made him feel stupid.

For his own part, he found she knew surprisingly little about aircraft, and he was delighted to share his passion for aviation and his growing technical expertise with her. She never seemed to be bored, although he could tell she failed to understand his fascination with flying.

"Maybe someday I'll go to OCS and be a pilot," he said, watching her as he did so. "Wouldn't that be something?" It was a dream he often entertained, but had not shared with anyone. Aspiring to being an officer was like being the smart kid in high school—you took too much flack from everyone. The fact that he even cared what other people said about him bothered him. He had a feeling it would never bother her.

"I've thought the same thing," she said, precisely spearing a grape in the middle. "Not flying, of course." A dreamy look stole over her face. "I want to be like Captain Bethlehem over on *Jeff*. Maybe command an aircraft carrier."

"Captain Bethlehem is an aviator," he pointed out. "You have to be to command an aircraft carrier."

Her eyes widened slightly at that, and he realized she had not known it. "A destroyer, then," she said calmly. "A ship—I don't care what kind. Any kind."

"The other ships are just our escorts."

She glared at him. "Escorts that the carrier can't be deployed without. Besides, I think it'd be neat, being on a smaller ship. In here, you might as well be working in an office building. I still get lost when I have to go somewhere new."

"I know what you mean." They chowed down in silence for several minutes. Williams went over his plan again. "Hey, are you going to the movie tonight?" he asked, his voice determinedly casual.

"Maybe. What is it? One of those slasher films again?"

"No. *Harry Potter*. I saw it a long time ago but it was pretty good."

"Oh, me, too! I love that movie." A smile spread across her face, then turned into a frown. "Except I have a mid-watch. If I don't get some sleep, I'll be dragging."

"You can sleep when you're dead," he said, repeating what a chief had told him a few weeks ago when he yawned in his presence. That startled her, and he continued. "Meet me down here at nineteen hundred. I'll even buy you a Coke. And we could get some popcorn out of the vending machine."

She stared him for a moment, an odd expression on her face. "You wouldn't be asking me out on a date, would you? Because you know that's not allowed on the ship."

He flushed. "No, of course not. We're friends, right?"

She didn't answer, just continued to stare at him. Finally, when he was starting to feel like a complete idiot, she said, "Sure. Only make it a little before seven, OK? I hate to stand in line."

The White House
1100 local (GMT −5)

The two Magruders waited in an office down the hallway from the Oval Office. Even though they'd both been here countless times, Tombstone always felt a stunning sense of humility at being summoned by the President. No matter that some individuals who had inhabited the historic building had shown themselves to be unworthy of the highest office in the land. No matter that party politics was never far from anyone's mind. This was still the White House, the embodiment of every dream and vision of America, the seat of power in the most powerful nation in the world. To be a part of those decisions, to walk these halls and advise the President, remained a rare honor for both of them.

"Sorry to keep you waiting," the Chief of Staff said as he stepped into the office. "The President would like to see you now." No apology for the two-hour wait was tendered and none was expected. The Magruders stood and followed him down the hall. Ahead of them, they saw a lean figure hurrying away. "Senator Hamlin," the COS confided. "The President will explain."

The President stood and walked around the desk to meet them in the middle of the room. "Thank you for coming." He motioned them to a comfortable seating arrangement away from the desk. A steward silently set a tray of coffee before them, then left, closing the door behind him. The Secret Service agents seemed to fade into the background.

"I have a serious problem," the President began, "one I hope you can help me solve." He outlined the events in Bull Run, pain in his voice as he mentioned the Smart children. "It's a major tragedy, one that should never have happened." The Magruders, still absorbing the details, murmured their agreements.

"My problem," the President continued, "is that I'm not sure what went wrong. You'd think after the intelligence fiasco surrounding 9/11, we'd have sorted the information flow out. Homeland Security Defense was supposed to have been the answer, but I don't think it's working. Not yet, anyway. The CIA and the FBI . . ." He paused, studying their faces for a moment, then nodded, evidently pleased by what he saw there. "No. I don't have to tell you about intelligence and territoriality, do I? Neither of those esteemed agencies has particularly liked joining a new team. I won't say that they're being actively obstructive—I'd have their asses if I could prove it—but I do think that's part of the problem. Selective intelligence sharing—and it's not working."

"Fire both agency heads and start over," the senior Magruder said bluntly.

"I wish it were that easy. But then I'm left with new leadership awaiting Senate confirmation, and I can't have that right now."

"Why not now?" Tombstone asked.

"The militias," the President answered. "Something like this happens and they go on full alert. We show any weakness right now and we're inviting another Wounded Knee or Waco."

"Do you have any evidence that they're planning something?"

"Enough to worry me," the President answered. "Which

brings me to the point. In the long run, HSD is going to be the answer. Jeremiah Horton is a decent fellow—he'll do the right thing. But something like this, integrating forces that aren't used to working together—well, frankly, the military has more experience at it than the civilian agencies do. That's where you come in."

"How?" Tombstone asked.

The President sighed. "This is a new war, Tombstone. We're used to law-enforcement activities inside the U.S., not war. Everything is going to have to change—everything. Including posse commitatus."

"Wow," the senior Magruder said, abruptly setting down his coffee mug. "That's a big step."

"No kidding," the President answered. "The concept of using military forces for law enforcement inside the U.S. is strictly prohibited. And I'm not going to get the law changed without proving that it's the right thing to do. So, I'm going to back-door a demonstration. I'm going to use your civilian company as a coordinator, and I'm going to ask you to draft contingency plans for a multiforce mission using both civilian law-enforcement and military assets. Your mission is to be prepared to put down any militia actions taken in response to this tragedy. You have my full authority and the support of the entire government as needed."

Both Magruders were silent for a moment, absorbing the radical idea. Then Tombstone asked, "Is there any precedent at all for this?"

The President shook his head. "You know the old saying. It's easier to ask forgiveness than permission. If the militias *are* up to something and you do stop it, then there'll be precedent."

"And if we don't?"

The President's face was cold. "Then there's always impeachment. And frankly, gentlemen, if that's what it takes to get us through this, I'm prepared to risk it."

USS United States
1800 local (GMT +3)

For the next few hours, Williams checked his watch every five minutes, wondering why time was moving so slowly. She always got to the chow line five minutes early—did that means she wanted to be five minutes early for the movie? Or earlier than that so they could make sure they got some popcorn? Finally, not wanting to leave it to chance, he slipped out and bought a box of microwavable popcorn at the ship store. Just in case she wanted more than one pack. Or in case there was another movie she wanted to see.

His aircraft was coming back from a routine surveillance patrol, and he had to be on deck after it landed, so he missed seeing her at the evening meal. He hurried through the post-flight checklist, made sure the bird was secure and all tie-downs were in place, then rushed down six decks to the vending machine. There was already a long line there.

He heard her call his name, and spotted her near the entrance to the galley. She held up two sodas. He slipped out of line to join her. He produced the popcorn.

She looked happy. "It looks like we're set." She led the way to the microwave, and they waited behind three other people to use it.

Finally, they were set. Again, he let her lead the way, and she selected a table about three quarters of the way back from the screen along a bulkhead. He slipped into the seat next to hers. The noise level in the galley was deafening, but abruptly died down as the lights dimmed and opening music started. "Just in time," she whispered, grabbing a handful of popcorn out of the bag.

She just looks like a kid. For some reason, he found that particularly appealing. Her gaze was fixed on the screen, her lips slightly parted and moist, spellbound by the opening credits. He helped himself to some popcorn, and over the next two hours, found that he was watching her as much as the movie. And he was quite certain which one he enjoyed more.

USS United States
2100 local (GMT +3)

Lance Corporal Barry Griffin was barely conscious of his
surroundings. Sometimes he was on field exercises in Alaska,
because that was the last time he remembered being cold, so
very cold. Other times, he knew he was on the ship, especially when the smell of food woke him. He came to recognize the few faces he saw—the corpsman, Evans, who he
dimly remembered from the galley, one of the nurses. The
doctors stayed so briefly and were so heavily masked that he
never formed a clear picture of their faces.

A fever, that's what it was, he finally realized. That was
the reason for the alternating hot and cold spells, the moments when it seemed certain he would suffocate in the overwhelming heat, those moments followed immediately by a
bone-chilling sweat as he threw back the blankets. At one
point he was caught in seaweed near the ocean floor, a re-
current dream during his dive training. He reached down for
his knife, but it hadn't been where it was supposed to be,
strapped on his leg. He jerked hard enough that the treach-
erous vegetation let loose of him, and he floated up to the
surface on a wave of morphine. The remnants of the seaweed
ran down his arm, and he was dimly aware of white shapes
moving around him. Fish? Or other divers? But why were
they in white? The prick of the IV needle being reinserted
in his arm went unnoticed. Later, when the morphine wore
off, he woke in pain to discover his arms tied to the railings
of his bed at the wrist and elbow.

"You were jerking around and pulled out your IV," the
corpsman said, patting him reassuringly on the shoulder.
"Standard procedure, just routine."

"Man, I feel like shit," Griffin murmured, exhausted by
the tremendous effort to speak.

"You've got the flu or something," the corpsman said quietly. "But they're getting it under control."

"The flu? Man, I feel like I'm dying." He drifted back off

into an unconsciousness that was not quite sleep.

The corpsman gazed down at him steadily, both pity and anger in his eyes. It wasn't the jarhead's fault, not really. He hadn't meant to contract a virus while ashore. If anybody was really at fault, it was the first sergeant, the guy who told Griffin to take off his clothes and shower down. They should've left their gear on until they got back to a safe area to become decontaminated, but the first sergeant had been so freaked by the possibility of bio weapons, he'd ignored his training and obeyed the compulsion to wash.

But maybe they would have been exposed anyway, even without that. There was no way to tell. It sure didn't make any sense to be pissed at the guy who was sick.

Yeah, you do feel like you're dying. That's because you are, buddy. They're not saying it but I can tell—you're getting supportive measures, some antibiotics—but it's not working. The fever's getting worse, and you're bleeding internally. Those red spots under your arm—they told me it was a bruise. Fat chance—like I believe that. It's petechia, subcutaneous bleeding you get when your platelets are crashing. Sooner or later, unless they can get a handle on this, you start bleeding and you don't stop. There are worse ways to go. I guess.

Over the last twenty-four hours, the fever had progressed rapidly. Nothing the doctors tried seemed to have any effect. Late-generation antibiotics were pumping full-steam into his system via three IVs, along with fluids to replace the lost blood and keep his blood pressure up. So far, they had been able to keep pace, but from what the corpsman could tell, the situation was getting worse. Unless he turned a corner soon, Griffin wasn't going to make it.

But I'm going to make it. Hell, I'm not sick and we're past the incubation period. No cramps, no headache—nothing. No fever. My blood counts look fine—did they really think I wouldn't read the chart that they leave in here?

Nevertheless, he and the first sergeant remained in isolation, with the rest of the men who'd been briefly exposed in the galley kept in a separate compartment. The first sergeant wasn't saying much, but the corpsman could see he was terrified. It was one thing to have an enemy you could reach out and touch, something you could train to defeat with weapons or superior physical force. It was another thing entirely to have something you couldn't even see kill you. Marines were among the worse patients anyway, but the first sergeant was too scared to cause any problems.

"How you feeling?" the corpsman asked. "You look OK."

"I'm fine." The first sergeant didn't bother to asking how *he* was, but the corpsman let it slide.

"If you were going to get sick it would have happened by now," the corpsman said, repeating what he had been saying for the last six hours. The first sergeant would never admit it, but the corpsman thought he took some comfort in the reassurances. "It hit him less than six hours after you guys came back. It's been six times that. This is just a safety precaution."

The first sergeant pointed at Griffin. "Safety precaution, with us stuck in here with with him?"

That was the one point the corpsman hadn't been able to figure out, either. If they really thought Griffin might have some sort of plaguelike disease, why would they leave anyone in the same room with him? There was only two conclusions: Either they thought what Griffin had was not contagious, or it was so serious that they were pretty sure neither the first sergeant or the corpsman would leave the isolation room alive.

The corpsman heard a small squeak, and turned around to see Griffin in a full-scale grand-mal seizure. His bed bucked violently as his massive body slammed against it, contracted into a sitting position, then slammed down again. One elbow restraint broke, then the wristband on the same arm. The IV popped loose, spewing a thin stream of liquid on the deck. Blood down ran down Griffin's arm. "Hold him down," the corpsman said, and darted to the head of the bed, trying to keep Griffin from striking his head against the bed railing.

"Hell, no," the first sergeant snapped. "Don't you ever

learn? That's what landed you a bed in here in the first place."

Finally, the convulsions subsided. Griffin lay limp and barely breathng on the sweat-stained sheets. The interior of the air-locked doors opened, and a doctor came in, hastily garbed.

Griffin's breathing took on an odd rhythm, and the corpsman felt his heart sink. Agonal breathing—the last stage before death. He glanced across at the doctor, and saw pity and understanding in her eyes. She shook her head solemnly.

Thirty minutes later, it was all over. Griffin took a long, shuddering breath, then simply stopped. The corpsman folded his hands peacefully on his chest.

The doctor said, "We'll try to move him as soon as we can. There are precautions we have to take. You understand."

"Yes, ma'am." She turned to look at the first sergeant. "If you were going to get sick, you would've done so by now. I'm going to move you to separate rooms, probably keep you in quarantine for another forty-eight hours. If you're showing no signs or symptoms after that, I'll consider releasing you." The first sergeant nodded his understanding, not looking at her, cowering in the corner.

The doctor turned to leave, then caught sight of the corpsman's hand. She grabbed his elbow, pulled him over to the sink, and dumped a bottle of hydrogen peroxide over his hand. He stared down, aghast, at the spatter of blood from the IV on his skin. "It's probably not transmitted by blood, whatever it is," she said.

He nodded, not believing her. Inhalation anthrax—okay, that's one that's not transmitted by contact. He tried to think of other examples, but his mind kept summoning up lists of diseases that *were* transmitted by blood. HIV, Ebola, the plague—just about anything. She was scrubbing his hand now with a small brush, scrubbing him as thoroughly as she would for surgery. When she finally finished, she rinsed his skin once again with hydrogen peroxide.

It's not transmitted by blood. It can't be. He stared after her as she left, hopeless.

ELEVEN

The White House
1230 local (GMT −5)

"Mr. President," the Director of Homeland Security said warmly, striding with confidence into the Oval Office. "Thank you for"—he caught sight of the man already seated in front of the President's desk, and finished, after a noticeable pause—"seeing me."

Jeremiah Horton was a large man who looked like the college linebacker he had been. He had a reputation as a gruff no-nonsense man, one who was more comfortable as a manager than as a leader. Like many men in the current Administration, he had had no military service. However, a distinguished career in the Senate had led to his appointment to the newly formed Homeland Security and Defense Office. He enjoyed the challenge of setting up the new cabinet-level post, and he prided himself on the exceptionally smooth integration of HSD with the rest of the President's Administration.

Nevertheless, the birth of HSD had not been without problems. Notably among them, the man he was now surprised to see. Carl Chassen, FBI director of operations, his counterpart—although a lesser rank, since his was not a Cabinet-level post—had been a continual thorn in his side. The FBI saw conspiracies everywhere. Most particularly now, they were focused on what they believed was a plot to strip the FBI of its powers in domestic law enforcement.

Publicly, HSD had repeatedly assured both the FBI and the public that nothing was further from the truth. HSD would merely serve as a clearinghouse, a coordinator of the various agencies having law-enforcement responsibilities within the U.S.

Privately, the struggle for control of domestic intelligence operations was another matter altogether. The FBI, the DEA, and the ATF all viewed every "coordinating policy" as an infringement on their territories. Each one guarded its turf jealously, sharing information with its sister agencies only when there was something they wanted in exchange or when they were forced to. In the last week, the situation had escalated, with the CIA treating a simple overture for cooperation of operations like a frontline assault. No matter that it had been a simple request for information coupled with an informal suggestion that HSD quite reasonably had an interest in those matters occurring overseas that were likely in the immediate future to affect the United States internally. No matter that the artificial boundaries created by legislation between the various agencies only serve to drain off resources that the fledgling HSD coveted. But last week, ah— that had been the kicker. The CIA, noting the HSD's growing stature within the Administration, seemed to have instituted a new policy of complete noncooperation. In at least one private conversation, the director of the CIA had blandly suggested that for security reasons it made more sense, in some situations originating overseas, for the CIA to be the lead agency when the action moved into the United States itself.

Horton had been outraged. The CIA's maneuver was clearly a grab for power, one that overstepped the bounds of its charter. The CIA was explicitly forbidden to have any role in domestic security. Yet here they were, suggesting that HSD was not to be trusted with highly classified and sensitive information developed from the CIA sources. No matter that everyone in HSD had undergone rigorous security screenings, and that their administrative procedures and security measures were modeled on the very best techniques now in use in other agencies. No, it was a daring move, but one that would fail. There was no way that the President would let the CIA assume control of any operations inside the United States.

The FBI, however, was another matter entirely. Horton knew that they were frothing at the mouth over HSD's charter role inside the United States. It was, the FBI had argued, the essence of *their* charter—law enforcement inside the United States, most particularly those matters that constituted crimes. And weren't *all* terrorist acts and preparation for them criminal acts? Why reinvent the wheel? The FBI was hoping, not so secretly, that Horton and his crew would fall on their faces. The FBI would be ready to step and to take over their role.

Chassen was the primary instigator. He had always been ruthlessly power-hungry, as far back as Horton could remember. Now, to see him sitting in on what Horton had fondly anticipated as a private meeting with the President was an unexpected slap in the face.

"Horton, come on in," the President said easily, pointedly ignoring the brief spasm of distaste that had floated across the other man's face. "We were just talking about the situation in the Middle East."

"Will there never be an end to it?" Horton said, shutting the door behind him and walking over to the unoccupied chair. He settled into it lightly with surprising grace. "If only they could settle their differences and bring some peace to that part of the world—I wonder if it will happen in our lifetime."

He saw similar expressions of cynicism on the face of both the President and the FBI director. "No. Of course not," the FBI director said, as though surprised Horton would even suggest it. "Why should they start now? War is the natural state of affairs for them."

"You have a cynical view of the world," Horton said stiffly.

"Don't you?" the President asked. "Come on, Jeremiah. Have you seen anything in the last twenty years—hell, make that the last two hundred years—to suggest that there's any possibility of peace in that region? Even if Israel disappeared, the Shiites and Suni Muslims would still fight. And they'd exterminate the same Palestinians they claim Israel is persecuting now, if indeed there are any such people, on their own."

Horton wished desperately he been in on whatever conversation had preceded his arrival. Clearly the President and the FBI director were singing the same tune, and he wondered what had led up to it. "One can always hope and pray for peace, Mr. President," he said gravely. "Is that what you wanted to see me about?"

"No, of course not," the President said, looking at Horton with a slightly bemused expression on his face. "Not unless I transferred you over to State and forgot about it."

Horton joined in the general laughter that followed that weak attempt at a joke. "I'll expect to see an increase in my travel budget, then," he added.

"Those frequent-flier miles to Idaho can really add up," the FBI director said.

Horton nodded gravely. "Bull Run, of course. I have to tell you, Mr. President, we don't like the way things are looking up there. From the reports we're getting, there's a good deal of potential for civil unrest. You know that with the mind-set up there and the militia presence, I wouldn't be surprised if—"

"It's not just the locals," Chassen interrupted. He shot Horton a sardonic look. "Abraham Carter—you know the name?"

Horton didn't but he had no intention of admitting it. "What is *his* involvement?" he asked, trying for a knowing, world-weary tone.

Chassen ignored the question. "Abraham Carter—with his son, he's active in the Free America Now organization.

We've been following their purchases and tracking their movements over the last month. All at once—Bull Run—and they go to ground."

"We're on the lookout for them." Horton said, as though it was old news.

"You won't find them."

"Because you didn't?"

"Exactly." Chassen turned back to the President, who wore an impatient expression. "Sir, our intelligence indicates they're planning a major move of some sort. Something to call attention to the government abuse of power in summarily executing that family and the kids. From what we know, it could be on the order of Oklahoma City."

"Or Waco. Or Ruby Ridge," Horton said. "For that matter, Bull Run."

"Gentlemen," the President snapped. "I did not ask for your presence in order to oversee a playground squabble. Frankly, we would have had this meeting earlier if I had had the time and patience. I, for one—and I'm the only one you have to worry about—am tired of seeing your infighting unfold on ACN. There will be no more of that—do I make myself clear?"

Horton's heart sank. He'd been expecting to be at the President's side as he dealt with Bull Run, and he was getting an ass-chewing instead. And in front of the FBI at that.

Both men were wise enough to not pretend ignorance. "OK," the President continued. "Now, Bull Run—a major foul-up all around. It's done, we screwed the pooch, and now we need to clean up after ourselves. No coverups, no casting blame, no turning this into political fodder. I will admit that the missions of HSD and the FBI overlap in a number of areas. I expect and I intended for there to be that overlap." Horton started to point out that Bull Run had been an FBI operation from start to finish. HSD, despite their protests—and a good thing that was now, in retrospect—had had no input into the mission. Neither the President nor the FBI knew that HSD had intended to mount a far more aggressive mission than the FBI had actually executed.

"We are going to learn from our mistakes," the President continued. "You know as well as I do that the whole concept of posse commitatus is under review now. I have signed an order authorizing a limited suspension of posse commitatus for the limited purpose of responding to anything else that may happen at Bull Run. Now, I don't want this misinterpreted, not by you or by the press. We screwed up. We'll take responsibility for it. But if Carter and his people are up to something"—and his tone of voice indicated that the President was more familiar with them than Horton was—"then we'll be ready for it. And because both of you have an ox to gore, particularly if military force is used inside the United States, I plan on using an independent entity to coordinate operations there."

"An independent agency?" Horton asked, incredulous.

"An independent *entity*," the President said, emphasizing the last word. "This will be a trial run integrating military active and reserve forces with all our intelligence and law-enforcement agencies to quell a potential civil disturbance. I'm taking the rather radical approach of assigning a a civilian defense contractor to conduct a threat analysis and propose an operational plan."

Horton's jaw dropped. "Civilians? What sort of civilians? You mean like military reserve officers?"

"In a manner of speaking. The initial planning stages will be under the control of a defense contractor known as Advanced Analysis."

The President waited, smiling slightly as he saw both men rapidly sift through their memories, trying to place the name. Chassen got it first, as the President had expected. "The Magruders, right? Nephew and uncle? They were in on that mission last year when we—"

"Need to know," the President cautioned, shooting the FBI director a sharp look.

Now Horton was seriously worried. What had the Magruders—and, yes, now he remembered who they were—been involved in that he didn't know about? That the FBI did?

Inside the United States, or outside? And if the latter, why did the FBI know at all?

"Between them, these two men have well over sixty years of combat experience," the President continued. "I was impressed with them both when they were on active duty, and even more so since then. So, to prevent what should be a relatively simple planning operation from turning into a turf war, they're my guys."

"But the actual execution of any plan—" Horton began.

The President cut him off. "May be completely unnecessary. If we get to that point—*if*—I'll make my decision then. Clear? And I might point out that one factor I will consider is how well both of you have worked with the Magruders." He fixed them with a steely glare. "You both work for me. You *do* remember that, don't you?"

"Of course, Mr. President," Horton murmured, echoed immediately by the FBI man.

"Well, then." The President leaned back in his chair and laced his fingers behind his head. "There's no need for either of you to contact the Magruders just yet. I told them that you are both completely at their disposal the moment they have any requirements. Information, resources, even advice— they ask for it, you ante up. Got it?"

A Cabinet-level appointee and he's treating me like I'm a schoolchild. Horton glanced over to see how the FBI was taking it, but could learn nothing from the man's expression.

Clearly, they were dismissed. Both men rose and almost in unison said, "Thank you, Mr. President." They filed out of the office.

They were silent until they were outside the Oval Office and well down the corridor. Then the FBI officer glanced up at Horton, a much larger man, and said, "Guess we just got sent to detention."

"It is a most unusual way of approaching it," Horton said stiffly. "I can only hope that the Magruders are up to it. All of their experiences are overseas. Frankly, I would be surprised if they could even locate Idaho on a map."

"Oh, I suspect they know where it is," Chassen said

calmly. "They both attended a school there—the nuclear trading prototype program, you know. It's always been in Idaho."

"Right, a few weeks on the Navy base in the middle of nowhere and they're experts on domestic terrorism," Horton snapped. He had not known there were any Navy bases in Idaho other than a few reserve facilities.

Chassen slapped Horton on the back, and Horton drew back, affronted. "Hey, look. We both just got handed our asses on a platter. I think we better try to play nice and get along, don't you? At least, that's what the boss wants."

"I would hardly call interagency cooperation a matter of playing nice."

The FBI director's smile vanished. "OK. Then don't play nice. I, for one, am going to do exactly what the President wants. And if I find out you're screwing things up or that you're holding out on the Magruders, I will personally kick your ass. And that, my friend, clearly does not fall within the definition of playing nice on the playground."

Fifteen minutes later, A. J. Bratton knew about the President's plan. Twenty minutes later, he had a plan of his own.

The United Nations
1300 local (GMT−5)

UN Ambassador Sarah Wexler thought of herself as a woman possessed of extensive reservoirs of patience and understanding, but even her resources—not so extensive as she believed—were being tested to the limit by the intransigence of certain nations. Pakistan, for one. India, for another. The squabbling over the borders, cultures, and atrocities each claimed the other had committed was a constant refrain in the United Nations. No matter that the Middle East was set to erupt again at any moment and that some dissident group had committed an act of war against an American carrier. No matter that North Korea was ranting about reunification again, that Russia's fledgling economy was failing and dragging the rest of the former Soviet Union down in turn, and that China had a large number of military assets circling the Spratley Islands. Any one of those situations could mean a serious worldwide crisis, and it wouldn't take much to set off any of those tinderboxes. And yet Pakistan and India aired their dirty laundry in public as thought it were the only issue into world. Hell, she was even more concerned about Chinese atrocities in Tibet that she was about India and Pakistan, and that was saying a lot.

It was getting worse every day, and today in particular had seen a spate of demands, requests, and accusations that had escalated to a feeding frenzy. Was there something about the alignment of the planets with a full moon or something? She was starting to believe that the entire world had chosen that particular morning to go completely insane.

There seemed to be no getting away from it. The ambassador from Pakistan was at her side now, long brown fingers plucking gently at her sleeve, his singsong voice grating on her ears in soft, confidential tones. "We would like to know where America stands," he said, obviously finishing up whatever argument she'd been ignoring. "I think there is some basis for claiming your attention on this matter."

"Of course," she murmured. "There are many matters on the calendar this month, though. And pressing problems around the world."

He drew back slightly. "The United States did not think Pakistan so inconsequential when it wished to invade Afghanistan."

"We did not invade Afghanistan."

He gazed at her steadily. "So many bombs, so many troops—and you did not invade?"

"As you well know," she said, her voice icy now, "we supported the Northern Alliance in retaking their country from a corrupt and repressive regime. I believe Pakistan has also benefited from the establishment of a more stable government in Afghanistan, has it not?"

The Pakistani shrugged. "To some extent. Less than your

government has benefited from our support, I believe."

"You believe wrong."

He studied her for moment, then his face turned ugly. "You will regret this, Madame Ambassador. You will regret it." He turned and stomped off, his back rigid with rage.

Wexler sighed as he went, and then turned to Brad, her aide. "That sounded like a threat to me."

"Me, too." Brad's gaze was still fixed on the Pakistani as he watched the other man make his way across the main assembly room. "Can we do anything about it?"

Wexler grimaced. "Not more security, if that's what you mean. I can barely go to the john by myself now as it is."

"So what you do think he meant?"

Wexler turned back to watch the Pakistani, who was gathering a loud, vocal crowd around him. They were speaking in a number of languages, but the gazes were all directed at her. "I don't know, but I expect we'll find out shortly." She paused for a moment, then, only half-kidding, asked, "Do you know anything about astrology?"

TWELVE

Greenfield slumped back in his chair and rubbed the corners of his eyes with his fingertips. His eyes felt dry and dusty. It was an all too familiar feeling, one he'd felt so often during Desert Storm. It was the result of too many hours substituting coffee for sleep. He leaned back in his chair and let the muscles relax, or at least tried to.

If he wanted to look like a tough guy, one of the ones who wanted to go for hours and days and years without ever sleeping, he would have to dip into the top right drawer of his desk. There he kept two essential items for any FBI field agent: Tums and Visine.

But what was the point? After this debacle, he wasn't even sure how much longer he had left at the FBI. It had been a total fiasco from beginning to end, and nobody was going to stop and remember that he'd been the voice of caution, that he'd questioned the plans and the information and the intelligence, that he'd argued against a nighttime surprise raid on the Smart residence.

No, what they'd remember was that he'd been the man on the ground, the man in command of a takedown that was starting to look an awful lot like Ruby Ridge. Somebody was going to have to pay for the failure, and Greenfield was pretty sure he knew who it would be.

Do I mind that much? Maybe I should retire, try to work out that disability claim. The way my back feels today, that sounds awful attractive.

Shame rushed through him. How could he think about his own future right now? Four people were dead, two of them children. And from the information that was coming out now, information they should have had before the raid, it was looking an awful lot like Kyle Smart, father of two and husband of Betsy, longtime resident of Bull Run, Idaho, hadn't done a damn thing wrong.

Hell of a way to make an example. At least they ought to find somebody who actually was a crook, even if you overlooked the fact that they died like that. At least you'd have a cold comfort of knowing in your heart of hearts that the son of a bitch was absolutely beyond the shadow of a doubt guilty, no matter what the courts and the lawyers said. A scumbag, one that the earth was better off without.

How do you ever rationalize killing kids?

More and more, it was starting to look like Mr. Kyle Smart was nothing more than a bitter, disillusioned farm boy. Sure, he might have turned into a serious threat, given time. He was heading in that direction. Maybe somewhere down the road he would have joined one of the vicious little hate circles springing up around the isolated parts of the country, taking comfort in finding other people like himself. And maybe he would've gone further than that, but probably never beyond the planning stage. Few of the groups were, by their very nature, capable of carrying out any coordinated plan of action. Under the slightest difference of opinion, they disintegrated into warring factions, like a drop of mercury under pressure.

Kyle Smart would never get to that point. Not now. Not him, not his two sons, not his wife. All because someone somewhere in the Bureau had screwed up royally by letting the Homeland Security folks in on the deal. If it had been a

Bureau decision alone, this never would have happened.

Maybe. Maybe not.

There was a short ring on the phone, signaling an internal call. He picked up the receiver and glanced at the status bar to make sure that the line was secure. "Greenfield."

"Come up and see me." The line went dead.

Nice guy. No hi, how are you, no name, no nothing. Just the command. Like everybody was supposed to recognize the cold, nasal accent from the Far Northeast immediately. A hell of an assumption.

Greenfield hauled his bulk out of the chair, silently vowing for perhaps the thousandth time he would get his butt to the gym more often.

The problem was that everyone did recognize that particular voice. No one mistook the voice of Carl Chassen, director of operations for the FBI, newly appointed to that post only six months ago and already making his mark on history as one of the most despotic ops directors ever.

Greenfield made his way up to the top floor, noting that the shabby government green paint on the walls was just ever so slightly less shabby at these levels. The carpet was cleaner, and might even have been laid within the last two Administrations.

He entered the director's reception area and offered Chassen's secretary a tired smile. She gazed at him sympathetically, her eyes showing their own signs of strain. "He's waiting for you." She gestured at the closed door behind her.

"Any advice?" he said halfheartedly. Janie Felts had on occasion made his job a little easier by giving him a hint about which way the wind was blowing, but not so now. Not that it was necessary. She looked away.

Hell of a nice lady, though. If I ever had more than just enough to cover rent and child support, I wouldn't mind taking her out. Assuming she'd even go out with a special agent.

He let himself into the office, bracing himself for the worst. Chassen never yelled. He didn't have to. The clinical precision with which he dissected his victims didn't require it.

"Sit down, Hank." Chassen's voice was cold—but then, wasn't it always?

Not "Have a seat, Hank," or "Thanks for coming right up," none of the social pleasantries that existed to make life flow just a little bit easier. They both knew Greenfield had no choice, that he would do as he was told. What was the point of rubbing his nose in it?

Greenfield sank into the available chair, suppressing a groan as he sank into it. He'd be damned if he'd let Chassen see him wince, not with what was coming.

"So. You blew it. I spent the morning at the White House taking the heat for it. Tell me why." Chassen leaned back in his chair and interlaced his hands behind his head. A dangerous sign, one that exposed his midsection, indicating subliminally that he had nothing to fear from Greenfield.

"It went badly."

Chassen arched one eyebrow at that and waited. It was a favorite tactic of his, saying nothing, provoking the agents into tumbling over their own words as they tried to fill the silence.

Greenfield was having none of it. He could wait as well. It was a skill born of long hours on stakeout as a junior officer, hours in which he could barely keep his eyes open. Then the sudden rush of adrenaline as the target appeared, when things started happening too fast to do more than react automatically to them.

He could feel the adrenaline course into his veins now, warning of the danger. It didn't matter that it was not physical, other than the fact he could end up a homeless bum on the street without his paycheck. The limbic system didn't distinguish between threats. It wasn't designed to.

"Understatement," said Chassen. Again, the silence.

I'll be damned if I'll talk. Not now. Nobody listened when I told them it would go wrong. Anything I say now will sound like an excuse. He settled for a noncommittal shrug.

"Well, then." Chassen leaned forward and clasped his

hands on the desk in front of him. "Under the circumstances, I'm sure you'd welcome an opportunity to redeem yourself." Again, the sardonic lift of one eyebrow. "You do well on this one, and a year from now nobody will remember Idaho."

Right. No chance of that. And even if everybody else in the world forgot, I'd still remember it. For a moment, he heard the screams again, mixing with the noise of the fire.

"The President has decided to assemble a special task force to deal with situations such as this," Chassen said, his voice betraying no opinion on the matter. "It will be composed of both American and Canadian military forces, as well as representatives from the appropriate law-enforcement agencies. Including, as deemed necessary, our brethren at the CIA. The President feels that we need to deal firmly with incidents such as these, bringing all of our assets to bear on a speedy and appropriate resolution. You'll be heading up our contingent for the next operation." Chassen stopped and waited, only a crease at the edge of his eyes betraying his amusement.

"When? And where?" Greenfield said, keeping his voice neutral.

"A few days from now. Back in Idaho. Since you're already familiar with the area, that will save you some time. You can hit the deck running, as they say in the Navy. You were in the Navy, weren't you?"

"Marine Corps." *As you well know, you bastard.*

"Yes, of course. Uncle Sam's Misguided Children. Well, then, you should be right at home." Chassen closed the folder he'd been studying and slid it across the desk to Greenfield. "The details aren't finalized, but this is a rough draft of the composition of forces and rules of engagement for the next operations. Also budgeting and manpower allocations. As you can see, we're throwing our full support behind this." Again that sly look of amusement.

Sure. All the resources of the Bureau. And that includes the one agent that's entirely expendable. That's what you call giving the President full support? Greenfield took the folder without speaking. He didn't open at. He waited.

Chassen appeared slightly unsettled. "Well, then. Study up on it and see me if you have any questions. You should be contacted by the military officer in charge within the next couple days to finalized details."

"Military officer?" Greenfield said, not moving. "We're on American soil."

"Of course, the whole issue of posse commitatus. I think you'll find that the whole doctrine will be changing shortly."

Since the failure of domestic intelligence agencies to predict the strike against the World Trade Center, there had been increasing talk in Congress about giving the military a freer hand in domestic security. The problem was that the country was founded on a doctrine known as *posse commitatus*, a doctrine that prevented using federal military forces inside the United States for law-enforcement activities. The National Guard units, which were state units reporting to the governor, were not considered in this category unless "federalized," i.e. called to active duty and placed into the military chain of command. The FBI had managed to work out some kinks in their operations with the National Guard to their mutual benefit, but other than some small cross-training, not with the regular military forces.

"So whose operation is it?" Greenfield asked again.

"Theirs. There'll be a military commander. You'll work for him."

"Is that legal?"

Chassen shrugged. "The President seems to think so. I imagine it will be a test case of sorts."

And no matter how it goes wrong, I'll take the fall for it. The Justice Department will say I should have known better, I should've cleared it through them. But the whole thing will be wrapped up in so many security classifications that there'll be no way to do that. I'm the sacrificial lamb.

"I see." Greenfield stood, paused for a moment, then headed for the door. He could almost feel Chassen smiling behind him.

THIRTEEN

Bull Run, Idaho
1900 local (GMT −7)

Drake placed her hands on her hips and glared at the Army officer standing in front of her. " 'No comment' isn't going to hack it right now. I want to know what's down the road. Barring that, I want to know why you won't let me go down and see for myself." Behind her, she could hear the familiar noises of the camera crew as they captured everything on tape.

The Army officer was stiff and correct. "I'm sorry, ma'am. A small plane crashed in the area, and the National Transportation Safety Board has ordered that no one be allowed into the area until they completed their initial survey."

"Right. What airport was it from? What kind of aircraft? Who is the pilot, and how experienced was he? Any passengers? What caused the incident?" Drake shot the questions at the man, hammering on his defenses.

"I'm sorry, ma'am. I don't know the answers to any of those questions. There will be a formal briefing held in three hours time. I'm sure the briefing officer will be able to answer your questions."

Three hours. Too late. I won't sit in what passes for a

*press room and quietly wait to get the same news that every-
one else is getting.*

She motioned to the cameraman, and said, "I want to do
a standup. Now." She positioned herself in the middle of the
road with the two Army jocks and a squad of men directly
behind her. No doubt one was waving to his mother as she
spoke.

"This is Pamela Drake, reporting from Bull Run, Idaho.
We have information to indicate that a tragedy along the lines
of Ruby Ridge has occurred in the valley behind me. As you
can see, it is accessible only via the road I'm standing on,
and Army officers are preventing anyone from entering the
area—or, presumably, from leaving the area if there's anyone
left alive to leave." She paused for a moment, then continued.
"As you can see, the men and women standing behind me
are armed. They are Army officers, if I'm not mistaken. Regular Army—not National Guard. The question now becomes
just what exactly is the Army doing? Their story is that
they're protecting the site of an aircraft mishap investigation.
The gentleman standing behind me does not even know
whether that's true or not. He's just carrying out orders. The
larger question is exactly what the Army's involvement in it
is. Was it a military aircraft? Or is this the beginning of
something bigger?"

She held still for moment, then made a chopping motion
with her hand. The red light atop the camera went out.

She turned back to the Army officer. "OK, we'll see you
in three hours. Where is the briefing being held?" She scribbled down the directions, although she had no intention of
being there. She managed to convey the impression of a disgruntled reporter but one that was willing to play by the
rules. To her advantage, the officer assigned to the area was
not part of the regular Army public affairs organization. Had
he been, he would have known immediately what she had in
mind.

Once they were all loaded up with the local affiliate and
headed back down the road, Pamela turned to her cameraman. "You ready?"

The reporter from the local affiliate looked at her uncertainly. "Ready for what?"

She waved him off impatiently. "None of your business. As soon as we get around the next corner, stop and let us out. Then be back here in three hours for the press conference. Other than that, I don't want to hear anything out of you. Got it?"

"What are you going to do?" the reporter asked.

"Got it?" she repeated, glaring at him. When he did not answer, she said, "Stop the van. Now!" The man driving ignored the local reporter and quickly brought the van to a halt. She and her cameraman jumped out, paused for a moment at the side of the road to survey the terrain. Then, without a backward glance, they began hiking up the hill.

An hour later, the two were on a peak overlooking Bull Run. Both were scratched, sweating, and bleeding in a few spots. The cameraman had even seen a couple of snakes, but he was being a trouper about it.

As Pamela surveyed the area, she gave a low whistle. He was already taping. "That doesn't look like a plane crashed there. Not unless it had damned good aim."

Below them, floodlights illuminated the charred remains of a small building. Two men were hosing down the remains. There were four Army vehicles there, including one that looked like an ambulance. All in all, the activity looked too military for the NTSB to be involved. Whatever had happened was already over, and this was simply the cleanup—or cover-up.

Pamela pulled out binoculars and focused on the area. What was it, a military facility? Or a civilian house? Whatever it had been, there was no evidence of any aircraft crashing into it, not the slightest trace of debris. Not that she had believed that from the very start.

In addition to a large number of military types, there were also a few civilians. Just behind the site, in an open field, she taught saw two helicopters. They were both powered down, waiting.

"You want to do a standup?" the cameraman asked.

She shook her head. "Not until we're further away. You never know how sound will carry in the mountains."

He shrugged. "Up to you."

"Let's just watch for a while. Be ready, in case anything starts happening." No sooner had she said that than there was a flurry of activity, and two men emerged from the burned-out remains of what had to be the basement. They carried with them three bright orange body bags that they very carefully passed up to a man standing at ground level. A priest appeared, made a few brief motions, and the bags were loaded into the ambulance.

The camera clicked as the cameraman recorded it all. Pamela just watched, barely able to breath from the anticipation.

"Don't move," a voice said quietly. "Don't move a muscle."

Both Pamela and her cameraman froze. They'd been in enough situations like this before to know that obeying was their best bet of staying alive.

"That's good—real good. Now, just keep it up while we have a brief look-see at your equipment." Pamela heard movement behind her, but did not turn her head to look. She heard her cameraman swear quietly as he was relieved of his equipment. Hands moved over her roughly, opened her pack, and she was subjected to a thorough pat-down.

"OK, you can get up. Let's move slowly." Drake did as she was told, turning slowly around to face the intruders. She sucked in a sharp breath and knew why the voice had sounded so familiar.

The man shook his head quickly, cautioning her to keep quiet. "Let's go down to my vehicle, shall we? Your story isn't here. But I can hook you up with the guys who are going to be in the middle of it. You ever heard of a guy by the name of Abraham Carter?"

As Pamela followed her CIA contact to his vehicle, she couldn't help smiling.

The Kuwait/Iraq border
Friday, September 14
1100 local (GMT+3)

Staff Sergeant Joe Parker hated the desert. Raised in the mountains of Kentucky, proficient with a firearm even before he learned his alphabet, he had grown up under the sheltering protection of the Appalachian Mountains. He knew how to lose himself in thickly wooded forests that climbed the sides of the mountains and the narrow valleys that stretched between them. He understood the rhythms of the sun, the way the weather affected the animals and the terrain, and how to use the light and the weather to his advantage.

But this—this damn desert—was as completely alien as the moon. Dawn came suddenly, no long lingering shadows to hide you. Night came on equally fast, one moment light, then boom—darkness. The abrupt demarcation between light and dark seemed as dangerous and alien to him as the flat terrain that stretched out to the horizons, unbroken by any rise in elevation other than the occasional sand dune. He felt exposed and naked on the bare flat land. In theory, he knew that his desert-colored camouflage and the other concealment measures that they took worked well, but in his heart he never believed it.

The one thing he was grateful for was that the terrain made patrols more straightforward, if more dangerous. You drove or flew over somewhere and you saw what you saw. There was no puzzling out the shadows of the trees, no looking for odd shapes along a wooded ridgeline.

Although he'd slowed down some in the last two years, the result of deteriorating cartilage in his knees, Parker still led area patrols from time to time, if only to keep his hand in and show the youngsters how it was done. At thirty-two, he was considered an old man in the service. The average age in the Army was twenty-two.

This day was no different from any other one. They had been transported by truck to the drop-off point along with their gear and then set out to patrol their area. Another patrol headed off the opposite direction, and they remained visible for a long time on the flat terrain.

Sweat sprang up immediately on the nape of his neck and traced small streams down his back. The perspiration would slow down later on as he became dehydrated and accustomed to the heat.

"On the horizon," his point man said, holding up a hand to stop their forward progress. "Look."

Parker squinted in the direction that his point indicated. He raised his binoculars to his eyes, silently damning the deterioration in his eyesight over the last decade. When he was the point's age, he could have seen it without the binos, too.

It was a small hump on the horizon, barely visible. Not moving, dark gray-green against the sand. A vehicle of some sort—nothing to indicate it was moving, no sand or clouds in the air around it.

"The intel photos showed a couple of abandoned trucks in the area," he said. "Might be one of them."

"Wonder if there's anything left in it," Point said.

"Worth looking at," Parker said. "Come on."

Kuwaiti air base
1230 local (GMT +3)

Captain Arless "Airless" Handshaw had been pulling alert for the last four hours, and he was getting pretty sick of it. They'd gone to an increased state of alert the day before, for some unknown reason probably having to do with satellite reconnaissance photos, and duty in the United States Air Force had begun to feel suspiciously like military service. With two F-15's on runway alert, that meant that the pilot and navigator-bombardier sat in the cockpit for four hours at a time, the aircraft connected to a huffer to supply electrical power, waiting for the word to go. The paperback he'd slipped into one pocket of his flight suit made the boredom bearable, but there was not much he could do about the heat.

Despite the supply of electrical power to the aircraft cooling system, the temperature inside the cockpit had been rising steadily over the last hour. It was, he suspected, somewhere around ninety-five degrees right now, but he avoided checking to make certain. He was miserable—no need to confirm it with instrumentation.

This was not how service in United States Air Force was supposed to be. Particularly not for pilots. Alerts should be pulled in air-conditioned bunkers sitting immediately adjacent to the airfield, the aircraft kept in the high state of readiness by the enlisted technicians. If necessary, the pilots could burst out of the bunker, clamber up the boarding ladders, finish off the preflights, and be airborne in well under five minutes.

So what was the point of sitting here? A few minutes here and there—yes, sure, he understood that could spell the difference between a successful mission and not, but he still felt that there had to be a less unpleasant way to do it.

"Flight One, Tower. Radio alert launch, rollout authorized." A stream of numbers followed, and the tower ended with the demand "Acknowledge."

He jumped at the first squawk, then slipped the paperback into his pocket and grabbed his grease pencil to jot down coordinates. "Flight One, acknowledge. Say again coordinates." He scribbled them down, and punched them into the onboard flight computer, verifying that the check sum matched up with the last digit of the sum of the other numbers. Coordinates were vitally important in this environment, where there were no landmarks or terrain to guide off. "Say again the composition?"

"Unknown. Reconnaissance launching right now, along with extraction. Provide air cover to extraction team, then join on Blue Leader for alternate attack profile."

Great. Baby-sitting the helicopter to get the troops out. By the time they got them safely out of the area, whatever it was that was kicking up sand would be flaming bits of metal on the desert. It wasn't that he begrudged the others the primary attack mission—hell, he had his chance at times—and sure, the troops deserved to get out safely. It was just that after sitting for four hours in the scalding cockpit, he ought to be entitled to a little more fun.

All around him, alert aircraft were spinning up, rolling out for the runway. He scanned the area behind them, watching as the helicopter at the far end of the field rose steadily into the air, then settled down and turned north. Nothing between here and there that should be a danger to it, at least not according to the briefing. Most of the antiair sites were little more that piles of molten metal now, although there was always a chance that someone had managed to sneak a mobile setup or Stinger into the area.

He gave the helicopter a slight head start, then launched and vectored over to it. He checked in with the helo pilot, confirmed good comms and their destination, watching with envy as the others streaked off to attack a truck convoy. As the helicopter progressed toward its target, he circled the airspace above, keeping a sharp eye out for any movement or trouble.

Fifteen minutes later, the primary mission was complete. The small band of Marines had boarded the helicopter in just a few seconds and the helo was heading for base. Freed from his baby-sitting duties, he checked in with Blue Leader One.

"Just about done," Blue Leader replied. "You want a piece of the action, you got to show up earlier."

"Like I had a choice." He shook his head, disgusted. Last out, last in. The others would be headed for the officers club by the time he got his bird buttoned up for the night.

"Join on us," Blue One directed, confirming his suspicions. With a sigh, he turned toward the other aircraft, about thirty miles away, and headed for the tail end of the pack.

Helicopter
1300 local (GMT +3)

"They sure took their sweet time," a corporal muttered, his voice barely audible over the hard *chop-chop* of the helicopter's blades. "Any longer and we would have to set up a base station."

"Wasn't bad," Parker corrected. "Sometimes they don't show up at all."

There wasn't much point in trying to carry on a casual conversation while in the helicopter. The noise drowned out just about everything, even if there had been anything to say. Each man was alone with his thoughts, seeing the images again of the blackened, distorted bodies rendered almost inhuman by the heat. It didn't take long for a dead body to spoil in this weather, even given the lack of moisture in the air. The bloody corpses swarming with flies, skin green and sagging, would remain with them for many days.

"What do you think happened to them?" the corporal shouted, oblivious to his squad mate's desire not to talk. "Were they dead?"

The staff sergeant shook his head, not because he didn't want to know but because he didn't want to face the possibility. There was something damn odd about the whole business, real damn odd, starting with the fact that the spooks had ordered in an air-retrieval mission instead of expecting them to hump it back to their rendezvous point.

1305 local (GMT+3)

"Looks like they missed one," Airless's bombardier remarked, touching the button to focus the display. "One truck, maybe. Not ours."

"You can tell that from the radar?"

"No. I asked. Everybody's safe and home in the barn."

"It's not moving," Airless said dubiously.

"Then even you ought to be able to hit it." His bombardier snorted at the gibe.

"What the hell." Airless put the F-15 into a hard turn, banking toward the target. Forty, maybe fifty seconds away—they'd shoot a quick round into it, watch the flames, and then at least feel like they'd done something for God and country. Not as satisfying as hitting a moving target, but better than nothing at all. "Control, diverting to investigate target of opportunity." Target of opportunity, hell. It was probably just a broken-down vehicle. Not much of a contribution to the war.

"Roger, acknowledge. Area clearance granted. Weapons free."

Well, that was something. At least no one was going to hassle him about wasting ammo on it. He felt slightly better.

"All yours," the bombardier said.

"I've got it." Like the bombardier could have done something about it anyway.

The target was dead ahead, alone. It looked like a normal two-ton truck. There was no movement around it. Might be playing possum—but Airless would have to check it out.

He swung around for another pass, dropping down and losing altitude, his hands placed over the controls ready to yank her into afterburner and grab some altitude if anything so much as shivered down there. But there was no reaction, not on the pass.

"At least they could move around some," his bombardier bitched.

"It's better than nothing." Airless swung around for the final pass, transferring his finger to the weapons selector switch. One missile—no more. He waited until the last possible moment and toggled it off. The F-15 shuddered slightly as the weapon left the wings. He broke hard to the right, clearing the area, putting distance between himself and what would soon be a fireball, turning back at the last moment so that they could both watch the impact.

"Yeah!" the bombardier said. The missile hit, and the truck disappeared in a fireball of glaring yellow and brilliant orange that seared the eyeballs. Black smoke boiled out from it, forming a pillar in the still air to match those further away on the horizon from the first team's attack.

"Control, felt a good one. One shot fired, one truck destroyed. Unless otherwise directed, I'm heading back to base." He waited, on the off chance at the controller might have another target for them, but was immediately disappointed with a crisp "Roger, acknowledge, return to base."

"Better than nothing," Airless said again, still feeling a slight sense of disappointment. "Better than nothing."

FOURTEEN

Tombstone Magruder surveyed the assembled crowd, matching the names he'd read in the briefing folder with faces. The crowd was broken into several small groups, each studiously ignoring the other. Clearly, the different law-enforcement agencies were not used to working with each other, or at least not as comfortable with it as the U.S. and the Canadian military personnel were. The military people mingled easily, exchanging stories of the last time they'd met and catching up on each others' careers.

Funny that folks from two different nations had more in common than the FBI and the CIA.

Or, at least the FBI and CIA want me to think that. The thought would bear exploring at a later date.

Finally, when he judged the time was right, Tombstone stepped up to the podium. Everyone immediately fell silent, the casual conversations mere gambits to cover for the fact that they were waiting for him to speak.

"Thank you all for getting here on such short notice," Tombstone began. "I'm Thomas Magruder, formerly of the

United States Navy. This is my uncle, Matthew Magruder." He gestured to his right, where his uncle was standing slightly behind him.

"Tombstone," one voice in the back called out, amused. "You still going by that?"

Tombstone smiled. "I suppose. I'll probably answer to it, anyway. OK, so now you know who I am. I know your names, but I haven't got those matched up with faces yet." *I do, but no point in letting you all know that, not if you're so intent on pretending you don't know each other.* He pointed to the right front corner of the group. "Start here, senior person introduce your people."

A bluff, rough-featured man stepped forward. He was wearing a sports jacket but looked uneasy in it. "Hank Greenfield, FBI." He introduced the man and woman with him, adding, "For what it's worth, we're familiar with the area. I was on site when the Smart incident went down."

Like they don't all know that already. But I like your style, putting it right out there on the table, no excuses. Tombstone studied him for a moment, taking his measure. *A no-nonsense sort of guy. I'll have a hell of a time getting paperwork out of him, but he'll be the top guy out in the field. I wonder just how much of that fiasco was actually your fault. Not as much as your people are laying on you, I bet.*

A man from the center of the group behind Greenfield stepped forward, a pleasant expression on his face. Instead of a sports coat, he wore a dark suit with a white shirt and red tie. *It looks completely natural on him, clearly tailored specifically to suit his athletic form.* "A. J. Bratton, CIA. Delighted to be on board, Admiral. Although, of course, we're just here in an advisory capacity."

"Right. I'll keep that in mind. And you might keep in mind that I'm not an admiral anymore—or at least, I'm just a retired one."

Bratton bristled slightly. "Of course. Our intelligence resources are at your disposal. Perhaps we can fill in some of the gaps in the database."

I'm sure." Out of the corner of his eye, Tombstone saw

Greenfield turn to glare at the CIA officer. Clearly the two knew each other, and clearly there was no love lost between them. Whether that was a matter of personal taste or an outgrowth of the long-standing rivalry between the CIA and the FBI, he didn't know yet. But, as closely as they would be working together, he was sure he would have an opportunity to find out.

"Captain Adam Sands," the Canadian officer in working uniform said, stepping forward. "I brought a couple of officers from my staff, the ones most used to working with you chaps. At least, they claim they can understand every accent in America." That produced a chuckle from the crowd. "Happy to be working with you again, Tombstone," the Canadian continued, using Tombstone's old nickname easily.

"And with you, too." From what Tombstone could remember, Sands was one tough cookie, sharp and driven. Tombstone particularly remembered his ability to remain completely unflustered no matter what the circumstances. There was more than a small trace of British reserve in the man, and Tombstone was glad to have him on the team.

The next man to stand up was a civilian. "Captain Bill Lawyers. I'm with the sheriff's department, and we cover this area along with the area you're concerned about. We're used to working with the other jurisdictions in the state, as well as with the Indian tribal authorities. There are a couple of hoops you have to jump through on tribal grounds, but for the most part they're pretty savvy. We can coordinate anything that needs to happen on federal lands. I've brought along Jim Horse Looking, from the Tribal Police."

"Welcome," Tombstone said. "Mr. Horse Looking, I wasn't expecting you, but it's good to have you on board." Something about the man's bearing made him examine the Indian more closely. "Former Marine?"

"Yes, sir. It still shows, does it?" The Indian's voice was low and quiet, almost diffident.

Tombstone nodded. "Yes, sir, it does."

There were a few other agencies present, including an attorney from the U.S. Attorney's office, a local district attor-

ney, and a public information specialist from the FBI who
promised to coordinate all interaction with the media the
minute they started showing up.

After all the introductions were completed, Tombstone
said, "Well, ladies and gentlemen. I suggest we start setting
up and staffing our organization, keeping in mind that we
need to be able to draw from all of the resources we have.
For the CIA folks, I expect you to let us know when we are
assigning you to something that might not be entirely appropriate. We'll keep you on the sidelines, in support roles, so
keep us honest."

Bratton waved his hand lazily, acknowledging the order.
"Not to worry, Admiral. We know what we're here for."

Tombstone studied for him for a moment, nonplussed. The
CIA had never been his favorite of government agencies,
having a tendency to secrecy and circuitous thinking that too
often got men on the front lines killed. Now, operating with
them in a joint task force, he was not entirely sure that he
trusted them.

"What's your next mission?" Bratton asked.

*Your. Not our. Whether he meant to or not, he's confirm-
ing my suspicions about the CIA's commitment to this project.*

"We don't know yet," Tombstone said offhandedly, being
careful not to let his face reflects his thoughts. Tombstone
took his nickname from the impassive expression normally
on his face.

"Then why are we all here?" Bratton said easily, indicating
that he thought it was a waste of time until there was an
actual mission.

"Best to iron things out *before* we have a specific mission," Greenfield observed gruffly. "Once the shooting starts,
there's no time for chain-of-command concerns." He shot
Tombstone a dark look. "Speaking of chain of command—
what is it?"

And there it was, right out on the table. No need to wonder
where Greenfield stood on any issue. Tombstone found his
admiration for the man deepening.

"Yes, do tell," Bratton said. The local man from the sheriff's department and the tribal police officer shared a dark look in the back.

"That's one of the concerns," Tombstone admitted.

"Posse commitatus," Greenfield said.

"Exactly. For right now, we're operating under the exception that allows military forces to coordinate training exercises and participate in dual disaster-relief exercises." Tombstone saw the cynical look on Greenfield's face and nodded. "I know. Exactly my position as well. But my information is that we're going to see some more direct guidance coming down from the White House in the next couple of days. It'll be his call as to how the chain of command works."

"His call as Commander in Chief? Or as Chief Executive?" Greenfield asked.

"Or as head of a sovereign nation?" Horse Looking paused, making his point clear. "If they cross into *our* lands, that becomes an issue, too."

"Will your nation require a formal declaration of war?" Bratton asked in a mocking tone of voice. "Surely you're not going to confuse the issue further with this sort of nonsense."

"If you plan on simply invading as your people did originally, perhaps we should. CIA, FBI—you are so fond of initials. We will not have the issue of Indian sovereignty simply treated as dispensable when you find it convenient."

"As soon as *your* people are self-supporting in some way besides gambling, you may be entitled to—"

"Gentlemen!" Tombstone snapped, cutting them off. "Enough of that. Officer Horse Looking, you have a point. I will depend on you to alert me to any potential issues. For the rest of you, as soon as I get any word, I'll pass it on. For now, since we do have authorization to conduct training exercises, we will stay off Indian lands. As far as our approach, I want to run this as if it was a military operation, but it's strictly a civilian one."

"But you're not military," Bratton observed. "And that makes it a bit awkward, doesn't it?"

"I am retired, as is my uncle," Tombstone acknowledged. "But we're both members of the Fleet Reserve, and there is at least an argument that we would still be considered military forces. Right now, though, we're here as representatives of Advanced Analysis to coordinate operations."

"I'd like to see the precedent for that," Greenfield said.

"There is none that I can think of, except perhaps in contracting federal prison security to outside organizations. But," Tombstone continued, "there's not much precedent for what were facing now, is there?"

That brought a hush to the room. None of them would ever forget where they had been on that day in September when cowardly terrorism had sent aircraft crashing into the World Trade Center and the Pentagon.

"So," Tombstone continued after a moment, "I'd ask you to cut me a little slack on the question of chain of command. For now, you can consider me the team leader, or officer in charge, or commanding officer, or whatever term you used to describe the person in charge. It may be that the President will decide that the FBI is better suited to control the operation."

"Not likely," someone said quietly in the back of the room. Greenfield's face turned red, but he had no comment.

Tombstone debated on whether or not to let the comment pass, then decided to tackle the issue head-on. "The first thing I'll require here is that you all put aside any previous interagency rivalries. We all know what happened at Bull Run, and I see no point in harping on it other than to review any operational lessons we may glean from it. It did not go well—understatement, right? Haven't all of you had an operation turned into a real clusterfuck right under your noses? I know I have." *And in one of those I lost my wife.* "So, I don't want to hear any cheap shots." He let that sink in, and then turned to Greenfield. "You and I don't know each other very well yet, although I suspect that will change over the next few weeks. At some point in the very near future, I'll expect a thorough and brutal rundown on what happened. My guess is you got shoved into moving before you wanted to move, probably based on pretty crappy intelligence. I'm not going to ask you to make excuses for what happened, but I do expect everybody to learn something from it. That okay with you?"

"Yeah." Greenfield was staring off in the distance somewhere, as though he was seeing Bull Run go down again. "And thanks for the sensitivity training, but I'd bet my ass that there's not a man in here who could say anything worse than what I've said to myself."

"Well, then." Tombstone turned back to the rest of the room. "We'll make up the following departments, I think. Administration, operations, intelligence, and logistics. If we need any other departments, we'll put them together as required. For now that ought to get us started."

"Any word on the first target?" Bratton asked again.

"No. Like I said, as soon as I hear something."

The men and women assembled soon sorted themselves out into four major groups, each one determining who was the senior person present and starting a list of requirements. Tombstone watched, fielded questions as they came to him, and was not surprised when Bratton eventually ambled over to him with a quizzical look on his face. "If you're going to run this as a military organization, then you're going to need an executive officer. Who've you got in mind?"

"You volunteering?" Tombstone asked.

Bratton smiled slightly. "Of course not, Admiral," he said, stressing the last word ever so slightly. "We're prohibited from assuming any direct command of operations inside the United States. Just like the military is."

Tombstone nodded, acknowledging the contradiction. "Things change. Like I said—you volunteering?"

Bratton held his gaze steadily, letting the pleasant, supercilious expression drop from his face. Tombstone, for the first time, saw the steel underneath the polished surface. This man had actual operational experience in many places that Tombstone was familiar with, and on some level he could sense that a lot of it had been more close-in and dirty than Tombstone had ever seen. "I could, I suppose," Bratton said finally. "But let's face it—you know I'm not used operating in this theater. Greenfield is." He nodded toward the FBI agent, immersed in setting up the operations department. "He'll be good for you there. And he's the only one who really has much experience inside the United States. Not to mention at Bull Run."

"Well, now that's impressive," Tombstone said. He didn't elaborate—he didn't have to. "I'll take your advice under consideration, Mr. Bratton. And I appreciate your insight. Let's just leave the matter open for now, how about it?"

The supercilious expression was back on Bratton's face. "You're the boss," he said in a good-natured voice. "Just thought I'd bring it up."

FIFTEEN

The Navy Intelligence petty officer conducting the third briefing of the staff sergeant was clearly at the end of a long day. He was thorough, the staff sergeant thought, going through the postmission checklist and asking every pertinent question, but it was obvious his heart wasn't in it. After all, the Sergeant had already conserved every question earlier. Still, he did his job. It was only when they got to the description of the truck and its deceased occupants that his ears pricked up.

"Ten, you say?" he asked, pausing from his scribbling, a look of interest on his face.

"Yes. I counted them." The staff sergeant repressed a shudder as the men's faces loomed before him, blackened and distorted. "Twice."

"And two in the front seat."

"Yes, that's right."

The sergeant put down his pencil and shut his eyes, rubbing his fingers at the corners. A frown creased his forehead and he sighed. "That doesn't make a lot of sense."

"Why not?"

"Because they've been using patrols composed of seven men. You've got twelve in the truck. That tells me it's not two patrols and it's not one. Were they all roughly in the same state of decomposition?"

"Looked like it."

"Were the keys in the truck?"

The staff sergeant stared at him. "I don't know. I didn't look."

"Think about it."

The staff sergeant shut his eyes, picturing the interior of the vehicle. Worn, more than it should have been. There had been a crack in the windshield, something they should have fixed. One side window missing, along with part of the instrument panel. And there, where the ignition should have been—"Gone," he said, opening his eyes. "No keys."

"No keys," the intelligence sergeant echoed, now frowning. He stood up abruptly and said, "Wait here. The intelligence officer is going to want to talk to you."

The officer. But why? Just because there weren't keys in the ignition? The staff sergeant ran through the possibilities, trying to decide what it was that alarmed the other sergeant. He had just concluded that he didn't know when the sergeant returned, an Army captain following him.

"Captain Henry," the officer said by way of introduction. He slid into the seat opposite the staff sergeant. "Sergeant has been telling me what happened. I have a few questions for you."

"Yes, sir?"

"When you examine the truck cab—no keys, right? Was it in gear or neutral? And was the parking brake set?"

The staff sergeant shut his eyes, visualizing the hellish interior once again. "Neutral, I think. And no parking brake. Not that they'd need it on that terrain."

"Shit." The officer stood, backing away from them. "Staff Sergeant, where are the rest of your men?"

"Probably at chow," the staff sergeant said, now growing alarmed. "You don't think that—?"

"I don't know." He grabbed his own sergeant by the arm,

and they backed away until they stood at the doorway. "You understand, I'll have to ask you not to leave this room." With that, he left. Moments later, the staff sergeant heard the loud-speaker summoning the rest of his squad to sick bay.

Cold fear ran through his veins. It all made sense now—the odd number of men, no keys, the truck left in neutral. It hadn't been driven there—it had been towed. And left to be discovered.

What had they been thinking? Why were they so certain that somebody would examine the damned thing before an air strike took it out? What were the odds of that? Had we been close enough to—to—

To catch it. Whatever they had, whatever they were infected with, whatever had killed them. How did they know we would be close enough to breathe the air, that we wouldn't take precautions—that we wouldn't be suspicious?

Biological warfare, the thing that struck terror into the hearts of most ground soldiers. If they could see it, they could kill it, and if they died trying, so be it. But this form of warfare, the invisible, deadly weapon of bacteria and spores, that was something else. You couldn't see it—you didn't even know when you were exposed. And once you had been exposed, there was very little you could do.

From outside the doors, he could hear the beginnings of an uproar. The receding steps on hard linoleum, the rustle of uniforms, muffled orders to clear the area. Still the staff sergeant waited, motionless. He knew the order to clear the area didn't apply to him.

Moments later, two soldiers clad in full NBC warfare gear came into the office. They walked over to him slowly and stood beside him. No words were necessary. "Lead the way, boys," he said, standing up. The movement made him slightly light-headed, and he felt a flash of annoyance at what he thought was fear. He rested one hand on the table to steady himself. But the blackness continued encroaching on his sight, narrowing his field of vision down to a narrow tunnel that seem to be filled by the two monstrous men. He staggered again, and after a moment's hesitation, one of them reached out and caught him by the elbow. The other darted to a telephone and punched the numbers in with fingers made clumsy by the gloves. "We'll need a gurney. And make sure the rest of the squad is in isolation—quarantine—immediately."

The staff sergeant heard the words coming as though from a long distance away. A loud buzzing filled his ears, drowning out everything else. He sank slowly to the floor, then crumpled. One of the soldiers unfolded him and stretched him out on his back. The staff sergeant coughed and the soldier jerked back.

By the time the gurney arrived, the staff sergeant had long since lost consciousness. Blood was seeping from his ears and nose and other orifices, and even the whites of his eyes were turning red. He was coughing up blood, too, when he had the strength to do so, but it continued to seep into his lungs at an alarming rate. No energy, no energy to fight it off. Slowly, quietly, he suffocated in his own blood.

Two days later, infectious disease specialists at Walter Reed Army Hospital would confirm what both the intelligence officer and his sergeant had suspected. The plague—the black death. And by that time, more than one hundred soldiers had been exposed to the deadly disease.

The United Nations
New York, New York
1300 local (GMT −5)

Wexler's voice, amplified by the microphone, rang out confident and sure. "I must ask this body to renew its longstanding resolution providing for a United Nations peacekeeping force in the Middle East. As to the justification, I think recent events provide more than enough. As you all know, our aircraft carrier, the USS *United States,* was attacked while in international waters outside the Persian Gulf.

Fortunately, due to the efforts of her crew, the damage was minimal. Additionally, we have credible evidence of stockpiles of biochemical weapons being maintained just across the Kuwaiti border. Both of those facts reflect the continuing instability in the region and the need for coordinated supervision to maintain law and order."

"Any response?" the Secretary General was from the Bahamas, and his musical accent provided a sharp contrast to her strident tones.

The delegate from Pakistan rose, pointedly turning away from Wexler and the American contingent. "Uh-oh," Brad whispered to her. "I think we're about to see some payback."

"No kidding," she murmured, keeping a neutral expression plastered on her face. Out of the corner of her eye, she saw the British ambassador stir uneasily.

Any opposition to the motion to extend the peacekeeping forces would be absolutely ludicrous. Pakistan was far closer to the region than the United States was, and if open warfare broke out, it would surely suffer just as much as anyone in the region. It was in Pakistan's interest to keep peace in the area, and she thought it was something that at least Pakistan and India could agree on.

"The ambassador from Pakistan," the Secretary General acknowledged.

"Pakistan wishes to add the following amendment to the bill as presented. As a matter of background, all the delegates are aware that the Middle East is not the only powerful region of the world currently in turmoil."

"Uh-oh," Brad murmured again. "I didn't believe he had the balls to do it, but he sure looks like he's going to try."

"Foremost among the troubled regions of the world today is the United States. As we are all aware, her own law-enforcement and civilian authorities have been overwhelmed by the recent acts of terrorism. Military troops are now deployed across the nation, suppressing the very constitutional rights that they purport to uphold. The rights of freedom of assembly and freedom of speech are no more than words to the current American regime, and all dissenters are being repressed just as vigorously as those in Afghanistan were."

Wexler responded, her voice amused. "Surely you're not suggesting that our women are now clad in burkas."

"I am merely pointing out that America suppresses dissidents more vigorously than almost any nation on earth. Under the circumstances, if we are to continue peacekeeping efforts in the Middle East, I would like to make a motion that a task force be deployed to the United States as well."

"No," Wexler said flatly. "Enough of this charade. We all know what is behind it. This didn't work last time and it will not work now. There will be no United Nations peacekeeping force inside United States."

The United Nations
2100 local (GMT +3)

After the ugly incident in the executive dining room, Wexler had no illusions about solidarity in support of the United States. True, Great Britain was standing by her side, and France and Italy were at least making nominal motions of support. Russia was being her usual unpredictable self, but Wexler suspected that it was more the result of being distracted by problems at home that any attempts to manipulate the situation. Most worrisome, China was silent.

China. No one knew better than she did that her personal relationship with its ambassador did not entitle her to an inside look at their foreign affairs policy. Regardless of their friendship, they were both professional diplomats, each serving the interests of their respective nations before allowing any personal considerations to intrude. Despite her understanding and resolve, at some level she was hurt.

There had been no need to discuss the matter with T'ing And indeed, they'd worked out a way of dealing with these matters between themselves, one that allowed each one to save face and avoid raising mutually disturbing issues. At times, when the issues simply became overwhelming, they avoided each other's company until the latest crisis had passed.

In their current unspoken protocol, T'ing himself should have raised the issue. He undoubtedly knew that the United States wanted to know his country's position on the outrageous Pakistani motion, and had he been able to comment, he would have done so. But his failure to even mention the matter led Wexler to suspect that there was more of an agenda than anyone knew. Perhaps it was another grab for the Spratley Islands. Perhaps it was the Korean issue, always a sore point in that part of the world. Or perhaps it was something entirely unrelated, an alliance that no Western mind could easily understand.

Whatever the reason, T'ing had not brought up China's position on Pakistan's motion. And, since he hadn't, Wexler wouldn't.

At any rate, she thought, surveying the assembled delegates, the matter was moot now. The matter had wended its way into subcommittee and out at record speed, and was scheduled for a vote this morning.

The President had called earlier that day to ask her how she thought it would go. It was one of the few times she had no ready answer for it, and she felt a personal sense of failure at that. There was too much ambiguity, too many problems in the world that might be bargaining chips for her to predict that outcome.

The British ambassador had clapped her reassuringly on the shoulder before proceeding to his seat. "Stiff upper lip and all that," he had murmured. The representative from Australia had also stopped by to offer a word of encouragement, saying, "No worries, mate," and grinning that broad smile that always amused her.

Still, it was easy to be nonchalant about it when you weren't the one forced into using veto power. It was easy to be charitable when you weren't the one who would have to exercise a veto.

The vote began. With every passing moment, Wexler's concern deepened. Even a short way into the roll call, it was clear that many of the smaller nations were going to be voting in favor of the Pakistani motion.

We're still fools in that way, aren't we? Just because we charge in and help their governments maintain order, provide them with extensive economic aid, back their IMF loans, and generally pretend that they are respected powers in their own rights, we expect some form of loyalty. But that's not the way the world works—it never happens. Nations respect power. Not friendship.

What bothered her most were the expressions of glee on some of the faces. It was clear that they were looking forward to turning the tables, to having the mightiest nation in the world dealing with foreign troops on her own soil. They'd tried this before, and it hadn't worked, but never had the United States experienced such internal turmoil as it was experiencing right now.

Not that it would happen. With the problem over delinquent dues resolved, the United States was now a full voting member of the Assembly and still possessed a veto power.

Finally, the Pakistani ambassador rose and turned to face Wexler as he cast his vote. "Pakistan votes in favor of the motion, joining with our brothers and sisters across the world who have suffered at the hands of American imperialism. Let this be a lesson to all powerful nations that those standards they apply to us must apply to them equally."

And that was the problem with the United Nations, she thought. It was the reason we set up a bicameral form of government in our own country, with the Senate having the same number of representatives from each state while the Congress reflects the population balance among states. Here, however, every pipsqueak nation in the world has one vote. No matter if they've lived off international welfare for their entire short-lived existences, they still get the same vote we do.

Finally, when the votes were tallied, the results clearly against the United States, Wexler rose. "The United States exercises its veto." She paused, considering whether she'd elaborate, and then decided against it. Everyone knew what she had just done and why she'd done it.

"The motion is defeated," the Secretary General announced. He gazed at Wexler, concern on his face. "This means the United Nations resolutions supporting coordinated action in the Middle East is also defeated. Does the United States understand that?"

"We do."

There was a longer silence. Then the Bahamian ambassador said, "Under the circumstances, I believe United Nations intervention in the Middle East is absolutely critical. Without our presence there, including the overwhelming support of the United States, we face a world in chaos. Accordingly, as a representative of more thoughtful voices, I call on the ambassador from the United States to reconsider her veto. I am willing to hold this vote opened for a period of time, allowing the ambassador to confer with your president. Additionally, the time during which the United States may exercise its veto is hereby extended. These departures from normal procedure will, I believe, allow this body to continue its work in the Middle East while granting disagreeing parties time to work out a more acceptable compromise." A storm of angry voices arose from the floor, needing no amplification to be heard. The Secretary General gazed out calmly at the protests. "So be it. This session is adjourned." He banged his gavel, stood, and swept out of the rear exit.

The chamber exploded into the chaos. At least a few of the delegates appeared prepared to attack Wexler personally, each one convinced that she herself was the force behind the Secretary General's action.

Wexler tried to tell them that she was as puzzled as they were, that she had had no warning herself. Surely that should have been evident from her reaction. However, the delegates were accustomed to her normal impassive expression, and simply thought her surprise was feigned.

The ambassador from Great Britain elbowed up next to her, adding his security forces to hers. "I suggest we leave now," he murmured, gently urging her toward the door. His own security force and hers quickly melted into one team and herded their charges out.

"What the heck was that?" Wexler asked as they exited the chamber and headed for an elevator. "How the hell did the SecGen come up with that little maneuver?"

The British ambassador regarded her fondly. "It wasn't so long ago that they were our colony," he said quietly. "And, contrary to most expectations, the current government is often inclined to take our advice. As you know, we still provide considerable assistance to them and, unlike Pakistan and other nations, they have not forgotten that." He fixed her with a stern look. "That skill is one that the United States needs to learn."

"Thanks." An elevator door opened, and her people broke away from the Brits and herded her into it. As the door closed, she saw the British ambassador smile.

SIXTEEN

Abraham Carter parked five miles down the road from the reserve center, pulling off on a road barely more than an animal track and following it until he was out of sight. Two trucks containing six other men followed him.

Abraham's truck had a radio dialed to the frequency of his strike force, and he carried a shotgun in addition to the side arm. None of that was unusual, not in Montana. In fact, it would have been out of the ordinary if a vehicle didn't have some firepower.

Jackson and two other men piled out of the truck and grabbed their gear from the back. Abraham watched them uneasily. This had to be done, and Jackson had insisted on taking the lead.

Jackson and his men took their time making their way from his father's truck to the reserve center. He and his companions, Bill Thornburg and Jack Mertz, had known each other since their teenage days. The other two men were completely trustworthy and eager to participate in the mission.

The reserve center was maintained by the National Guard and the U.S. Army Reserve, with troops from both forces sharing the facility. The Army provided uniforms, equipment, and some operating funds. In exchange, the Montana National Guard was subject to mobilization and federalization, a process during which it would cease to become a state law-enforcement agency and become part of the federal military forces. A small Naval Reserve unit was temporarily attached as well, its prior reserve center a victim of the latest round of base closures.

The three-acre tract was nestled between two mountain ranges on a relatively flat bit of terrain. It was surrounded by a six-foot chain-link fence that had been there since shortly after the Korean War. In the last few years, the support posts had been extended and razor wire curled around the top rail. There had been some talk of installing motion sensors and pressure sensors along with remote-surveillance TV, but Montana was exceptionally low on the reserve funding list.

At each quarter of the reserve compound, a large street-lamp illuminated an area both inside and outside the compound. Large stretches of the area surrounding the building itself were still in darkness, and clumps of trees partially shielded the building from view. There were two gates, one in front of the reserve center and intended primarily for passenger vehicles and smaller trucks, the other reached via a side road to the north of the compound and used by heavy equipment such as flatbed trucks, Marine assault vehicles, and two Army Corps of Engineers bulldozers.

Jackson stopped in a swath of bushes just outside the fence and surveyed the parking lot. "Just like they said—but two cars there, not one." Jackson said. Prior to 9/11, the building had been unattended after normal working hours. In case of an emergency or mobilization order, the caller was advised by the answering machine to contact the duty officer via his pager. Now, most reserve centers were manned 24-7 by at least one body. This late at night, Jackson had been expecting to see just one car, that of the duty officer.

"They didn't say anything about two people," Thornburg said. "But that's not a problem."

Jackson grunted. No, it wasn't a problem, but he didn't like it. Faulty intelligence was the major downfall of most operations, and he was particularly determined that this would go exactly as planned.

"Could be somebody's car just broke down over the weekend," Jack suggested. "We can check if there's dust on the windshield, see if it's broken."

"Good idea. But it's under the lights." The parking lot had a separate set of streetlights and every inch of it was illuminated. "What if somebody decides he needs something out of his car? No, we go in like we planned. If somebody else turns up, we deal with it." Jackson's voice was grim.

They went in the way that they had briefed, circling the compound through the brush and trees to approach the heavy equipment yard. There, the large trucks and vehicles were parked near the fence close to each other and provided additional shadows. Jackson took the wire cutters and unhesitatingly made the first cut in the chain link. They retreated to a safe distance and waited for twenty minutes, but nothing happened. Their source had been accurate. There were no ground pressure sensors or sensors on the fence to alarm whoever was inside the reserve center. They returned, cut enough strands to open a hole, and slid into the heavy vehicle yard.

Like the parking lot, the concrete lot that housed large equipment for several units was well illuminated, but badly planned. Several vehicles were parked in such a manner as to provide a continuous trail of shadows to cover their approach. It was not entirely accidental. The same source that had provided the details on the compound security was also part of the motor pool.

He had also provided a key, both to the back door and the administrative section, where the duty personnel usually stayed. Jackson and his men moved quietly, three large, camouflaged figures out of place in the white passageway with well-waxed floors. The double doors that separated the administrative section from the drill hall were steel-paneled with two windows, one on each side. Jackson and his men crouched down so as not to be seen as they used their key. The door opened easily.

Yeoman Second Class Anthony Hillman looked up as the door opened. He froze for just a moment, then slammed away from his desk and started running. Probably for the duty room, Jackson thought. There'll be a telephone there.

Hillman was fast, but the three men caught him easily. Jackson slammed him against the wall and put a knife to his throat. "The keys to the armory—now."

"I don't have them," Hillman said, his voice a little shakier than he would have liked.

"Sure you do." Jackson pressed the tip of the knife into Hillman's throat. Hillman moaned as the blade penetrated the skin. Rough hands moved over him, plunging into the pockets of his uniform. Thornburg pulled out a ring of keys.

"Well, well. Let's go see if these fit the armory. I hope not. I would hate to think you'd lied to me." Jackson twisted Hillman's arm behind his back and marched him to the armory. After fumbling through half the keys, Thornburg found one that fit. The door swung open. They were confronted by a steel cage secured with another lock. Thornburg tried all the keys, then shrugged. Hillman had been partially accurate, anyway. "Only the gunner's mates have that one" Hillman said, his voice a little stronger. Sure, he was still scared, real scared, but he was pissed, too.

"I have a key," Mertz announced. He pulled out his .45 and shot the lock. The bullet destroyed the lock, ricocheted once, then buried itself in the cement wall.

"Go get the truck," Jackson ordered. "I'll keep our new friend company." He shoved Hillman down the floor and stood over him, a faint smile on his face as he aimed his own .45 at the petty officer's face.

Tombstone's command post
0400 local (GMT −7)

Greenfield appeared to be completely fascinated by the condition of his fingernails as he listened to Tombstone speak. Finally, when the former admiral was finished, he looked up. "Why me?"

"Why not?" Tombstone asked. "The FBI is more familiar with this sort of operation than anyone else."

"I sure am." There was no mistaking the bitterness in Greenfield's voice.

"Would you like some more time to feel sorry for yourself?"

Greenfield finally looked up. "Try again, mister. The only people I feel sorry for are those three who died in the fire. I see those kids every time I turn around. Or I see an adult that looks like they will ten years from now. I've seen their pictures in the paper. I know what they looked like. That wasn't how they looked the last time I saw them."

"Then keep it from happening again. Take on the XO billet."

"That an order?"

Tombstone shrugged. "If you want it to be. Call it a request for now."

"Try Bratton. That's more his style."

"He suggested you."

Greenfield nodded. "That makes sense. It's to the CIA's advantage if this goes wrong."

"Maybe I made a mistake," Tombstone said in an entirely different tone of voice.

"That would make two of us. Look, it's not that I don't appreciate it. But I couldn't keep things from going wrong when I was in charge of the operation. You're asking me to step into the number-two position and take responsibility for your decisions."

"No." Tombstone's voice was firm. "That's what happened to you before. I'm asking you to make sure that my decisions and orders are carried out. That's all. Any shit rolls uphill in my organization, buddy. That's evidently not the case in the FBI."

Tombstone turned and stalked away. He hadn't gone more than ten steps when Greenfield said, "OK. I'll do it."

Tombstone stopped. "Good. The first thing you do, set up communications with whatever state and local agencies there are around here. Something is going to go down—it's just a matter of when."

Montana Reserve Center
0400 local (GMT—7)

Seaman Greg Vincent Hedges completed his security round and was heading back toward the building when he saw a shadow move. He froze where he was, his eyes focused on the spot, and then saw a man moving between the shadows. His right hand went to his belt where he normally carried a .45. In civilian life, Seaman Hedges was with the Butte Police Department. But security patrols at the reserve center were armed with nothing more than a walkie-talkie. He had it riding on his left hip, and he reached out and turned it off, hoping the click the switch made wouldn't be audible. He slid to his right, finding a shadow of his own to provide cover, and watched.

There were three of them, all in camouflage and armed. He saw them make their way to the reserve center, unlock the back door, and disappear from sight. Hedges made a slow, careful circuit of the area himself, more skillfully than the three men had done. When he was certain there were no others waiting, he put a truck between himself and the reserve center and pulled out a cell phone. He dialed 911.

"So which one of those cars out front is yours?" Jackson asked heartily, as though making conversation.

"The white Toyota."

"And the other car?"

They don't know Hedges is here. A surge of hope ran through him. "I don't know. Somebody left it here last weekend." But he was a little too slow in answering to be believable.

"Just left it here, huh? You're not standing a very tight watch if you don't know who it belongs to."

"I haven't read the pass-down log yet. Maybe there's something about it in there." As soon as the words left his lips, Hillman regretted it. Because the pass-down log was sitting right next to his duty log, and the duty log would show that there were two people, not one, in the building. Fortunately, the intruder didn't appear inclined to want to examine it.

Just then, Mertz and Thornburg returned. "Ready to go. They leave the keys in the trucks."

Jackson nodded. "Good. Let's get a move on. You, too," he added, motioning at Hillman. "Load up the weapons and ammo into the deuce-and-a-halves. It won't take long—half an hour and we're out of here."

Hillman tried to believe that they were going to leave him alive.

Hedges filled in the dispatcher in clipped phrases, adding, "Tell them I'm in the heavy equipment compound. I don't want to get shot. Once I see them approach, I will step out in the open with my hands up. I have my ID on me."

"Roger, copy all. Units will be responding—what?" The dispatcher broke off as she listened to someone off-line. "There'll be a slight delay in the assistance, Greg. We have to call in another agency."

"Look, I know this is on federal lands, but we've got a situation going down," Hedges snapped. "We don't have time to wait for the feds to roll out of bed."

"From what I can tell, they've been waiting for your call."

Montana Reserve Center
0410 local (GMT−7)

Fear pulled Hillman in different directions. Every time he looked into the intruders' faces, a shiver ran through him, terminating somewhere about six inches below his belly button. Their faces were not that easy to make out, not with all that camouflage paint. Surely they didn't think that he would be able to recognize them. Disobeying any order was unthinkable, yet at the same time, he was desperately certain he knew what would happen when they were done. The only reason he was alive right now was to serve as slave labor loading the trucks. When that was done, he could only be a liability to them.

Finally, the last two shotguns were loaded in the back of the truck. The ammunition had been loaded first to keep it near the center of gravity. At the intruder's command, Hillman climbed into the back of the truck and helped pull a tarp over the load. It wouldn't offer much concealment if they were stopped, but it would keep rain off it if a storm came up. Given the moldy, rotten condition of the tarp enclosing the back of the truck, that might be all the protection it had.

Ammunition. Weapons. Ammunition. Weapons. The thought kept running through his head that there had to be some way to capitalize on the proximity of the two. *Grab a shotgun, jam a cartridge in it.* No, damn it, he should've thought of that when he was loading the ammo and somehow slipped a couple of rounds into his pocket.

He bent down and tugged on the tarp as though making sure it covered part of the load, his fingers scrambling underneath it and closing on a box of shotgun shells. Two of them watched him, their faces impassive. He tried to pretend he was fumbling with the rope, but couldn't manage to do it.

One of them motioned slightly with a weapon. "Quit fucking with it. It's done." His words had a resounding finality to them.

*I can grab it and use it as a club. I can get at least one
of them before they—no, I can't. Maybe they're not going to
kill me. That's why they have the camouflage on.*

They certainly had not been cautious about letting him see
their faces. Why didn't they care, then? The grab for the
shotgun was looking better and better.

The man who climbed up in the truck with him grabbed
him by the shoulder and shoved him toward the tailgate.
"Out."

On the ground, the leader of the gang took charge again.
"Back in the reserve center. I'm going to lock you in the
armory. Somebody will come by eventually to let you out, I
guess."

A vast sense of relief flooded Hillman. That was it. They
would lock him up. It would be hours before his relief arrived, and they would be far away by then. They were probably ex-military themselves and correctly figured that the
watch would change at 0800.

Hillman led the way back into the reserve center, so weak
from relief that he could barely walk. The leader followed
him while the other two stayed at the truck. Back in the
reserve center, he walked docilely to the armory. The sooner
he got there, the sooner they would lock him up and go away.
Right now, he could think of nothing beside that.

As he stepped into the weapons cage, he turned to face
the leader. He kept his gaze fixed on the floor to reassure the
man that there was no way he could identify him, none at
all.

The leader stepped in the cage with him. In one smooth
motion, he drew his .45 and shot Hillman in the head. The
young petty officer's body slammed into the back wall, splat-
tering the pale-green government paint with gore.

Jackson trotted back out to the trucks, shaking his head in
annoyance. The first shot to take the lock off had left him
slightly deafened, and the second shot had compounded the
problem. Maybe he should have shot the sailor in the drill
hall where there was more open space to dissipate the sound.
But that wouldn't have had the same impact on those who

found him as the armory would. Or would it? Surely they wouldn't think that incompetent excuse for a soldier had died defending the armory.

It had to be inside somewhere, that was the problem. Even in a part of the country that was normally well armed, some-body might be curious about gunshots coming from the re-serve center. Jackson experienced a quiet moment of pride that he even thought of that—many wouldn't.

Thornburg and Mertz had the trucks started and turned toward the gate. One of them had already snipped the chain holding the gate, and it was pulled open. Jackson jumped into the passenger seat of Thornburg's vehicle and said, "Let's go."

Thornburg gave him a grin and gunned the engine. He let it idle down and then shifted into first gear. He stopped, squinted, then stuck his head out the window. The grin faded into a scowl.

"What is it?" Jackson demanded, still barely able to hear. "Sirens."

Hedges had heard the gunshot and started to break cover and run forward. He knew with sick certainty what had happened, and swore silently at his own impotence. He should have run out and jumped one of them, maybe lured one of them off—somehow, he ought to been able to do something. Even with-out his gun.

You couldn't do anything except die with him and you know it. Wait for the backup.

He could hear the sirens, marginally louder now, their fre-quency increasing as they approached. But the trucks were gunning their engines. As he watched, one rolled out and headed for the gate.

Get to the gate. You can hold it shut, you can, one part of his mind insisted.

No. You can't. They'll simply run you down. No Tianan-men Square standoff with these guys.

Inspiration seized him. The lead truck would pass within thirty feet of his location, the second one about twenty feet behind it. There was a risk, but not a large one. The shadows covered this portion of the compound and the gate, and all he needed was a little luck.

He let the second truck pass, took a deep breath, then ran out from the shadows to fall in behind it. Adrenaline flooded his system, giving him the extra energy needed to dart forward, jump, and grab the second truck's tailgate. He let his arms do the work then, his feet providing traction where they could as the truck picked up speed. He hauled himself into the back of the deuce-and-a-half and slipped under the canvas cover. Inside, it was pitch black, and he prayed that the night was dark enough that the man in front of them would not be able to see him moving.

He fumbled around in the darkness until he located a box of shotgun shells, then quietly felt under the canvas until he found a weapon. There was no sign that the driver noticed anything was amiss. He caressed the shotgun, feeling a whole lot better about what was starting to sound like a stupid plan.

Better, but not good enough. There had to be—yes, there was. His fingers closed around a .45 handgun. Now where was the ammo? It took a little longer, but finally he located it. The noise from the diesel engines and the truck rattling covered the sound as he loaded both weapons.

So now what? He contemplated dropping the tailgate and shoving the rest of the weapons and ammunition out of the truck, rejecting the idea almost at once. Too much noise, and it would pose a hazard for other people on the road. No, better to keep everything all in one place: the perp, the evidence, and the cop.

Through a small sliding window that separated the driver's compartment from the rest of the truck, he could see that the distance to the lead truck was increasing. Sooner or later, the driver would notice he was falling behind and speed up. It had to be now.

In one clean motion, he broke the glass and shoved the business end of the shotgun through it into the driver's compartment. The truck careened wildly and almost turned over, but the driver fought it back onto the road.

"Pull over," Hedges said, shouting to be heard over the noise. "Both hands on the steering wheel, asshole."

Either the driver didn't hear so well or he was terminally stupid. He was already reaching for the handgun on the seat.

Shit. This isn't going well. Time seemed to slow, almost stop. The driver's fingers closed around the gun. It would be an awkward angle, almost impossible to do any aiming, but Hedges wasn't willing to take any chances. He pointed the shotgun down and pulled the trigger.

The driver's arm below the elbow disappeared in a hurricane of blood that blew back through the window, temporarily blinding Hedges. He jerked the shotgun back and jumped, sacrificing any skill or grace he might have possessed in a frantic effort to make it to the tailgate. He bounced off the side of the truck as it went into a spin. Screams of pain and anguish were now audible from the front seat. It was impossible to stand up, and he had only a few seconds before the truck overturned or crashed into a tree. Hedges pulled him himself up amid the shifting cargo, gathered his feet under him, and made one final jump. He hit the canvas cover in the back of the truck, and for a moment he thought he was trapped.

Then the old, sun-bleached fabric parted, releasing him from the dangerous confines of the truck. He flew through the air, instinct taking over. By sheer luck, he hit the dirt beside the road and tucked and rolled. He took most of the impact on his shoulder and felt something give way. He tumbled through brush, chin tucked, arms covering his face as branches and shrubs tore at him. Finally, what seemed like hours later, he came to a stop.

Silence. The truck, where was it? He tried to shove himself up, but his right arm wasn't bearing any weight. He collapsed on his side, rolled over, and tried again. Finally, in the dim starlight, he could see a dark shape further into the brush up ahead. The engine was silent.

I'll find him. Find him and kill him for what he did. Hedges moved forward, still running on adrenaline and instinct, vengeance his only goal.

With each move came the pain, and that restored him to sanity. He had not covered more than ten feet toward the truck before he stopped, pulled out a cell phone, and dialed 911. In the distance, the sirens were growing louder.

0430 local (GMT −7)

Any moment now. Abraham glanced at his watch again, reassuring himself that they were still not late, that everything was going according to plan. It wasn't like him to have a case of nerves during an operation. But then again, he usually wasn't quite so far from the action.

Oh, he had no doubt Jackson could pull off getting the ammunition and weapons. They'd done so too many times in the past. Sure, the Army investigated and tried to crack down, but these military facilities in remote areas of the country were little more than sieves. Firepower leaked out of them and into the surrounding hills, and rather than face the embarrassment, the Army simply marked equipment off as lost, expended, or stolen.

It wasn't the operation that worried him. It had been the look on his son's face. He knew Jackson was chafing under the restrictions placed on him, that he longed for greater responsibility within the organization. He had somehow gotten it in his mind that it would take a dramatic gesture to prove himself worthy. Abraham had tried to dispel the notion, stressing the need to remain covert and appear simply as members of the community. While Jackson outwardly agreed with that principle, Abraham knew his son too well to believe him.

Finally, he heard the dull roar of the truck echoing through the mountains. It was coming closer now, approaching far too fast. It was a decent road, but still, a two-ton truck was an unwieldy monster.

Moments later, the truck drove by, traveling at approximately sixty miles an hour down the narrow road. Abraham swore and yanked down the microphone from its mount on the ceiling.

"Red Dog One, this is Red Dog Leader. Interrogative your status?"

There was no answer. He tried again, this time adding, "Report!"

Jackson's voice answered, unsteady as he jounced around in the truck. "No problems. Go ahead and head out. We'll rendezvous as planned."

"Slow down," Abraham ordered. "You'll just call attention to yourself going that fast."

There was no answer. Swearing, Abraham put his truck into gear and headed down the road after his troops. An old Army adage sprang to mind: Lead, follow, or get the hell out of the way.

Highway
0430 local (GMT −7)

Thornburg's headlights flickered wildly in the rearview mirror and caught Jackson's attention. He leaned forward to stare at the mirror, and then rolled down the window and stuck his head out. "What the hell is he doing?"

"I don't know." Mertz took his gaze off the road in front of him long enough to check the rearview mirror. "Flat tire, maybe. That's all we need right now."

"Are there spares?"

Mertz shook his head. "I didn't notice any."

Jackson swore quietly. "We better slow down and let him catch up, see what's wrong."

The lights careened off the right side of the rearview mirror and disappeared. "Stop!" Jackson snapped. "Damned idiot. Turn around—we'll have to go back and get him. I think we can get most of his gear on this truck."

Mertz obediently slowed the vehicle and then started to turn. Alarm bells went off in Jackson's mind. There was no traffic on the road, no indication that anyone but the kid in the reserve center had seen them. But the other car—what if—? "Pull over."

He'd made a mistake, perhaps a serious one. What if there had been someone else in the reserve compound? Could they have done something to the second truck? Or had they ambushed Thornburg on his way out? Was that even possible?

He closed his eyes for a moment, ignoring Mertz's quizzical look. A very long shot, but it was possible. So now what? Could they risk everything to go back and see what had happened to Thornburg?

No. They couldn't.

Thornburg had probably had a flat tire. That had to be it. But there was a small possibility that he had been ambushed, and that was a chance they could not take. One truckload of weapons was better than none.

"Forget him," Jackson said finally. He glanced over, and saw understanding dawn on the other man's face.

"So what do we do now?"

"Turn around and take the alternate route to the east." Jackson thought furiously for a moment and continued. "On the off chance that he's been compromised, we're going to take the long way around. Make sure no one is following us. Then, when we're sure were clean, we'll stop at the caves, unload the armory, then head for HQ." Seeing a look of doubt on Mertz's face, he said, "There were bound to be casualties, Jack. You knew that."

Mertz shrugged as though it didn't matter. "You're the boss." He turned the truck around and started back the way they'd been headed.

Jackson smiled. *Not the boss. The leader. There's a difference, and someday you'll understand that.*

SEVENTEEN

Tombstone's command post
0600 local (GMT−7)

"No kidding," Greenfield said into the phone, and his tone of voice caught Tombstone's attention immediately. He left the aerial charts he was looking at and walked over to the corner of the room that had been designated as Greenfield's office. There was a look of concentration on the man's face as he listened, as though every atom of his being was devoted to straining out every morsel of information from the conversation. His side of the call had that peculiarly stilted rhythm of someone who's the recipient of news. "Where?" A long pause, then, "When?" Finally, a look of grim pleasure spread across Greenfield's face and he said, "How do we get there?"

He turned to Tombstone, something in his bearing making him look like a very dangerous man. "We got them. At least part of them. If you still have any connections in the government, you better pull them now. And later on, too, because one very tough, smart cop from Butte just saved us a hell of a lot of trouble."

Abraham Carter and his men parked their vehicles a safe way from the compound and followed the well-concealed trail back to HQ. As they approached the front entrance, he saw a small figure seated on the porch, alone and apparently unarmed. He motioned most of the men into concealment and went forward with only one other man.

"Hello," a woman's voice said, confident and sure of her welcome. "I've been waiting for you. I'm Pamela Drake." Behind her, her cameraman held out his hands, palm up, to show he was unarmed.

Thirty minutes later, after Drake had proffered an entirely fabricated story of her success in locating them, Carter holstered his pistol. "Okay. You're here. For now." He turned to face his men and continued. "You all know what we're up against. There's a good chance they're onto us now. Or least, we have indications that they are." No one questioned that statement. They all knew that the organization far above their level had agents planted in every federal law-enforcement agency.

"You think you'll have to make a stand here?" Drake asked.

Carter shot her an annoyed look. "Maybe. They'll know the trucks and weapons are missing. If they find out we're here, they'll make the connection."

There were some murmurs of agreement, and then they fell silent. "So what do we do?" one asked.

"We wait until Jackson gets the trucks here or until we hear from him. Then we move out."

"And if the Feds turn up?" Drake persisted.

"We hold them off long enough for the trucks to get away, if it comes to that. It won't be an easy thing. They'll likely have helicopters and air assets to help track them, probably infrared as well."

"What are the odds they'll come here?" another asked.

"I don't know." He glanced outside. The sky was already starting to lighten. "But I think we'll find out soon."

Tombstone's command post
0635 local (GMT −7)

Greenfield snapped his cell phone shut. Tombstone was still not accustomed to the wolfish expression the man's face had taken on. "What is it?"

"Our Butte cop. He managed to snag a ride on one of the trucks and took down the driver. Jumped out the back just before it rolled over. The driver is still alive, but just barely. The cop's okay."

"Where?"

"About twenty miles from here, out on a pretty isolated road. The other truck started to come back to look, but evidently it changed its mind and headed east. The state fellows are scrambling now."

"Patrol cars?"

Greenfield nodded. "Air, too, as soon as they can get the birds warmed up. Be nice if we could avoid scaring these guys off and find out where they're headed." He glanced at his watch. "Every second we wait is going to make it harder to find them. The country out here . . ." He let his voice trail off, indicating the rugged landscape around him. "Mountains, ravines, caves are everywhere. They could disappear real easily."

"Let's not wait for them," Tombstone said. "We've got those air assets lined up, right? They're supposed to be on fifteen-minute standby—let's just see how well the reserves can put their money where their mouth is." He turned to the operations officer, who he knew had had some aviation experience. "You talked to the air reserve center?"

The man nodded. "It's an Air National Guard unit about thirty miles from here. They said they have helicopter and surface-search aircraft on standby."

"Get them airborne. Coordinate an intercept vector with Greenfield." Tombstone caught himself—he had almost said, "the XO."

"Can do." The operations officer snapped open his cell phone, consulted a scrap of paper, and a punched in a telephone number. He walked away from the two men to talk to the air reserve operations officer on the other end.

"Pretty nice," Greenfield said grudgingly. "Air assets, all the manpower you want—hell, I bet we could even submit a pretty fancy restaurant bill on your expense account."

Tombstone regarded him steadily. "And you're thinking that if you had had this much support, Bull Run would have gone differently."

The warrior look faded from Greenfield's face. Suddenly, he looked years older. "Maybe. Maybe not." He stared off into space, as though watching the operation unfold again. "I had enough assets on site—more than enough. It was the intelligence that sucked."

"Speaking of intelligence, who took the trucks?" Tombstone asked. "Any idea?"

Greenfield shrugged, clearly putting the Bull Run incident away. "It could be a number of folks. From the style of it, it could be the Carters. We think they've been involved in a number of weapons raids and it's always a middle-of-the-night, paramilitary sort of thing. Camouflage uniforms, the whole nine yards. Most of the other militias just pilfer the stuff. Out in this part of the country, they have enough contacts to make that happen. They usually don't have to kill people to get what they want."

"Pilfer?"

"They steal it. They all have people inside the active duty and reserve organizations. How hard is it to make stuff disappear?" Greenfield's voice held a note of bitterness. "So, yeah, my money is on the Carters."

"So where do you think they're headed?" Tombstone asked.

"I don't know. That's why we need to find that other truck. They probably have a base camp somewhere and eventually that's where they'll go. They need bodies to carry the guns."

Bratton strolled up, a look of mild interest on his face. "Lands End, probably."

"Lands End what?" Tombstone asked. Greenfield simply scowled.

"Lands End, Idaho. They have a base camp there. Sort of a training facility—it's been up and running about six months now. Abraham Carter was headed up there yesterday, so if Junior is running, that's where I bet he will head."

"Why didn't you tell me this yesterday?" Tombstone asked.

"Because—" Bratton started

"Because," Greenfield interrupted, his voice harsh, "sharing information doesn't necessarily mean the same thing to the CIA as it does to you and me. Before this, it wasn't relevant, was it?"

"No, it wasn't," Bratton said calmly.

"And now it is," Tombstone said.

"That's it exactly." Bratton nodded his head. "Sharing information doesn't mean dumping everything we have in front of you. It means that when we've got something that's pertinent to your operation, we let you know, if we can do so without endangering an agent's life."

"You have someone inside the organization?" Greenfield asked. Bratton did not answer.

I see how it is. They're going to cooperate, but not go out of their way unless they have to. Tombstone filed that bit of information away for later discussion with the CIA agent. Out loud, he asked, "Do you know the layout of this Lands End?"

Bratton nodded. "Here." He passed over a few pieces of paper with drawings on them, diagrams of an area of land and an interior diagram of a house. "We can probably get in relatively unobserved coming in this way," he said, tracing out a route through the woods behind the house. "But it's a long haul—it runs right along the base of these mountains and would be pretty easy to keep under observation. Going over the mountains isn't practical, and the other approaches are all clear-cut. We can get there, but whether we can do it covertly is a big question mark."

"OK, that's it," Tombstone said. "For now, we'll operate on the assumption that the Carters were behind the reserve center raid. Ops, get our air assets looking for that truck. Greenfield, call off the state boys—I don't want them spooking that truck." He raised his voice slightly. "Bug out, folks. I want everything critical packed and in the vehicles in fifteen minutes. We're headed for Lands End."

"And then we wait," Greenfield added. "This time, we wait."

Just outside Bull Run
0700 local (GMT −7)

Jackson Carter pounded on the window that separated him from the truck's cab. It slid back and he shouted, "Take the next left! We need to get this stuff in the caves and get to HQ."

The driver said nothing. Jackson studied the road behind him, searching for any sign of pursuit. "OK, keep a sharp eye out, but I think we've lost them. Another twenty minutes, and we'll be at the cave. Ten minutes to off-load and then we're history." Jackson put his head back and let loose a loud, fierce war cry.

Finally, Jackson stopped his howling. Mertz had a sickly smile pasted on his face. "This is just the beginning, buddy," Jackson said. "This is just the beginning."

EIGHTEEN

Despite what Air Force pilots thought, pulling Alert Five on board an aircraft carrier was considerably more unpleasant than sitting in an F-15 ashore. The black tarmac nonskid reflected up the heat, assaulting the aircraft with shimmering waves from every direction. The smaller huffers, rarely used in the Navy, were overwhelmed almost immediately trying to provide cooling air. The pilots sweated inside G-suits, silently damning the Iraqis who had forced them to bake in their own sweat. It was one thing to want to fly, to risk being killed on a combat mission—another matter entirely to sweat to death on the deck of an aircraft carrier.

Fastball was probably the least patient of any of the pilots of the squadron, Rat reflected. He had been bitching for the last twenty minutes, complaining about everything possible on board the ship, and had now regressed to reciting indignities he had suffered while in Navy ROTC. Given enough time, she was sure she would hear all the details of how unfair his potty training had been.

She tried to concentrate on the book she'd brought with her, but his whining voice interfered with her concentration.

Finally, when she could stand it no longer, she snapped, "Is it at all possible you could maintain radio silence long enough for me to finish this chapter? I've read the same page five times."

"Well, excuuuuuuuse me," Fastball said, seriously aggrieved. "Pardon me for assuming that perhaps some light conversation would make time go by faster. I guess I should never have assumed thought that the RIO I fly with every day would be interested in talking to me."

"Talking, maybe. Listening to you whine, no."

"Doesn't Commander Busby ever whine?"

She had wondered how long it would take him to get to the heart of it. Every time she disagreed with him, he began making sardonic remarks about her possible relationship with Busby. It had been going on for a week now, and she was getting damned tired of it.

"Well, doesn't he?" Fastball asked again, unaware of how dangerously close he was to the edge of her temper.

"No, now that you should mention it. He doesn't. I suppose he has better things to do with his time than complain about every detail of Navy life," she snapped.

"I knew you were seeing him," Fastball said, satisfaction in his voice. "Don't bother denying it anymore."

"And just how the hell do you 'see' someone on board an aircraft carrier?" She snapped.

"I guess you should tell me. He's senior enough to rate a private stateroom, right? And senior enough to be able to manage his own schedule."

"You got something to say?" Rat demanded.

From behind, she could see him shrug. Then he turned back to glare at her, turning as far as the ejection harness would allow him. "I'm not the only one, you know. Everybody sees you two at chow. Busby's showing up in the dirty-shirt mess all the time these days. Before, you never saw him outside of the flag mess. And you two all chummy, sitting by yourselves—you're a helluva cheap date, Rat."

She loosened her harness and reached forward to smack him on the side of his helmet. He let out a yelp and tried to turn to reach her, but the seat blocked his movement.

"Who I eat with is none of your business. And neither is what I do in my off hours. Not unless and until it begins affecting my performance in the cockpit. And if you got a complaint in that department, I suggest you take it up with CAG."

"Jesus, Rat. I'm just trying to look out for you."

"What are you, my big brother?"

"No. Just a guy who knows how other guys talk. And there's a lot of talk going around, Rat. You may not be doing anything, but when you come out of his cabin late at night with that stupid shit-eating grin on your face, it doesn't help matters any."

"You're jealous." She stated it as a fact, not a question.

He shook his head. "No. Don't flatter yourself. But you might keep in mind that what you do reflects on me, too. We're a team. Or at least I thought we were."

Not just jealousy. She realized that in a flash. No, she been closer to the mark when she'd called him a big brother. She had a sudden flash of insight. Sure, he would have heard the remarks—she'd overheard some of them herself. But she'd let them pass, not deigning to acknowledge them. Fastball wouldn't—he was constitutionally incapable of avoiding a fight. He would stick up for her, and probably had taken a lot of crap over it. No matter that nothing inappropriate had happened between her and Lab Rat. Nothing would, not while they were on the ship. But someday, when liberty ashore was a reality again, when they were both sure about how they felt, there was a very good chance that—

"You're right," she said finally. "I ought to avoid the *appearance* of impropriety, too."

Stunned silence from the forward seat greeted her admission.

"And you know there's nothing going on." Again, she stated it as a fact.

"Yeah, I know," he muttered. "You're too much of a tight ass to get laid on the ship, aren't you? Or maybe anywhere?"

She bit back a sharp reply, recognizing the outburst of

testosterone for what it was. A few moments later, she was greeted with, "Sorry about that."

CVIC
1520 local (GMT +3)

Petty Officer Carl Ellison loved his job. He was a tall, well-built man with broad shoulders that had carried him through a stellar career as a high school quarterback. He stayed in shape working out with the Marines in the gym. He had large, bold features, the overall impression of sheer physical prowess muted only by a full, sensitive mouth.

Despite his appearance, Carl was at heart a bookish fellow. As one of the more junior members of the intelligence team, he read all the incoming traffic, picking out messages of immediate importance and arranging the others for the watch officers who prepared their daily briefs. Most traffic readers simply glanced at the subject line and tossed them in the appropriate pile.

Not Carl Ellison. He read every detail, savoring the feeling of being on the inside of the war, looking forward to when he would be the one on the other end generating those reports. He could already imagine the tight, crisp, and understated phrases he would use in place of the sometimes wordy prose he was required to file.

It was his habit to skim through all the messages first, noting the subject lines, so he could pull out anything of urgent importance. This time, one third of the way through the two-inch stack, he froze. The subject line struck immediate terror into his heart, and all thoughts of his later career drafting messages went out the window.

Possible biological weapons use, confidence medium. Confidence medium—that meant they had more than a mere rumor. At least one fact or background or history to back it up. He took the message out of the stack, absorbing it in one large gulp, then going back to read it more carefully a second time. By the time he started reading it the third time, he was already on his feet and headed for the commander's office.

Commander Busby felt his gut tense when he saw the look on Ellison's face. He had been pleasantly surprised to find out that his temperament and that of the petty officer were closely matched, despite the disparity in their physical appearances. He was nurturing the young man along, hoping someday soon he would apply to one of the number of college education programs the Navy sponsored.

"Biological weapons," Ellison said as he passed the message to Busby. "Medium-confidence report."

That was all Busby really needed to know, but he scanned the message anyway for the details. This particular weapon came in the form of a two-ton truck abandoned in the middle of the desert, discovered by an Army patrol that had inspected the contents. In it, they had found twelve bodies, black and swollen in death, the features distorted. A bit of canny work by an intelligence specialist had given the warning before the situation could become disastrous—and later, blood samples taken from the patrol who'd investigated it brought terrifying news.

The black plague. Certain death in the Middle Ages, somewhat treatable these days by modern methods, but by no means always curable. It spread rapidly from airborne exposure, symptoms coming on quickly, its victims almost immediately debilitated by raging fever and painful muscles and bleeding.

"They caught them in the chow line," Busby said softly, horror in his voice. "My God, the close quarters—they must have infected another fifty people, minimum." He scanned the remainder of the message, looking for the details of the evacuation plan, and saw that anyone exposed to a member of the squad was currently on a large transport headed for the States. But for some it would be too late.

A buzzer sounded, capturing their attention. Busby picked up the red phone on his desk, the one that connected him directly to TFCC.

"Intelligence, Combat. We've received a Warning Order, sir. We're to stand by to conduct precision strikes again suspected Iraqi biological-weapons sites. They're requiring a preliminary plan within the next six hours."

"Roger," Busby responded. "Assemble the rapid-response team in the admiral's conference room. I'm on my way."

He pulled out the folder that contained the contingency plans already drafted, thankful that they had done their homework. The bare bones of such a mission were already sketched out, accompanied by a floppy disk containing the details formatted as a message. Manning, missions, cycles, and requirements—it was all laid out, merely waiting to be tinkered with to fit the particular targets designated. He silently thanked Senior Chief Armstrong's foresight, since he had been the one to make sure all the plans had been updated.

By the time he got to the conference room, the rest of the team was assembled. Strike, operations, supply, maintenance, and representatives from each squadron, generally the squadron commanding officer. There was a brief flurry as they discussed the message among themselves, and then a sharp, "Attention on deck," that brought them all to their feet as the admiral walked in.

"Carry on," Coyote said immediately, indicating they should return to their seats. He walked to the front of the room, passed a scribbled piece of paper to the operations officer and said, "These are the initial targets from JCS. This is being handled at the highest level. I don't have to tell you that the intelligence that brought us this information cost several lives." He glanced over at Busby, as though he might have additional information on the deaths. "So, let's get on it. I'd like to see strike details in an hour and have the completed answer ready to go out half an hour later. Any problem with that?" He glanced around the table, confirming that there was not. "Very well." He turned and stalked out of the conference room, barely giving them time to come to their feet again.

It took the team only forty-five minutes to put together the first draft of the plan. Exactly 106 minutes after they had received the initial order; their response to the warning order left the ship.

To their credit, the watch team at JCS was no slouch, either. After a brief phone conference with Fifth Fleet, the response came back: *Execute*.

Tomcat
1600 local (GMT+3)

Fastball and Rat's argument was interrupted by word of a possible mission. It had not come over a radio circuit from the Air Boss or over the 1MC. Instead, a young airman had climbed up the boarding ladder, motioned to them to undo the cockpit, and filled them in on the details. The more informal channels moved far faster than the official ones.

From the moment he heard the news, Fastball was ready to go. Rat, the more experienced, began her preparations as well.

Finally, when the order came, they were ready.

"We're going first," Fastball crowed as he increased power to the engines and waggled the control surfaces for a final check. The catapult officer stepped forward and made a motion with his hands, indicating that Fastball should cycle all of his control surfaces. He did so, circling the stick, and was rewarded with a thumbs-up, indicating that all control surfaces appeared functional. There were a final few details on the radio, and then the catapult officer snapped off a sharp salute. Fastball returned it, immediately dropping his hand back to the controls and increasing the engines to full military power. Seconds later, a massive force shoved him back in his seat.

The bone-rattling run down to the end of the catapult always seemed to go on for far longer than it actually took to launch that much metal into the air at a speed capable of sustaining lift. As they shot off the bow, the Tomcat sank momentarily, fighting to remain airborne. Fastball dealt with the familiar clutch of panic that he always suffered at this point as he contemplated the possibility that insufficient pres-

sure at the catapult had given them a soft cat shot and insufficient airspeed.

Seconds later, the Tomcat caught the air, fought her way
back above the bow, and gained speed steadily in response
to the full throttle. Fastball heard Rat's sigh of relief and
echoed it. He let the Tomcat gain more speed and made sure
they were going to continue flying, then slid her into a steep
climb. She was now fully under his control, responsive to
the slightest twitches of his fingers, a melding of man and
machine. In the back, he heard Rat grumbling, but he ignored
her. Later, when they had targets to destroy, what she had
to say might be important. For now, she was just a passenger.

CVIC
1620 local (GMT+3)

"All flights airborne," a voice over the speaker announced.

"Good hunting, ladies and gents," Lab Rat said softly.
"Good hunting."

Fastball's Tomcat
1621 local (GMT+3)

"Skeeter, get over here," Fastball ordered. He heard a sigh
over the circuit he shared with his wingman, and then the
other Tomcat slid snugly into position.

"That close enough for you?" a slow drawl asked.

"That will do. Now stay there," Fastball ordered. "Rat,
give me a vector."

"First target, bearing three-two-zero, range forty-five
miles," she answered. Even as she spoke, Fastball was putting the Tomcat into a hard turn, coming to base course.

It was a site they knew well, one that they had briefed
countless times. It had been on the top of their list of potential biological-weapons facilities for the last month, and

small bits of information continued to increase the probability that that was what it was.

And why do we wait until people die to destroy it? We knew what it was—why didn't we take it out?

He shrugged, putting the question out of his mind. Those decisions were made way above his pay grade, but someday . . . Fastball viewed their failure to destroy this target as the sort of cowardly behavior that he'd come to expect from most Administrations. Maybe they were afraid they'd hit a baby-food factory instead of a real biological-weapons site. Maybe they *did* know more than he did about the targets, about what could go wrong with a preemptive strike. Well, to hell with them. When he was senior enough to be making the calls, he'd call the strikes like he saw them.

"Two," Skeeter acknowledged, following suit at Fastball's command. His Tomcat appeared to hang motionless in the sky at exactly the right distance from Fastball.

Five minutes later, Fastball announced, "Feet dry. Visual on target."

The facility was located just off the coast, a complex of concrete buildings and piping that resembled a refinery. Rat had studied its outlines hour after hour, committing its shape from every angle to memory. Now, as she craned forward to get a look at it, she felt a reassuring sense of familiarity.

"Concur, target," she acknowledged. "Descend to angels two on approach."

"I know, I know," Fastball muttered. "Didn't we brief this enough times?"

"Just follow the checklist, Fastball," she said wearily.

"Why don't you just leave the flying to me? If you want to do something useful, watch for antiair missiles," he said sharply, putting the Tomcat into a sharp descent.

There was always a wild card, wasn't there? Intelligence could do a lot, but they could not keep up with every single movement of small weapons on the land. There was no intelligence about fixed antiair weapons sites, but there was every possibility that there could be a man stationed on the roof with a Stinger tube or a mobile air setup. Even a few machine guns could exact serious damage if they manage to connect with the fuel tank. No bombing run, not even the ones conducted at the training range, was ever entirely safe.

Fastball kept his gaze fixed on the target, at the exact position that he wanted to nail. He absorbed the information displayed on his HUD unconsciously, integrating it with what his eyes told him and correlating the two pictures.

"Five seconds," Rat announced. "Four, three, two—mark!"

The heavy jet jolted upward as the five-hundred-pound bomb left the wing, lofted into the air on a trajectory destined to take it right into the center of the complex. Moments later, Skeeter released his weapon as well, and the two Tomcats peeled away from the approach path in opposite directions to avoid mutual interference. They went buster at right angles to the target for a few moments, gaining maximum distance, and then converged back on base course.

"Good hit," Rat shouted, turning around to watch the fireball behind them. "Secondaries, too, I think."

"Nice job," Skeeter's RIO agreed.

"Then it's back to the barn, boys and girls," Fastball announced, self-satisfaction in his voice. "I think we earned ourselves the couple days off Alert Five."

USS United States
1625 local (GMT +3)

"I want some answers, and I want them now!" Admiral Jette swore, slamming his fist down on the heavy conference room table. "*Jefferson*'s got her strikes already launched, weapons in the air, and you people haven't even finished up the answer to the warning order. Anyone mind explaining this little discrepancy to me? Is there a really damn good reason that we can't be first off the mark?"

No one spoke. Every officer seated at the admiral's table knew the answer, but they had learned from hard experience that the emperor did not appreciate being told he had no clothes on.

"What about it, Strike?" the admiral asked, directing his comments to the air strike officer. "What's your excuse?"

Of all the officers there, Strike was the most experienced. He'd been on numerous cruises in this area, served on Fifth Fleet battle staff and as the force operations officer on board a command and control ship, and had forgotten more about the Middle East than most of the others had ever learned. Additionally, he had just decided to retire. His oldest daughter, age ten; had been diagnosed with multiple sclerosis and was not doing well. In all good conscience, as much as he loved flying, he could not leave his wife to bear the burden alone. This was his last cruise, although no one knew it yet.

"The problem is, Admiral, that we weren't ready," he said bluntly, locking his gaze on the admiral's angry eyes. "If we had a notional flight schedule ready to go, if we left a little bit of flexibility in our plans, then this whole thing would have run much more smoothly."

"Are you telling me you can't do your job?" the admiral demanded, his voice low and menacing. "Would you like me to relieve you now or shall I wait for a court-martial to decide your incompetence?"

"I'm not incompetent, sir. With all due respect, I'm probably the most competent strike officer you'll ever see. And it is my considered professional opinion that the staff is not up to speed." Strike's voice was firm as he spoke. He could feel the waves of shock and apprehension surging out from the other officers, but he ignored them. Sure, he could have used some moral support, but why ask them to sink their careers along with his? They were good men and women, most of them, and the Navy would need them to balance out idiots such as the man wearing the stars in front of him.

"I want aircraft in the air within thirty minutes," the admiral said. "No excuses. Thirty minutes." He held up the two sheets of paper he'd been handed, the staff's first cut on their commander's plan. "I am releasing this. You want flexibility, you'll get flexibility. Get those aircraft in the air *now* and you can make changes as need be while they're en route. Think your pilots can handle that, or do they need to have their hands held all the way to the target?"

"My pilots can handle anything," the senior commanding officer present said. "We're ready, sir."

And fuck you, too, buddy, Strike thought. *Go ahead, suck up. But see who has to pull your ass out of the fire. And in the end, you won't be the one that suffers. Your pilots will, and God help them all.*

The admiral's answer came back just as promptly as Coyote's had, although with a cautionary note to verify all intelligence prior to launch. Fifteen minutes later, the first of the Alert Five aircraft of *United States* launched.

Tomcat 101
1645 local (GMT +3)

Commander Lauren took the first flight himself. His motivation was not an avid desire for attaboys or a greedy grab for more stick time. Lauren had had more than his share of combat missions, and was second only to Strike in number of traps on board a carrier. He chose a less experienced pilot-RIO team for his wingman.

Lauren was a tall, stocky man with a shock of silver hair that made him easily visible in any crowd. A sprinkle of freckles across his nose, coupled with bright blue disingenuous eyes, often led people to underestimate him. No one who had ever served with him or flown with him ever made that mistake more than once.

"*States,* this is Renegade Leader," he said, toggling his mike on. "Be advised we are feet-dry and ten miles from designated target. You have any intel updates for me?"

"Renegade One, *States.* We're working on it, sir. If there's a modification, we should have it to you in about five minutes."

Five minutes. Thanks, fella. I'll already be in range if there are any new antiair sites in the area. "Roger, *States,* acknowledged." *But I'll be damned if I let you hear me sweat it out.*

A small red symbol began blinking on his HUD, and the ESM warning gear in the rear seat simultaneously erupted with incessant beeping. "Fire control radar," his RIO announced. "I think we got a SAM site dead ahead."

"It figures," Lauren said. Generally, you could detect a hostile radar at about one and one half times the range that the radar could detect *you.* They gave him some time, if not a lot, to try to turn and make his way around the edges of the radar's detection envelope. "That's it, bearing zero-six-zero?"

"Affirmative. I think if you—"

"Already on it," the pilot said laconically, swinging the Tomcat ninety degrees off base course. "Let me know when we start losing signal strength."

"Roger." The ESM beeping stopped as the Tomcat opened range from the site.

"Renegade One, *States.* Be advised there's a possible SAM site to the northeast of your current location."

"Roger, got it." *Thanks a lot, guys. Too little, too late.* "Interrogative our target status?"

"Renegade One, new target designation to you." And a new symbol popped into being on his HUD, labeled with bearing and range information. "Intelligence confirms probable biological-weapons site, with possible warhead capabilities. No known antiair defenses in the area."

"No *known*? That's not very reassuring."

A new voice came on the circuit, one he recognized immediately as the admiral's. "Nothing about combat missions is supposed to be reassuring, mister."

Just what I need, him sitting in TFCC and micromanaging the final run. Wonder if he'll give a weapons-release countdown for me?

"Got it," his RIO said. "Come right to about ten degrees. That shit is coming in from the side. We can make a hard turn, come in right over it, and get out of that radar's range before they get a handle on us. The range should be long enough for a spoof to work." The ESM system had active countermeasures, ones that could intercept a targeting radar and transmit a return signal that would convince the threat radar that its target was somewhere else.

"In theory, at least," the pilot noted.

"Yeah. In theory."

I remember this target. Not a lot to look at. It's on the side of a hill, built back into it. A helluva target for a five-hundred-pound dumb bomb. Something like that, we need a daisy-buster. But it's a come-as-you-are fight and what we have will have to do. Maybe we can damage the entrance enough to hole up anybody back in the buried part of it.

"Commencing final run," he said, turning the aircraft to put it on the path indicated on his HUD. From here on in, it was a matter of coordinating electronic information and visual, using his experience to release the dumb bomb exactly at the right moment to loft it onto the target. Sort of like throwing a softball, he mused. And in this case, he would have to rely on his eyes and experience to tell him what alterations in the flight plan he had to make to compensate for the hill. The plan called for him to nail the center of the target, but that clearly wasn't going to work. He needed to strike near the entrance.

"I've got a visual," he announced a few seconds later, as the dull brown before him resolved into a sloping hill with a concrete building set on the side. It merged into the hill, but his eyes recognized the setup from the intelligence photos.

"Roger, concur," his RIO said.

"Two," his wingman acknowledged.

In a few words, Lauren sketched out additional instructions for his less-experienced wingman, hoping that the other pilot was enough of a stick to do some fine-tuning to the release point.

All once the ESM gear erupted into warnings. "SAM site, SAM site," his RIO shouted, his voice tight and under control. "Drop it and get us out of here!"

"No," the pilot said. "We're not close enough, and I'll be

damned if I'm going home with these babies on my wings. Five more seconds—now!"

The aircraft jolted as the five-hundred-pound bombs left the wings, heading down toward the target, following the aircraft's course and descending in a parabolic arc. Lauren broke off to the right, his wingman following, and kicked in afterburners to clear the area.

"They're launching, they're launching," his wingman shouted over the circuit. "I have a visual on two—no, *three* missiles!"

"Settle down," the pilot ordered sharply. "Keep your eyes opened, you'll be okay. The SAMs are slow and clumsy—you can avoid it if you stay on your toes. Just like in school, Joe."

He rolled his Tomcat inverted and stared back the way they'd come. Yes, he could see them now, his vision preternaturally sharpened by the knowledge that they were there. Two long, white telephone poles rising up from the ground, beam-on to them now but already turning to follow them, the third one not yet visible. At least they didn't have fighters. Ground-based missiles were a helluva lot easier to handle.

"It's got me, it's got me," his wingman shouted as the ESM gear stuttered into a harder, faster tone, indicating that one of the missiles had detected him on its own radar and was locking on. "Chaff, flares—commencing evasive maneuvers."

The air around them was suddenly cluttered with strips of metal foil and burning flares, all designed to throw the missile off its target. The countermeasures gear kicked in automatically, intercepting the radar signals from the missile seeker head, delaying them, and transmitting them back, attempting to fool the small computer mind into thinking that the aircraft was somewhere else.

"It's got us, too," his own RIO said. "Wait for it, wait for it—break right, break right!" The pilot did as the RIO ordered, popping out chaff and flares as he did.

"I lost it—no, it's reacquiring, coming back on me—break

right, break right," his wingman shouted, swinging his Tom-cat around as the missile turned away from the chaff and flares. For whatever reason, this particular missile was te-nacious. Lauren had his own problems to deal with, though. His own nemesis had reacquired and was turning to meet him.

There's something to be said for the Hornet. Damn, I wish I had their turning radius right now. He jerked his Tomcat around almost in midair and was rewarded with, "It's falling off," from his RIO. Evidently their maneuvers had exhausted the missile's fuel and it was tumbling back to earth. *Be damned fine if it fell back on that bastard target.*

"Come on, come on," he heard his wingman chanting. The G-forces were distorting his words. The pilot was fighting to stay conscious as he put his aircraft into a hard, diving turn. "Joe, easy!" Lauren said. "Change altitude, increase closure without so many Gs—acknowledge!"

"I'm trying," the voice said, even more sluggishly. "It's not—"

Suddenly, below Lauren and to his right, a fireball ex-ploded where moments before had been a Tomcat. "Joe," he shouted, as though raising his voice to reach across the dis-tance between them and save his junior wingman. "Answer me!"

"That was him," his RIO said softly, shock in his voice. "Those weren't that hard to avoid." He began to swear softly.

Shit, double shit. I've got to go see.

He put his Tomcat into a hard turn that headed directly for the fireball. He had to see if there were any parachutes. The odds of it were slim to none, but as long as there was a chance that his wingman and his RIO had gotten out just before the hit, that somehow he had managed to eject them in the moments before the missile hit, Lauren had to check.

The air below the fireball was already littered with burning pieces of fuselage that fell through the air like a shower of meteors. Lauren stayed around the edges, careful to avoid the secondary explosions and shrapnel, and rolled inverted to check the air below them. "Anything?" he asked his RIO, already knowing what the answer was. "Anything at all?"

"Renegade One, *States,*" the TAO's voice said over tactical. "Interrogative the status of your wingman?"

"No chutes," the pilot said shortly, his voice emotionless. "I'm coming back for another check, but I don't think he made it."

Silence on the circuit, and then the admiral came back on. "Get your ass back here, mister. Now."

"Just a few more minutes, sir. Just in case—"

"Don't you people understand what orders are? I said now!"

The silence that followed on the normally busy circuit had an entirely different quality to it. Shock, horror, even more than the death of his wingman had occasioned. It was unthinkable that a pilot leave a wingman before he was absolutely and morally convinced that there were no parachutes in the air. It violated every tenet of the warrior's code, the one that both he and the admiral had been raised on.

That could be no explanation, no justification. This was not the time for an argument. Instead, the pilot simply ignored the man with the stars and began his futile orbit once again.

CVIC United States
1650 local (GMT+3)

The intelligence specialists and officers listen to the exchanges closely, each one secretly glad he did not have to deal with the admiral. They saw what the pilot was doing—everyone in the LINK saw Lauren continue his search of the airspace for his wingman or a parachute. They saw and applauded him, hoping that they themselves would have the courage to do just that if it ever came down to it.

Just then, the telephone rang. The specialist picked it up and passed it to the intelligence officer. "Met, sir."

The intelligence officer took the call, saying, "We're a little bit busy right now for a weather report."

"Not for this one," a grim voice announced. "You guys have any idea what surface winds are doing right now?"

"No," the intelligence officer said, dismay on his face. He was no dummy—there was only one reason for the meteorologist to be calling up right now with that particular inquiry. "But—"

"But, nothing. You better get this aircraft carrier turned around and headed south right now," Met said. "Because, according to my calculations, if there was any biological agent released in that strike, it's going to be coming across our deck in about fifteen minutes."

Hornet 101
1745 local (GMT +3)

Even if he had not known it from Admiral Jette's voice, by the time the pilot was on final, he knew he was in serious trouble. But he was fresh from a combat mission and losing his wingman, and the kind of trouble he was facing didn't bother him all that much. Sure, the admiral could shaft him on his fitness reports, recommend that he never be promoted, and even try to relieve him of command. None of it was mortal danger—except to his career. And that seemed a very unimportant matter compared to losing his wingman.

He could hear the tension in the air boss's voice as he turned onto final, traced its echo in the LSO's terse orders, and saw it in the strange, rebellious face of the plane captain who helped him out of his ejection harness. By now, the entire story would have made the rounds throughout the ship. And, as far as he knew, there was not a single aviator—strike that, a single sailor of any type—who would have done anything other than what he did. Oh, maybe some of them wouldn't speak up, worried about the effect on their own careers. But inside, where it counted, he knew that each one desperately hoped that if their situations were reversed, he would have made the same choice that Lauren did.

Once the post-shutdown checklist was complete, he leaned

back against the ejection seat, breathing deeply. The real
world came crashing back in. In a few moments, he would
have to face the admiral and accept responsibility for disobeying the admiral's orders.

*But damn it, he never should have asked me to leave. I
wasn't in immediate danger. There was no reason to order
me to leave the scene.*

*Unless there was something you didn't know. Maybe he
had some intelligence about another attack, maybe there was
some reason for his outrageous order.*

*No. Because if he had, I would have heard it in their
voices now. Nothing stays secret for long on a carrier.*

The plane captain, her face almost completely obscured by
goggles and her cranial helmet, was deftly unfastening his
ejection harness and inserting the cotter pins into the ejection
seat, which would prevent it from accidentally being activated while the aircraft was on the deck. He noticed her in
ways that he normally wouldn't have. The slight curl of hair
that escaped from her cranial to hang down over her forehead. The smooth, unlined skin below the goggles, the quick
smile that threatened to break out into a full grin at any
second. Her mouth was delicate, a deep red color that no
cosmetic could mimic. He was seized by the sudden urge to
grab her hands in his and kiss her, to feel contact with a
woman. It was a natural aftermath of combat, particularly
when you'd lost someone.

She seemed to sense his interest, and a slight flush rose
on her cheeks. Her hands moved more slowly, lingering over
the straps as she unfastened them. She paused for a moment,
then pulled her goggles away from her eyes and settled them
on the top of her cranial helmet. Her eyes, he saw, were
ringed with red circles where the rubber from the goggles
pressed into delicate skin. Her eyes were a dark, tawny
brown, deep and full of sympathy. Her face was unmarked
yet by life, other than by what the Navy had taught her.
Purplish circles under her eyes reflected the long hours she
kept.

"Sir," she said, her voice barely above a whisper. "Sir?"

"Yes, Airman Carmichael?" he asked, proud that his voice was kind and level. He remembered her now, the details of his interview with her when she checked on board and reported to the squadron. A smart kid, one with a lot of potential. Her A school had been aviation electronics, and she would soon rotate out of the line division and into her rating work center. He remembered that she seemed to be shy, exceptionally reserved, and he'd thought her rather sweet at the time.

"Sir, I just wanted to say—what happened up there—" Her voice trailed off. He held up a hand to stop her.

"What happened up there was—" He stopped suddenly, unable to make the party-line explanation come to his lips. He couldn't lie to her, not to those dark brown eyes gazing into his, hurt, wanting to know why the world wasn't working the way it ought to. "What happened up there," he began again, even more gently but with a tremendous sense of release, "was really shitty." Both of them knew he wasn't talking about the loss of his wingman. "We lost two good men today. I searched every bit of the area—there was no sign of them. They never even knew what hit them." For some reason, that seemed to ease her mind. He wondered whether he could have lived with himself if he had not stayed on station to look one last time for his wingman.

"It's hard, isn't it, sir?"

For one insane moment, he thought she was talking about his dick, which was indeed demanding to be heard. "Yes, it is," he said gravely, fervently grateful that he had paused before answering. "It's always hard when you lose someone."

"The admiral is a shit." Something had changed in her voice, a hard note at odds with the delicate face in front of him. She flushed immediately, all too aware that she was way out of line, and looked away.

"I won't tell him you said that," he said gravely, deeply gratified at some level that even this young airman understood the difference between right and wrong. "As long as you promise not to tell him that I think he's a shit, too."

Her face snapped around to his, a look of shock on her face. Then a hard, tight mile smile crept across her full lips, aging her immediately by a decade. "Our secret, Captain." Somehow even her voice seemed deeper.

"Agreed." Then he looked down at the ejection harness, and said, "Now help me get this damn thing off, okay? I've got an execution to attend." He gave her the same tight smile she'd proffered just moments earlier, cementing the bond between them.

Later, waiting in the hallway passageway outside the admiral's office, he held her face in his mind, drawing strength from her expression.

USS Jefferson
1755 local (GMT +3)

Lab Rat stared at the speaker overhead, listening to the horrific details coming across it, each one spoken in a flat, neutral voice with no trace of emotion. The winds across the Persian Gulf had shifted, and now traced a direct line from the recently destroyed biochemical site to the USS *United States*. Given that the bunker had been lodged in the side of a hill, and that there was no indication of secondary explosions or complete destruction that might have incinerated any biochem weapons, it was possible that whatever hell had been housed there was now being carried by the wind toward the ship.

"Of course, there are civilian cities along the dispersal path as well," the admiral continued in a flat, detached voice. "Should there in fact be Iraqi chemical or biological weapons being dispersed, my medical staff advises me that we can expect significant collateral damage. I have already released an OPREP-3 report to JCS summarizing those attacks."

"Dear God," Coyote said, disbelief in his voice. "What do you need? Medical support? I'll have that coordinated if there's anything you need."

"The offer is appreciated," the admiral said. His tone deep-

ened and he began to sound even more formal. "The ship
has drilled very extensively for this very possibility, and is
currently buttoned up as tight as she can get. The captain has
every confidence that between the saltwater wash-down system and the positive pressure maintained inside the hull,
there will be no danger of exposure."

The captain—now why did he say it that way? He should
have said that *he* was confident. Let the troops hear it in his
voice, feel it in their bones from the way he talked. *That's
why you get paid the big bucks, Admiral—to stand out there
in front and give your troops something to follow.*

"Under the circumstances, we have commenced a precau-
tionary emergency destruction of some older material," the
admiral continued, his voice still unnaturally calm. "However, most of the corporate knowledge resides inside the
minds of our more senior officers. Rather than risk losing
that experience, I have decided to—"

*No. He can't be thinking that. He wouldn't dare. He
wouldn't dare.*

"—to evacuate senior staff from the ship's company and
my own staff. There will be three CODs departing in approximately forty-five minutes en route to Kuwait, where we
will check in with Fifth Fleet. I would expect that we will
refuel and transfer to the USS *Jefferson,* leaving a portion of
the officers at its fleet headquarters."

There was dead silence on the circuit. Coyote struggled
for words, fighting down his disbelief. Diplomacy had never
been his strong point, and any traces of it that he had managed to acquire now deserted him. "You mean you're going
to run?" he asked over the circuit, his voice incredulous.
"You're going to leave your battle group there while you get
your own ass to safety?" More silence. Coyote thought that
he really ought to be wishing he had not said that, but
couldn't convince himself of it.

The man was a coward. He had just announced it on a
secure circuit that was broadcast to every command center
and every commanding officer and captain in his battle

group. Faced with the unthinkable, the admiral was going to run.

"Pending other orders from Fifth Fleet staff, expect our COD on board early tomorrow morning." It was as though Coyote had not spoken.

"No way, asshole," Coyote said, all traces of civility gone from his voice.

"I can still coordinate the movements of my battle group, given access to sufficient communication circuits, and—"

"It will be a cold day in hell," Coyote said, his voice burning with outrage and scorn, "when I let a coward on board my ship to direct his people from a safe position. When you get ashore in Kuwait, you better plan on staying there, because if you or your aircraft approach USS *Jefferson,* I will have you shot down. You read me?"

"Admiral?" Coyote's TAO said, disbelief in his voice. "I think we have a problem."

NINETEEN

Tombstone's command post
2000 local (GMT −7)

The daylight was starting to fade when the first glitch appeared. Hank Greenfield came up to Tombstone and said quietly, "A word, if you will." Tombstone followed him out away from the rest of the agents.

"What's up?"

Greenfield shook his head. "The Air National Guard elements won't support us. Said they're worried about this federal pursuit issue. That last robbery from the reserve center shook them up some, and they're claiming that we don't have any intelligence about what we're facing. Their CO said it's too risky for the helicopters to commit."

Tombstone swore quietly. "Why didn't they tell us before?"

"They said they just found out themselves. Evidently the war is being fought back in D.C. as well. Seems not everyone approves of the President's idea." Greenfield shot him a look that said, "And neither do I."

"Then we'll move without the helicopters," Tombstone said.

"Not a good idea. We can lose them too easily in the hills

in this terrain. I recommend we reschedule until we can firm up the intelligence and air support."

Tombstone studied him for a moment. Greenfield knew what it was to move in on a position like this without adequate intelligence. That had been his downfall at Bull Run. Under normal circumstances, Tombstone would have agreed to reschedule the mission.

But these weren't normal circumstances. Somewhere in this area was a large stash of weapons and ammunition and rocket launchers, and they needed to be eliminated immediately.

Tombstone's legal advisor had suggested halfheartedly that they apply for a search warrant, but hadn't pressed the issue. They all knew the odds of getting any state or federal judge to issue a warrant when the whole issue of Fourth Amendment rights and hot pursuit ran smack up against posse commitatus. After Bull Run, any judge would probably want to see stone tablets carried by Moses before he signed off on a search warrant.

"So we'll cover both the trucks and Carter's HQ ourselves," Tombstone said.

"Aren't you listening to me? If we break off assets to cover the trucks, we won't have enough people to adequately cover Carter's HQ. And we're likely to lose the trucks in the hills. Both ends of this will be catastrophes."

"So we get some more people," Tombstone said.

"Can they get here in fifteen minutes?"

"No."

"Then they might as well not get here."

"How long will it take us to get there?" Tombstone asked.

"Around two hours, maybe a little more. As long as the weather holds," Greenfield answered, glancing up at the sky. "The prediction says scattered thundershowers. That'll complicate everything, of course."

"And may ground our airpower anyway. Look. I know what you're saying, and I don't want another Bull Run any more than you do. But it's time to rock and roll. Get everybody packed up and set a covert watch around Carter's HQ.

Sooner or later, he's going to go to the trucks or they will come to him. That buys us a little time, enough to get the air problem and manpower problem solved."

"And if they don't head for HQ?"

"Then we concentrate on Carter. Cut the head off the snake." A sudden thought occurred to Tombstone. "Get me a cell phone. I think I may have an answer to our airpower problem."

Jackson's truck
2010 local (GMT −7)

After two hours of winding their way along treacherously narrow roads, the truck pulled into a clearing. Except for the narrow access road with overhanging trees, the area was surrounded by sharp peaks and rugged terrain.

Mertz pulled in and backed the truck up to a pile of brush. Jackson hopped out and started hauling it away. Mertz shut the truck down and joined him. Fifteen minutes later, they'd cleared away the entrance to a small opening in the rock.

"Let's get it all out," Jackson said. He grabbed a case of ammo and slid in through the opening. At first, it appeared to be no more than a narrow crevasse in the cliff, but ten feet later it widened into an open cavern of around five hundred square feet. It was dry and smelled of old dirt. Cases of MREs and bottled water were stacked neatly along one side, sleeping bags and packs along another. Jackson picked a space near the entrance and set the crate down. Thirty minutes later, the two men had unloaded all the weapons and ammo. They stopped for a moment to admire their handiwork.

"Pretty, ain't it?" Mertz said finally. "Seems a shame to leave it here."

"Yeah." Jackson grabbed a rocket launcher and slung it over his shoulder. "Find some rounds for this."

"I thought it was all 'sposed to stay here. That's what your daddy said."

"Change of plans." Jackson patted the rocket launcher fondly. "These babies pack a round that will take out an armored vehicle. They're a lot more effective than what we've got if we have to deal with any pursuit problems."

"What kind of pursuit problems?" Mertz asked suspiciously. "There weren't nobody following us."

"And we're going to keep it that way."

"But your daddy—"

"I'm on-scene commander. I'll deal with him when we get back to HQ. And this little baby will make sure that we do."

TWENTY

Tombstone had spent most of the two hours and twenty minutes it took to get to Carter's HQ on his cell phone. Just as they pulled into their staging area some two miles from the compound, he'd finished scribbling a list of names and phone numbers he'd just gotten from the Navy Reserve Air detailer. He'd smiled slightly as he wrote the names down, the memories of the time he'd served with each man and woman clear and vivid. Better to have those on his mind than Bull Run.

They trekked through rugged terrain, moving slowly and quietly, avoiding the sentries Greenfield's scouts had found. Bratton had provided no more detailed information, but he'd nodded matter-of-factly as the scouts reported each listening post. Finally, they were in position.

"Are you sure this is it?" Tombstone asked, his voice a whisper.

"That's always the question, isn't it?" Greenfield said. He studied the small farmhouse they were encircling. It was too much like the last time, too much like the Smarts' place.

Like it, but with differences. Cinder-block building instead of wood-frame, with a sturdy two-story wooden barn about a half a mile away. With his binoculars, Greenfield could see fresh tire tracks leading into it. The missing National Guard trucks and weapons, he was willing to bet. There was none of the small, wild rustlings that indicated livestock and other animals somewhere nearby. None of the fresh, pungent smell of them, either. What manure he did smell was old. Whatever this place was now, it was not an active farm.

Cinder blocks. At least it won't burn.

The house backed up to a stretch of trees, partially sheltered from northern winds by them. There were no lights on, but Greenfield knew in a way he could not describe that whoever was inside was awake and watching them.

"This is it," Greenfield said, certainty in his voice. "It's not like last time—this one I'm sure of."

Tombstone studied him for a moment, seeing the strain in the man's face. He glanced back at the farmhouse, then at his second in command. For a moment, he had doubts about what he had done, putting Greenfield in this position. Maybe he would have been better off with someone not tainted by the Smart incident.

But no—after this many years of experience in leading men, Tombstone knew when someone was about to crack and when they weren't. Greenfield was certain of what was inside, and watching him now, the way he moved with quiet competence, the confidence in his voice, Tombstone was, too.

"OK. Let's let them know we're here," Tombstone said.

Greenfield smiled, and it was not a pleasant sight. "Call me crazy, but I think they already know."

"Yeah, maybe. Get the snipers in position. Let's send them a wake-up call."

Lands End
2315 local (GMT −7)

Behind the glass, the windows were boarded up. The first tear-gas rounds fired shattered the glass and cracked the boards, but remained outside the house. Even from there, gas drifted into the house, and the men inside reached for their gas masks.

"They'll know soon that it didn't work," Abraham said quietly. "Be ready." He glanced around at the faces and saw that they were nervous but determined.

"They took the first shot," Abraham continued. "I want the rest of the world to know exactly how they conduct their operations." He turned to the latest visitor to the compound and fixed her with a cold glare. "And you'll tell them, Ms. Drake, won't you? Every detail."

Drake kept her voice flat and level. "Every detail." Her voice was muffled by a gas mask.

"If they start firing immediately, get your ass down the ladder." He pointed at the open hatch in the middle of the kitchen floor. "I showed you the back way out—get moving. We'll be right behind you. We don't intend to go down like they did at Bull Run."

For that, Pamela was immensely grateful.

2320 local (GMT−7)

Tombstone swore silently as the tear-gas canisters bounced off the windows and fell to the ground. "Which way is the wind blowing?"

"Away from us," Greenfield said dryly. "I've done this a few times, you know."

"Yeah. Looks like they have, too. So what's next?"

"We start talking." He picked up a bullhorn and handed it to Tombstone. "Would you care to do the honors?"

2325 local (GMT−7)

"Attention inside the house. Abraham Carter, you are surrounded. Put down your weapons and come out with your hands up."

Drake started. *Tombstone! What the hell are* you *doing here?* She started to speak, then thought better of it. They weren't telling her everything they knew. Why should she?

"Back door," Abraham ordered. One of his lieutenants moved a rug aside and jerked on a metal ring attached to the floorboard. A hatch swung up from the floor. "Down the hole, Drake. And stay back from the ladder. When we start moving out, it's going to happen fast."

Drake started to resist, but Abraham reached out and slapped her across face hard enough to make her yelp involuntarily. "I will remind you that the condition of your being allowed to remain here as an observer was predicated on obeying my orders without argument. Now move." He pulled back the slide on his 9mm and chambered a round.

Pamela glared at him, anger written in every line of her face and body. But she stepped back, still facing him, until she reached the ladder, then proceeded down it. Abraham watched her go, and then turned to the rest of the men. "Tough little thing, isn't she?"

"Carter, this is your second warning. You have five minutes to lay down your weapons and surrender. Your immediate cooperation is required to avoid serious consequences."

"Don't answer," Abraham said. He examined the firing hole carved out of one board, tried to see if he could see them. They were maintaining good firing discipline, he noted. There was no reflected light, no sudden flaring of matches or cigarette lighters to give them away. Still, once the shooting started, Abraham would know exactly where they were.

He turned to Drake. "They're bluffing. Right now, they're trying to decide whether to go with the firepower or simply wait us out. Those are the two standard tactics, that and negotiating. They figure we'll get low on food and water eventually and start making small compromises to get some. Or they'll open fire all at once with the heavy stuff."

"Which approach do you expected they'll choose?" Drake asked.

"I think they'll try to wait us out," Abraham said. "They don't know where the trucks are yet."

"And what was in the trucks that is so important?" Drake asked.

"Supplies. Things the movement needs. We went to a lot of trouble to get them to give them up that easily."

"So is this a suicide mission?"

Abraham shook his head. "To paraphrase General Patton, the whole point of war is not to die for your country. It's to make the other son of a bitch die for his. That's why we have the back way out. And that's how you know that Kyle Smart wasn't one of us. He wasn't prepared."

Abraham picked up a walkie-talkie. "Red Team, Team Leader. Prepare to move out."

2330 local (GMT –7)

The sound of the diesel engine starting cut through the still night air. Greenfield turned on Tombstone, enraged. "Now you've pushed them into trying to make a break for it before we've got enough assets in place. I told you before and you didn't listen—this isn't a military operation. This is law enforcement. The sooner you get that through your head, the fewer people will have to die because of your arrogance."

Tombstone turned to him, his face hard and cold. "If you were in the Navy, I would—"

"I'm not. And you can't. You're right on the edge of having a fuck-up happen right here, Magruder. Get your head out of your ass and pull your people back. It's not going to take much for one of them to start shooting to cover their escape. Once one fires, you can kiss your ass good-bye, because the rest will follow suit. And then it's Bull Run all over again. Do you really want that?"

Tombstone reined in his anger, forcing himself to consider the possibility that Greenfield was right. He had sent men and women to their deaths many times when he was in the Navy, sent them out on missions knowing that the probability of their returning was minimal. Was this any different?

Yes. It was. He was on unfamiliar terrain, not only physically but legally. Only a fool failed to listen to his advisors.

Without a word, Tombstone picked up the bullhorn. "Hold your fire. Weapons down, safeties on. I want a representative from each post back here for a briefing." Turning to face the compound, he said, "Attention inside the house. Be advised that if you attempt to leave in other than the manner I have outlined, we will open fire. If there are any casualties *on either side*, you will all be accessories to murder."

2331 local (GMT −7)

"Accessories to murder—now that's a laugh. Maybe even a threat," Abraham said.

"That was Tombstone Magruder," a voice said from below the floor. It was Drake, speaking up to offer her opinion. "I'd take him seriously if I were you."

"You know the man?" Abraham asked.

"I do."

"Get up here." Drake scrambled up the ladder. He grabbed her and marched her over to the door. "Tell him you're in here."

She glared at him, and for a moment he admired her sheer balls. "I won't. That wasn't part of the deal."

He pinched her hard on the butt. She yelped.

He picked up the bullhorn and turned toward the front door. "You hear that, Magruder? That's a friend of yours— Pamela Drake. I believe you two are acquainted. Be advised that if you opened fire on us, she'll take the first round and it won't necessarily be from your people."

"She knows better than to be in there," a cold voice answered immediately. "It's not going to stop me, Carter."

"Oh, I'm willing to bet it will," Carter said to the other men. "Let's up the ante. Gag her and tie her up."

"No! I won't—" Drake's voice was cut off abruptly as a rag was stuffed in her mouth and secured by duct tape. She was tossed roughly into chair, her hands taped behind her and her feet bound to the legs of the chair. She struggled, but it made no difference at all.

"*Now* we're out of here," Abraham said. He led the other men down the ladder and into the basement.

Tombstone's command post
2333 local (GMT −7)

Greenfield groaned. "If they have a hostage, that puts a different slant on things."

"We can't let it change anything," Tombstone said. Despite his resolute tone of voice, there was an anguished look at his eyes. "If we do, then they win every time."

"Let me call in our hostage negotiation team."

"Like you said earlier—no time. Something's going on in there."

"You *cannot* take chances with the lives of the hostages," Greenville said clearly and forcefully, as those speaking to a slow learner. "You cannot. That's not the way it works in the United States of America. Not my America, anyway."

"And that's the point, isn't it? They think it's their America—you think it's yours. The question is who wins." Tombstone looked around at the rest of the group and said, "I need options, people."

An Army sergeant stepped forward. "Sir, if we can get a microphone in close enough, we might be able to hear what's going on. That might help."

"Good idea. How can you get a microphone up close?"

The Army sergeant turned to study the equipment stacked around them. "Cable, a microphone—get a couple of people to cut me down some small trees, sir, and lash them together. I can get close enough to use them like a boom. It may not work, but it's worth a shot."

"Do it."

Relief surged thought the crowd as pent-up energy was released. To be doing something, *anything*, was better than waiting. Greenfield watched them work together, improving the makeshift boom on the fly. Twenty minutes later, it was done.

"On my way," the Army sergeant said. He crept along a gully until he was at the closest approach to the house. Slowly, carefully, he extended the boom, shoving the microphone closer and closer. Finally, he lifted it slightly so it sat against the window.

Forty feet away, men and women crowded around the speaker, hardly daring to breath as they waited for any sound. There was nothing. They listened for twenty minutes, with nothing but silence. Finally, frustrated, Tombstone called the sergeant back.

"Have you done this sort of thing before?" he asked.

The sergeant nodded. "Yes, sir. But with better equipment. Still, this gear is good enough to pick up anything going on inside. If you're not hearing anything, I'd say there's nobody in there. Nobody can hold still that long without coughing, moving, bumping into something. Especially not men under pressure like this."

"They're gone?" Greenfield asked.

"Sounds that way to me, sir."

Suddenly, something banged against the front door. Slides locked back and rounds were chambered as everyone turned to stare. There was another hard knock from the inside, and a muffled scream as though someone were—

"It's Pamela," Tombstone said suddenly. "Pamela, gagged. God, how many times have I wanted to do that?"

"A slow approach, with shields," Greenfield advised. He motioned to the riot-control gear. "It won't stop everything, but it may deflect enough rounds to keep you alive."

"Did you hear the man?" Tombstone snapped. "They're not there anymore."

Tombstone could hear Greenfield behind him issuing a flurry of orders, directing the teams to fan out to search for the escaping militants. There wasn't a lot they could do at this point without air support, but they had to try.

Air support—and why had that fallen through? A sudden,

ugly suspicion surfaced in Tombstone's mind. Was it possible? He turned to Greenfield. "Which Air National Guard unit did you contact for support?"

"The local one. I was trying to arrange it informally, but when that fell through, I tried the Air Force Reserve. They were still bucking it around in channels, trying to figure out the funding."

"You said a lot of these men have connections to the National Guard. Is it possible that somebody derailed the cooperation on that end?"

Greenfield scowled. "Yeah, it's real possible. That exact thought occurred to me. I didn't push it, because the last thing I need in the air is a pilot and crew not really looking for the bad guys. If anything, they could be spotters and reveal our location."

"You don't know who you can trust, do you? But I do." Tombstone picked up his cell phone and punched in a number. He glanced over at the Army communications specialist. "Have you got HF abilities on that?"

"Yes, sir. All I need is a frequency."

Tombstone reeled off a string of numbers from memory, then said, "Set it up. Let me know when it's done." The tech punched in a couple of numbers, then gave Tombstone a thumbs-up. Tombstone spoke into the cell phone. "Navy Detachment One, I need speak to your operations officer. Code Cosmic One."

There was a stunned silence from the other end; then a young female voice quickly recovered and said, "Code Cosmic One, aye. Wait. Out."

Tombstone let his hand holding the microphone drop to his side. "Now we wait."

"What was that all about?" Greenfield asked.

Tombstone gazed at him impassively. "An old friend."

2340 local (GMT −7)

Jackson was sweating heavily, which alarmed Mertz. He'd never seen Jackson so much as break a sweat under any circumstances.

"Red Team One—execute!" his father's voice snapped over the walkie-talkie.

Jackson took a deep breath. His voice trembled ever so slightly as he said, "Okay. This is it. I'll open the doors."

Naval Air Reserve Center, Butte
2345 local (GMT −7)

Commander Michael Fields had duty, and he was taking advantage of the otherwise wasted day and night to catch up on his desk work. He had just polished off four inches of paperwork when a young airman burst into his office and said, "Sir, I need you on the clear tactical circuit. Priority Cosmic One."

"What the hell?" Fields shoved himself away from his desk and headed for the radio room at a trot. Just why would anyone be calling up at this sleepy backwater training station with that sort of priority? It didn't make sense.

"Unknown caller, this is the operations officer," Fields said into the mike. "Interrogative your authority?"

"Fields?" the voice said incredulously, and something in it sounded familiar to him. "Don't use my name on this circuit, but I think you know who this is. In fact, I think I bailed your butt out of trouble a couple of times, young man."

"Holy shit," Fields breathed. Rekeying the mike, he said, "Yes, I think I do know who this is. What can I do for you?" He carefully avoided saying sir or admiral.

"I need two attack helicopters, maybe an S-3, and anything else you can get airborne with guns on it. And I need them now. How fast can you scramble them?"

"This isn't exactly an attack base," Fields said. "It'll take me"—he glanced over at the airman, who was already juggling aircraft spots and crews—"about fifteen minutes if everything works right. We have a training mission just ready to launch, and I can chop them to your control."

"What composition?"

"Two helicopters, but they're guns-only capability. An S-3, too. How will that do?"

"The load-out on the S-3?"

Fields glanced at the airman. She pointed at an entry on the schedule and said, "Just guns, sir."

Fields relayed the information, and was answered with, "That will do just fine." The familiar voice reeled off a frequency, and said, "We'll be operating in the clear. Unavoidable, but there's no way around it."

"Any chance you have some SINGAARS gear there?" Fields asked.

"Yes, as a matter of fact I do," the voice answered, sounding slightly surprised. "I'm not sure it's configured correctly—give me a channel and a setting. We have the military code-of-the-day information."

Fields turned to the airman. "Get the communications officer up here. I think we're just about to jury-rig ourselves a secure circuit."

TWENTY-ONE

Tombstone's command post
2345 local (GMT −7)

Greenfield's radio crackled to life. "Team Leader, Team One. The doors to the barn are open. I see one truck—looks like our target."

Greenfield scowled. "They're making a run for it."

"Sounds like it," Tombstone agreed. "Where is everybody?"

"We've got a couple of routes blocked, but not everybody is in position. At least it's not dark yet."

"It's dark down there in the valleys," Tombstone pointed out. "With the cloud cover, it'll be a dark night, too."

"Team Leader, Team One! They're rolling, sir. A two-ton truck, headed out from the barn and southbound."

"Move, people!" Tombstone snapped.

Greenfield changed channels on his radio, and was snapping out orders to the lookouts and strike elements positioned further out. All their careful planning, all their preparation—all gone to shit.

Inside the tunnel
2348 local (GMT −7)

Just when he thought he could stand it no more, Abraham Carter felt a trickle of fresh air on his forehead. At first he thought he was imagining it. It seemed like they'd been in the tunnel for hours and hours, although it could not have been more than fifteen minutes.

There it was again, this time unmistakable. The blackness around him seemed to be softening slightly, and he thought he could see a faint glimmer of light ahead. Yes, it had to be—the end of the tunnel. Energy surged through him.

He picked up his pace, now frantic to be free. The steel toes of his boot bit deeper into the soft ground, his fingers scrabbling over dirt and an occasional stone. The tunnel itself was supported by cross-beams and timbers at intervals, but they had not completely prevented small slides of dirt from caving in from the sides.

The dead, underground silence was breaking up, too. He thought he could hear night sounds, the wind blowing across the entrance, branches creaking, and small animals moving through the brush. And another sound—what was it?

Trucks. Big ones. Jackson.

No. Surely not. They couldn't be—

The rumbling grew louder, now clearly audible over every noise he thought he'd heard from the outside. It was Jackson and his men, taking advantage of the break in the action to flee.

"Hurry!" he shouted, the ground around him absorbing his words. A chunk of the wall ahead broke off, each particle distinct in the beam from his flashlight. "We have to get out of here."

The rumbling grew louder. Now he could feel the vibrations through his fingertips and legs where they rested on the dirt. He moved even faster, in his haste kicking dirt into the faces of the men behind him, provoking a spate of curses. He ignored them, unable to concentrate on anything other than the awful possibility now forming in his mind.

The sound was even lower now. The men behind him recognized it and seemed to catch his fear. They crowded up behind him, stamping on his feet and Achilles tendons, trying to push past him in the passageway built for only one man. Panic set in, driving all rational thought from their minds. Trickles of debris came from every direction, and the air was thick with suspended particles. It was harder to breathe. But the light, ah, the light—there it was, clear evidence that safety was just fifteen feet ahead.

Abraham lashed out viciously with hit right foot, kicking the man behind him. He could barely hear the shout of pain over the all-consuming noise of the trucks overhead. It was getting harder to move now as the loose dirt accumulated along the bottom of the passageway, sucking at his legs and hands, trying to embrace him. Sheer terror overwhelmed him. It was like swimming now, and his progress slowed. The cries from the men behind him grew softer as he piled up dirt in his wake.

Suddenly, there was a huge jolt overhead. The dirt rained down, coming in larger chunks now, mixed with rocks, and it hurt when it struck him. He couldn't breathe.

But he could go without air long enough to reach the entrance if only—

The passage in front of him collapsed, blocking off the traces of light that had been his only hope. He took a deep breath, trying to suck in as much oxygen as he could, and dug frantically at the dirt in front of him. Every bit he removed was immediately replaced by more dirt falling from overhead.

For just a moment, his oxygen-starved brain entertained the possibility of digging straight up, burrowing his way to the surface instead of trying to clear the passageway. But the tunnel was fifteen feet deep here, and one part of his mind knew it was hopeless.

One last violent cataclysm of sound and the remainder of the tunnel caved in. Crushing weight pressed in on him from all sides. It crept into his nostrils and mouth, forcing its way down into his lungs, hard and gritty against his open eyes, devouring him. He tried to scream, but there was nowhere for the air in his lungs to go, not with the dirt pressing in on him. He struggled, still hoping, still believing that he could make his way through it, until the last bit of life faded from his body.

Tombstone's HQ
2348 local (GMT−7)

"I am in pursuit of the lead vehicle. He's made it to the junction and is turning left." Suddenly, a barrage of gunfire echoed around the mountains, coming to them both over the radio and through the air. "They've got automatic weapons!" a man shouted. "Taking fire—we're hit, we're hit!" The circuit went dead.

Subsequent reports came in from the other pursuit units. It was the same story in each confrontation. Tombstone's troops were massively underpowered when confronting the firepower of the militia. The rounds fired by the militia smashed their engine blocks, immediately immobilizing the pursuit vehicles. Had the helicopters been there, they might have been able to stand back and track the vehicles by infrared, but the danger would have been significant.

"Come on!" Tombstone shouted, heading for his vehicle. "They're not getting away!"

He hopped into the driver's seat and fired the vehicle up. His second in command plopped himself into the passenger seat, drawing his side arm as he did. "This is not a good idea. A very not-good idea."

"You'd let them get away?" Tombstone asked, disbelievingly.

Greenfield grunted. "Listen, you heard what happened. They've got armor-piercing rounds. Even assuming we can get past the wreckage on the road, what makes you think you're so invulnerable? This isn't an aircraft you're driving, Magruder. It's a ground vehicle—a tough one, one built for trouble, but no match for rounds designed to take out a tank."

Tombstone slammed the vehicle into gear and pulled away, tires kicking out dirt. He pulled onto the road and accelerated, heading toward the junction.

Greenfield tried again. "This is a mountain road, not airspace. You can't maneuver, not with the drop-off on either side. You looked at the map. You know what the terrain looks like. It's no go, Admiral. It's a suicide mission, and one that won't hurt them one little bit."

Tombstone slammed on the brakes. "So what do you recommend?"

"We get law enforcement involved in it now. They've committed crimes—they're clearly in our jurisdiction. We have evidence—hard evidence—that they are in possession of stolen ammunition from the reserve center. With that, it's not going to be a problem to find probable cause for a search warrant."

"A search warrant—lot of good that will do. We get a fancy piece of paper with a judge's signature on it. Meanwhile, they're out there with those weapons and ammunition, and by the time we can catch up with them, it's going to be distributed out to every little group of crackpots in every part of the country. That's what you recommend?"

Greenfield's voice was hard. "Welcome to the world of domestic law enforcement, Admiral."

Jackson's truck
2349 local (GMT−7)

The truck nosed down hard as the ground sank away beneath it. Mertz shifted into low gear and stomped down on the accelerator. After a heart-wrenching moment, the truck grabbed traction and jerked itself out of the ditch.

"Keep going!" Jackson shouted. "We're almost out of here!"

Mertz shifted to a higher gear and jammed the accelerator down, achieving a suicidal speed. The road before them seemed to be moving as it was caught in the bouncing head-lights from the truck. Mertz hung on to the steering wheel grimly while the violent motion of the truck threatened to throw him across the cab.

The tunnel. It had to be the tunnel. Jackson had walked the path between the barn and the road too many times not to know that there was no ditch there.

Had they gotten out? Or had they still been in the tunnel when it caved in. Jackson felt his world spiraling out of control. It wasn't supposed to happen this way—it wasn't!

Tombstone's command post
2351 local (GMT −7)

"Team Leader, this is Viking 709, over." The laconic voice coming in over the secure portable gear gave every impression that the pilot hooked up with retired admirals wading through brush every day.

Tombstone took the mike. "Roger, 709, Team Leader. Interrogative your position?"

"About five miles out, sir, angels five. You ought to be hearing us about now."

"Copy five miles—and your weapons load-out?" Tombstone asked.

"Guns, flares—that's all we have. Team Leader, our skipper just told us to get airborne and chop to your control. Any chance you can fill us in on what we're doing here?"

"Roger, sure can, Viking. Apologies for the mystery, but we were on an open circuit."

"And now we're not." The pilot's voice left little doubt in anyone's mind that he wanted to be filled in and *now*. Tombstone felt a surge of anger. Just who did this little pup think he was, questioning the orders of—

Okay, okay. This little pup was an aircraft commander who'd launched on his skipper's orders, but deserved some more information before he started shooting. Fair enough. He probably didn't even know it was Tombstone.

Tombstone sketched in the situation for the pilot, wondering for a split second whether or not it was possible that this young man was somehow involved in one of the militias. He pushed aside the thought—at some point, you had to start trusting somebody, and it might as well be now.

"Okay, so I'm looking for a deuce-and-a-half," the pilot acknowledged. "I've flown enough ground support to do that. You got someone who knows the lingo?"

"More than one," Tombstone said. He passed the mike to Greenfield. "As a former Marine, this ought to be right up your alley."

Jackson's truck
2354 local (GMT −7)

A new noise caught Jackson's attention. "Aircraft. We're okay as long as were under the trees, but as soon as we—"

Suddenly, a large chunk of the road in front of them exploded. It threw up a solid wall of dirt and rocks and shattered trees that momentarily hung suspended in front of them, then fell to the ground.

Mertz swerved hard to the right, trying to avoid it. A tree loomed up in front of the truck and he screamed, hauling the truck back onto the road again. The engine screamed, over-revved, freewheeling, with the tires no longer in contact with the ground. For one long moment, they were airborne. Jackson felt his stomach lurch up into his throat.

They hit the ground with a bone-shattering jolt, landing on the right two tires. The truck hung there for a moment, as though deciding whether or not to remain in that position, then rolled over several times before pitching up against the tree. The engine died, evidently abused beyond its limits.

Silence, broken only by the sound of branches snapping as the truck settled to the ground. Jackson Carter lost consciousness.

He came to a few moments later, and then tried to figure out what happened. He knew where he was, what he was doing, but exactly how they had gone from careening down the road to lying on their side wasn't clear. He looked over at his companion, still seat-belted in. "Mertz?"

There was no reply. Carter turned toward him, stifling a groan as strained back and neck muscles protested vigorously. The other man was lying against his shoulder harness, blood trickling from one corner of his mouth. The left side of his head was smashed. He was not breathing. Still, Carter reached out and felt for a pulse. There was none.

Shit. He settled back against the seat belt holding him and contemplated just remaining there. His legs were almost in Mertz's lap, and the belt supported him sprawled against the seat. He could think of no reason to move.

The noise of a helicopter overhead brought him back to full consciousness. He forced himself to care about the situation, and reached with stiff fingers to the shoulder harness and belt buckle. It was jammed in position by his weight hanging on it. Swearing, he pulled a combat knife out of its sheath and cut the straps.

He fell down in a heap on the interior left side of the truck, landing on Mertz. For a moment he rested, wondering if his legs would support him. Then, as the sound of the helicopters grew closer, he forced himself to extend his legs. He was standing inside the truck cabin, his head poking out of the shattered right-hand window.

The door. If it's not jammed—He shoved, putting all of his weight into it, and the heavy metal door complained and moved up. With a resounding thud barely audible over the noise of the helicopters, it fell back against the body of the truck. He grabbed the sides of the opening and pulled himself up, finding footholds on the dashboard and in the seat. Every muscle in his body was screaming that as bad as the pain was now, it would be worse in the immediate future. He ignored it, grateful for the training that enabled him to do so.

Moments later, he was free of the truck. The sound of a helicopter was receding slightly. He took a deep breath of fresh air, smelled the distinctive odor of diesel fuel. A new sense of urgency overtook him. He lowered himself carefully from the side of the truck, trying not to damage his body any further, and hobbled off the path. With each step, his muscles eased slightly. While he could no longer move with the easy grace that he was accustomed to, at least he could walk.

The Carter compound
2358 local (GMT−7)

Drake struggled furiously against the bindings, but there was no give to the duct tape that held her hands together and her legs to the chair.

She could hear her cameraman swearing quietly as he struggled with his own bindings.

She had covered too many of these sorts of situations overseas not to know what was coming next. Eventually, there would be a takedown, a violent, no-holds-barred approach on the house. And unless the Americans were a good deal more cautious about it than their contemporaries overseas, there was a good chance she would not survive.

This can't be happening here. It doesn't happen in America. Afghanistan, the Middle East, China. Not here.

She heard a quiet movement out front and froze. *Any second now.* If only she had some way of calling out a warning, of telling them that she was still inside and that the men they were after were gone.

The door in front of her slammed back and bounced off the wall behind it. Men dressed in dark colors were outlined in the door frame. She held her breath, waiting for the first bullet.

The men moved rapidly, spreading out in all directions. One grabbed her chair, dragged it outside, and threw it to the ground. He was fast, so fast—moments later, a knife was sliding along her skin, cutting into the duct tape. He ripped it off her mouth.

"Where are they?" he asked, wasting no time.

"Gone. There's a tunnel."

"Do you know where it goes?"

"No. I was only in it for moment. It looked pretty long."

"Medic!" he shouted. He proceeded to unbind her hands and her legs. "They'll take good care of you." With that, he disappeared into the open door.

Two other men approached her, one carrying a small bag. "I'm OK," she said, trying to stand up.

Gentle hands held her down. "We'll be the judge of that."

"Pamela," a familiar voice said. She turned to see Tombstone kneeling next to her. When had he walked up? She must be more shook up than she thought. "Are you okay?"

She nodded, all at once unable to trust her voice. This wasn't the first time she'd almost died covering a story, but it was the first time she'd felt so completely violated, so helpless.

"Get her back to the truck," Tombstone said. "Is there anything you can tell us?"

"Tunnel. About ten men." Her voice was shaky. She took a deep breath, alarmed at the shuddering that was spreading throughout her body.

"Did they say where they were going?"

She shook her head.

"Anything else you can tell me?" Tombstone asked again, examining her closely. Clearly, he wasn't used to seeing her shook up.

"No." Pushing away the two medics, she struggled to her feet, assisted by Tombstone's hand on her elbow. "Thanks. For getting me out."

Tombstone kept his hand on her elbow and for just a second, she saw a trace of the man she had once been engaged to, her lover, the man he'd been before he'd lost Tomboy. But it disappeared to be replaced by the new, sterner Tombstone that had emerged over the last several years.

"All right, then."

He turned to head to the house, but she called out to him. "Tombstone. I meant it. Thanks. And—uh—is my cameraman here?"

● ● ●

"I want live air," Drake snapped into her cell phone. "I have the whole story—every bit of it. I was *there*."

"I understand, Miss Drake." the long-suffering evening producer said. "It's a dynamite story. But we're on live feed from the Middle East right now."

"Is there any blood? Right now, this second, I mean?" Drake demanded.

"We're not sure, but it looks like a big strike against some shore stations."

"I don't care what it *looks* like. You know the rule: 'If it bleeds, it leads.' And right now, Idaho is a whole lot bloodier than a bunch of bombs hitting sand in the Middle East, at least at this very second. And seconds are what count."

"Okay, okay. Stand by. We'll feed you as breaking news in four minutes."

"Okay, and I want two minutes," Drake said.

"Shit, no. I got bombs falling over there. Thirty seconds."

"Ninety."

"Done."

Drake snapped her cell phone shut and turned to her cameraman. "On in four for ninety." He just nodded—he'd worked with her often enough to know that as long as he did his part, she'd be letter-perfect with hers.

Drake shut her eyes, mentally outlining her report. Ninety seconds—thirty better than she'd been willing to settle for, but still not enough time for everything. They'd already uploaded the footage they'd taken from the hill overlooking the Smarts' and the coverage during her meetings with Carter. There'd be some outside footage of the compound—damn, she needed visuals! Sure, she could stand in front of the camera and talk, but viewers these days went for the visuals, not the talking heads, and there was only so much of the stark landscape around them that they'd want to see.

Just then, she heard someone shout, "We found them. Ten of them, in the tunnel!"

"Any survivors?" Tombstone asked.

"No."

Ah. She felt a mixed surge of relief and pity that Abraham Carter and his men had not made it out.

If it bleeds, it leads. And just what could be more interesting in the Middle East right now than this?

TWENTY-TWO

Viking 701
Sunday, September 16
0100 local (GMT +3)

Well to the west and south of the fighters now plunging toward the coast, Commander "Rabies" Grill surveyed the ocean below him. Funny how after enough time spent staring down at water, you can pretty much figure out where you were even without your navigation gear. This nasty, dark body of water below him, for instance. It could never be mistaken for the clear dark blue surface of the Pacific, which seemed so deep and inaccessible. It was, Rabies thought, the most indifferent to human presence of all the bodies of water.

The Atlantic, now, that was a different matter. Crossing time to Europe was around a week to ten days, depending on how fast the admiral wanted to get there. Just off the coast of the U.S., there were the silty brown coastal waters, then the sudden, clear green path of the Gulf Stream as it made its way north, arced east near Greenland and Iceland, then headed back south along the coast off England and Wales, carrying with it rich nutrients from the East Coast through the Arctic realms. The boundary between the Gulf Stream and the Atlantic Ocean was usually fairly clear, occasionally muddied by a few eddies that spun off from the Gulf Stream. Sometimes Rabies could even believe that he felt the line of mountains that ran down through the middle of the Atlantic Ocean, the Mid-Atlantic Ridge that almost divided the ocean into two bodies of water. Even with their jagged points well below the surface, they were a major factor in acoustic transmission and submarine detection.

And then there was the Med, ah, the Med. It wasn't that Rabies liked the water that much—it was what it represented. Warm, sun-drenched islands, Italian food, Greek food, every imaginable cuisine brought to the coast of this ancient sea by the inhabitants of Europe and elsewhere.

While it might be a gourmand's dream, as the busiest bit of water in the world the Mediterranean was a submariner's nightmare. It was loud, noisy, and shallow. The water was dark green and brown, occasionally blue in the deeper parts, and in some places you could almost see the bottom. There were other problems with finding submarines in that area as well. The mouth of the Mediterranean was one of the strangest environments for acoustics in the world. Cold water flowed into the Mediterranean along the bottom, while warm water flowed out along the top, creating such turbulence near the mouth that any detections were virtually impossible. The salinity, too, differed widely between the two, as the salt water pouring out of the Med mixed with the salt water from the sea. The oceans were largely homogeneous when it came to salinity, but the Med was the one place that wasn't, along with the Dead Sea, which was so dense and salty that it was virtually impossible to avoid floating. Not that that mattered to Rabies—there were no submarines in the Dead Sea.

Yet, when he thought about it, the Red Sea had to rank right up as his least favorite ASW environment. It was deeper than the Med, but the bottom was littered with wrecks and uncharted obstructions, all of which interfered with MAD and sonobuoy detections. The United States had made considerable strides in charting all the obstructions, but there was still a long way to go. Every country in this part of the world seemed to put up oil pipelines overnight, and the new ones were hardly ever annotated on the charts, even though the quartermasters did their best to keep up.

And then there were the drilling rigs. The ones far off-shore—and even the ones near the shore—radiated broadband noise that shot through the entire spectrum, blanking out many useful frequencies. Normally, you could filter some background noise out, but there were so much of it here that you risked losing too much signal along with the interference.

Oh, well. Tough for him, but even worse for the submariners who tried to work in these waters and the Persian Gulf. For decades, it had been conventional wisdom that no submarine could operate in the Persian Gulf. During Desert Storm and Desert Shield, the United States Navy had proved everyone wrong. While the submariners despised working in shallow waters, they reported their exploits with such smugness that most of the other warfare communities wanted to smack them.

The latest intelligence reports speculated that the Iranians might have just received a shipment of minisubmarines from North Korea via China. The small ten-man-crewed boats were ideally suited to operating in these constrained waters. They were powered by a battery charged by a closed-circuit diesel engine, and unless they were charging those batteries or on the surface, they were virtually undetectable. They could cover long ranges with their late-generation battery technology, moving slowly but inexorably toward their targets.

There were two major shortcomings with mini-submarines. First, the accommodations made for the human crew who sailed in them were abysmal. Second, the mini-sub had limited storage capacity for weapons. From what he knew of the Iranian sailors, he doubted that the government placed very much emphasis on the first problem. In fact, he wouldn't have been surprised to learn that berthing space had been sacrificed for torpedo storage.

Still, there were worse things, weren't there? After all, most of their missions lasted no longer than a few days, and while conditions might be unpleasant, the crew could at least survive without decent beds. And really, if you got right down to it, the life expectancy of the crew after firing a missile was short enough that bunk beds weren't what you might call a necessity of life. He patted his control stick fondly, thinking about the torpedoes and antiship missiles slung under his wings. At least, if he had anything to say about it, their life span would be short. It was like what they said in the Russian Navy—the Soviet Navy back then—with radiation sickness rampant among submariners due to inadequate shielding on the early-generation reactors. It was a standing joke that there was no family tradition of submarine service like there was the United States Navy. Soviet sailors who spent much time at all on board nuclear subs were often sterile.

"Anything?" he asked over the ICS, although he already knew the answer. If there'd been the slightest hint of a contact, his TACCO and enlisted technicians would have him dancing to their tune by now. Although he was the pilot in command, the TACCO in the back, a few years his senior, was mission commander. Unless a decision involved safety of flight or safety of crew, the TACCO's word was law.

Rabies didn't like it much, but on balance it made little difference. After all, if he wanted to head back to ship, there wasn't much anybody was going to do to stop him.

"Nothing yet," the bored voice of the TACCO replied. "Let's give this pattern another fifteen minutes, then move it to the south a bit. They may be near the entrance, lurking around that new pipeline down there."

"Roger," Rabies said cheerfully. He glanced at his copilot, a young woman on her first cruise. "It's always like this, you know. Like watching grass grow."

"Could be worse. We could be assigned surface surveillance," she answered.

Rabies shuddered. "Bite your tongue." There were few things that the Viking pilot liked less than flying down near to the surface and buzzing commercial ships looking for identifying characteristics and recording the rigging. For one thing, whoever painted the ships usually had lousy handwriting. And for another, it wasn't that unusual to find that some nations made frequent military use of their commercial fleets. All too often, there was some raghead hiding behind a couple of containers with a Stinger propped up on his shoulder ready to take out the first American he saw.

No, hunting submarines was what they were for. But the youngsters had to do their time on surface surveillance and taking tracking—he had put his time in when he was a junior pilot.

"Rabies, head south," the TACCO said, his voice a notch higher than it had been before. "You got the mark." A new symbol appeared on Rabies's display, indicating a fly-to point from the TACCO.

"You got something?" he asked.

"Maybe. Faint indications of a diesel engine—it fits for the one they may have on board, according to the intelligence summary. But it's real intermittent and long-range—we won't know until we get closer. It's worth looking at, though."

That final assessment, Rabies knew, came from the enlisted technicians. Although the TACCO was in tactical command and Rabies might be the pilot in charge, all the people on board knew who really held the keys to their success. It was the first-class petty officer seated next to the TACCO, the one with the finely trained eyes and ears who could sniff out the sound patterns made by machinery from among noise, signals from noise, submarines from surface ships, and friend from enemy.

AW-1 Greenberg, the antisubmarine warfare specialist flying this mission with them, was exceptionally good, even among the elite community of aviation subhunters. He had recently completed a tour with the intelligence staff in San Diego, and was completely familiar with all the intelligence that was too highly classified to ever make it to the fleet. That was probably why the XO had him on this mission, hoping they could pull something out of their ass on this one. Because if there was anything that made a carrier nervous, it was having undetected submarines in the area. What you couldn't see, you couldn't kill, and the only thing that worried them more than submarines was chemical or biological weapons.

"Dropping two," Rabies said, nodding at the copilot. She dropped a sonobuoy at the indicated point, then watched as he navigated from point to point as directed by the TACCO. When he finished, the electronic plot indicated a long line of sonobuoys.

"All buoys cold and sweet," Greenberg reported, indicating that each of the new sonobuoys deployed was working properly but not detecting any contacts. "Hold it—*got it*. Buoy thirty-four, sir. Buster." Buster meant bust your ass getting there.

"Let's go get them," Rabies said gleefully. He put the Viking into a sharp turn heading east. They were at the very edge of their assigned area, maybe just a touch closer to the coast than he would like, but well outside of the known Iraqi shore-based missile ranges.

Known ranges. He wondered if anyone else noticed that little phrase.

"I'm holding a diesel engine, a couple of pumps, sir," Greenberg said, his tension evident only in the fact that his voice was a little faster than normal. "Could we make a pass and check out the surface?"

"You got it," Rabies said, putting the aircraft into a descent. It was a sanity check of sorts, to take a good look at the surface of the ocean where you thought you had a submarine to make sure there were no ships in the area that corresponded to it. It was an especially necessary precaution in the Mediterranean, the Red Sea, and the Persian Gulf, all of which had heavy merchant traffic.

Hornet 102
0110 (GMT+3)

Thor sat ramrod straight in his ejection seat, his head turned so that he could watch the catapult officer. He circled the stick, got a thumbs-up in return, and nodded with grim satisfaction. Of course the Hornet's control surfaces worked well. They always did. The light, easily maintained fighter was always in perfect condition—at least, the ones that he flew were. The Marine Corps quality-assurance technicians made certain of that.

On signal, he eased the throttles forward to full military power. They clicked past the detente and into afterburner. The catapult officer stood, snapped off a sharp, proper salute, then crouched down and touched the deck and pressed the pickle. In the space of a microsecond, Thor returned the salute, faced forward, and braced himself.

As always, the first jolt was hardly impressive. An instant later, what began as a gentle jolt changed into crushing pressure on his chest as the light fighter slammed down the catapult. The Hornet rattled, steam boiling up from the shuttle, clumsy and ungainly while still bound to the carrier by the shuttle, yearning to be away from the steel and in her natural element. Finally, when the noise had built to an almost unbearable level, he felt the sudden, sickening drop and release of pressure that told him he was airborne.

Now, the trick was to stay that way. He let her grab the air and pick up speed before putting her in a steep climb, heading for altitude to wait for his wingman to join on him. Ten seconds later, he heard the announcement that his wingman was airborne. Precise, exactly as scheduled—just the way the Marine Corps liked it.

They joined up with the ease of two pilots long used to working with each other and headed for the fighter sponge. It was a designated bit of airspace where the fighters would assemble in an orderly stack, waiting till the flight was at full composition, then breaking off into fighting pairs to seek out and engage the enemy. It took far less time to actually execute than explain, and soon Hornets were peeling away from the stack.

"Hornet 102, vector. Bearing zero-seven-zero, range ten. Probable Forger. Good hunting." The E-2's voice reeled off initial vectors for the rest of the flight, disbursing them along different angles of the approaching wave of aircraft.

"Going to be hot," Red Tail remarked. "Damned SAM sites. They ought to let Special Forces loose on them." Understood, but not voiced, was the assumption that if Marine units had been ordered to destroy or neutralize the SAM sites, there would have been no question about it.

"Just like playing dodge-'em ball in grade school," Thor said. "You ever play that?"

"No, not that I recall. What was it?"

"You take about thirty of those damn red bouncy balls, you know, the kind you never see anywhere except grade school. Maybe a volleyball or two. Put them all in the center of the gym and divide the kids up into two sides. At the whistle, everybody races out and grabs a ball, streaks back to the line, and then does his damnedest to nail somebody on the other side with a ball. Hell of a lot of fun, as long as you keep moving."

"I like the sound of that," his wingman said, his voice studiedly casual. They both knew they were simply making conversation for something to do while they waited. "Maybe we should get a gang up on the flight deck to play."

"No. Have to be the hanger bay. We'd lose too many balls over the side."

"Good point. Still, it sounds like fun."

The topic of childhood games exhausted for the moment, both fell silent. On their HUDs they could see the array of Hornets, the spacing between them increasing as they headed toward feet-dry. Once they were dry, they didn't know exactly what waited. They thought they did, but you could never be certain until you were actually in the middle of a furball.

"Tallyho," Red Tail said, his voice tight. "You see it?"

"Yeah, I got it. Take high."

Red Tail peeled off and ascended, dropping back into the classic fighting-pair position. Thor descended slightly, the two targets heading for them now visible.

Most of the world's combat air fleets had learned their tactics from watching the United States Navy and Marine

Corps, so it was no surprise when opponents assumed a similar disposition. Thor felt a hard sense of amusement tugging at the corner of his mouth. "You may know what it looks like but you ain't got a clue how to use it," he said softly. "Come on, asshole. Bring it on."

Forger One
0110 local (GMT+3)

Abdul's gut tightened as he surveyed the line of American aircraft heading toward his shore. He felt a moment of shame and then dismissed it. It did not matter what he felt—what matter was what he did. And, whatever else happened, he expected there to be a lot fewer Hornets in the air when he was done.

"Wait," the ground-intercept controller snapped over the common circuit. "Maintain your positions. They must be within range of our support forces. Do not engage over open water."

The line of death, the pilots had taken to calling it, even though the commander had indicated it was to be called the line of glory. But all of them knew what would happen if they ventured over that line themselves. The shore-based missile operators were not sufficiently skilled in telling the difference between enemy aircraft and their own, and there was every chance they would be taken out with friendly fire. Any Iraqi pilot who wanted to stay alive had better plan on staying behind the line of death.

Oh, but in front of it—that was where the glory would be. It troubled him on some level that his commanders felt that they needed to rely on missile sites rather than the fighters. There had been some discussion of the Republican Guard during Desert Storm and Desert Shield, and how they'd had cut and run at the first contact with the enemy.

But we are not ground forces. We are pilots, born, bred, and trained for this mission. We will not run.

Hornet 102
0111 local (GMT +3)

Without being entirely aware of it, Thor absorbed the information displayed on his HUD. There was something about the formation that bothered him, bothered him on a level he couldn't entirely grasp. There was a long line of antiaircraft sites along the coast, spaced with a regularity that resembled the Maginot Line. Then, just behind that, a line of aircraft laid out in a straight-line geometric pattern. Their intent was obvious—have the shore installations take the first shot, then follow up with their fighters to take out whatever made it through that line. The entire concept of layered defense was something United States Navy had worked on for decades.

It's too even. That's the problem. Well, that won't last. As soon as the fur starts flying, even the best plan goes out the window. But, as they say, an average plan executed immediately and violently is better than a great plan executed too late.

"Little shits," Red Tail said conversationally over tactical. "Guess we scared them, huh?"

"Yeah. Looks like they've got orders to stay well back. I wonder what we could do that would get them out here."

"Don't know, man. Maybe we'll have to go in and drag them out."

Drag them out. Easier said than done. For all of his bravado, Thor knew that getting past the overlapping shore antiaircraft sites would take some doing.

The shore sites themselves were marked with black Xs, each one labeled with the target designation. Shaded green circles radiated out from each X, some quite regular, others irregular. Those represented the detection ranges of the radars as corrected for terrain, atmospheric conditions, and other known obstructions. Within the green, there was a smaller area crosshatched in red, indicating the kill zone. Within the red area, the radars had an eight-percent chance of being able to put a missile in your vicinity. Of course, whether you were there when the missile arrived at the spot was another matter altogether. Finally, just outside the green area, about half the distance from the side, was a yellow dotted line. This represented the counterdetection range, the range at which Thor could expect to detect pulses from the shore radar before the radar detector saw Thor. In general, counterdetection ranges were one and a half times as large as detection ranges.

Overall, the shore sites provided a solid interlocking stretch of green along the coast. There was no way to avoid going into it unless you went far to the north and came in that way, and that wasn't going to happen.

Fortunately, there was an answer. Two Wild Weasel teams armed with antiradiation missiles were leading the pack, going in slightly ahead of the conventional fighters. Each one carried missiles that would home in on the shore-site radar signals. Even if the transmitters were then turned off, the missiles would remember their location and head directly for the antennas that were radiating signals. In theory, at least, the antiradiation—or HARM—missiles would cut a swath of destruction through the antiaircraft installations, enabling Thor and his cohorts to get inland.

"I hold you on course, on time," the voice of the E-2 Hawkeye backseater said. "Estimate thirty seconds until you're within range."

"Roger," Thor acknowledged. "Stand by, boys and girls— Mom has the keys to the playground."

Viking 701
0120 local (GMT −7)

Sure enough, as they descended through the cloud cover, Rabies' radar picked up a small lozenge of a contact. He banked, spiraling around down toward it, and caught the glint of sunlight reflecting off a metal hull. "Some gunboat," he complained. "Well, that's too bad."

"I don't think so, sir. This isn't sound from a surface ship.

No way." Greenberg's voice was confident. "It's way too deep."

"You sure, Greenie?" Rabies asked doubtfully, playing the wet blanket even though his pulse was already beating faster at the tone of Greenberg's voice. "Lots of merchant traffic down there."

"This is *not* a merchant," Greenberg said, his voice not the slightest bit defensive. "It's a submarine. And it's mine."

"All right, then!" Rabies turned to his copilot. "Call it in!"

"Aye, aye, sir," she said. She glanced wistfully at the controls in his hand, sighed, then picked up the mike.

"Okay, okay," Rabies grumbled. "I did promise, didn't I? Your aircraft." He waited till her hands were on the controls and she had positive control of the Viking.

"My aircraft," she acknowledged. Rabies picked up the mike.

It was his own damned fault, wasn't it? He had told her she could fly the next pattern. After all, that was why they put a senior pilot together with a new pilot, wasn't it? To give the youngsters some experience, to let them practice under an expert pilot before sending them out with a green team. That's the way it was in the Navy—you trained your own replacement.

And Lord knows, if anyone deserved a chance, this kid did. She had good reflexes and even better airmanship skills, not to mentioned a healthy dose of common sense. She even knew a fair amount about submarine acoustics, and that was saying a lot. Most Viking pilots like to emphasize the fact that they were pilots—jet pilots—not four-eyed geeks who read intelligence summaries and studied sound-velocity profiles. They were jet pilots, by God, and nobody was going to forget it.

But she'd always been interested in the technical details of acoustics and classification, so much so that Rabies was almost embarrassed for her. Rabies had even begun to suspect that at heart she was just as much of a geek as Greenberg was.

Rabies called the carrier, filling them in on the detection

although the data was already flooding onto their screens via the secure link. The TAO on the carrier already knew exactly where each one of the Viking's sonobuoys were, and they could even get real-time transmission from each one via a link with Viking to display the contact in the ASW module.

But there was nothing like eyes on a target to get a good, accurate picture of what was going on. Even in the data link, sometimes the details were lost, some of the fine details that had alerted Greenberg to the presence of a submarine.

As he spoke to the carrier, Rabies kept an eye on his copilot and the progress they made between the fly-to points. Just as he anticipated, she handled the aircraft as though it was an extension of her body, deftly maneuvering from point to point with minimal fuel usage and popping out sonobuoys at precisely the right moment to land exactly where the TACCO wanted them.

"All buoys sweet and hot," Greenberg sang out, no trace of smugness in his voice. Rabies understood—as did Greenberg—that there had never been actually any question about whether or not there was a submarine there. Rabies was just doing his job, and Greenberg had known indisputably that he was right. There had been no contest.

"Roger, Viking," the carrier acknowledged. "Maintain firing solution on contact at this time. I repeat, maintain firing solution."

"What the hell?" his copilot asked. She glanced over Rabies, the question plain on her face. Why they hell weren't they putting a couple of fish in the water to take the bastard out? After all, they had a strike inbound on the shore installation, didn't they? Did anyone really believe that this little bastard was just out here for a walk in the park? Not possible, not this close to the carrier. Although the minisub was still too far to attack, it wouldn't be long before it was within range of the carrier, and that was assuming that the information they had about weapons ranges was accurate.

"There are a couple of nations around here that have minisubs," Rabies said, distaste in his voice. "It's possible it could be somebody else's. They're going to verify that there are no neutrals or friendlies in the area through some top-level channels. If they don't get an all-clear, we don't get weapons-free."

It was his copilot who summed up what they were all feeling. "If they close within weapons range of *Jefferson*, we don't have a choice.

TWENTY-THREE

Hamish pulled the thin T-shirt away from his body, stretching it and then letting it snap back. The movement of the air over his skin at least gave the illusion of a cooling breeze, though nothing could be further from the truth. With the humidity hovering around ninety percent and the temperature still higher than ninety degrees, there was no way the sweat on his body was going to dry.

Given a choice, Hamish preferred the dry baking heat of the interior where he'd grown up. Although temperatures could soar dangerously high before you realized it, the fact that you were sweating reminded you to stay hydrated. Here, the climate defeated the body's natural cooling mechanism.

But it wasn't like he had a choice, was it? The orders from the mullah had been clear—every man over the age of fourteen was to report to the nearest military commander for mobilization. The very young and the very old were left behind to watch over the women. Hamish felt a pang of envy that he tried to shut away. Even the youngest male child had authority over any woman he might see. With the older men gone, he would have been a veritable god in his house, his every whim obeyed. His mother would not have dared to give him those long, deep stares that she sometimes gave him when he tried to exercise his God-given authority over her. She would not move so slowly, but quickly, like she did for his father. And his sisters—well, without being more specific, it would be a long time before either one of them saw the outside of the house.

And for more reasons than just petty vengeance, he assured himself. It was not right that they should be out in public, even clad in their heavy veils and burquas. There were too many bad influences about, foreigners who roamed the streets as though they had a right to be there, imported from other countries to do the hard labor and distasteful tasks. Not so many now as there had been before, before the days of war with America. But still, sufficient.

Sufficient to ruin lives.

His oldest sister's face flashed into his mind, the way he remembered it when he was young. Dark hair, darker eyes, skin so translucent that it seemed impossible it could contain a body like his. Indeed, he was convinced that her body was nothing like his, not with the dirt and grime and sweat that clung to him and the other men every day. She was faintly scented, always cool and gentle. When his mother was not available, it was from her that he sought comfort. Nothing had been the same since she had left.

Since she had died.

She had been outside the house, coming home from the market, with his two other sisters. Their mother had not gone that day, and he blamed the old woman for what had followed. The evil crone would have known to stick to the busy streets, to have been home before evening started. As it was, as the sky grew dark, the family had started to worry.

Finally, just before full darkness set in, his two younger sisters stumbled into the door. Their burquas were torn and a shocking expanse of skin showed. They had lost their veils, and pale white ovals of faces stared out at him from the black robes. His youngest sister had a bruise showing on one cheek, and the other had a split lip, a few drops of dried blood still on her neck and hand.

The two girls were rightly terrified of being punished, and it took a while to get the story out. Finally, when his father had forced the details from them, he picked up his gun and left, taking Hamish's two older brothers with him.

They had left him in charge, but there seemed to be precious little he could do to maintain control. He was outnumbered now with the older men gone, and the appearance of the servants on the scene served only to add to the cacophony. He tried to shout, to be heard above the screaming, but his mother had rounded on him, stared at him for a moment, then, without speaking, slapped him smartly across the face.

He had never seen a woman strike a man, nor even heard a woman raise her voice to one. The shock stopped him where he stood, and he could do nothing except stare in disbelief as his mother gathered up his sisters and the female servants and retreated to the women's quarters. The door shut firmly behind them.

For a few moments, he felt like crying. His sisters—one missing, two clearly hurt, all the men gone—and now, to be barred from whatever else was going on. It was almost too much for a nine-year-old boy to take. His eyes filled with tears and he felt the beginnings of a sob shake his body.

But what if his father came home and saw him like that? The humiliation and pain he suffered at his mother's hands would be nothing compared to what would happen then. So, he regained control of himself, forcing his features into the stern, angry mask he'd seen so often on his father's face, and settled down to wait. The more he thought of it, the more he convinced himself that he had sent the women to their own quarters to deal with things. Yes, that's what his father would have done. The memory of the stinging slap across his face retreated.

Two hours later, his father and his brothers returned. They brought with them the lifeless body of his older sister. He almost started to cry again when he saw her hanging limp and lifeless over his older brother's shoulder, a rag doll who apparently weighed no more than a sack of grain. His brother pushed open the door to the women's quarters and tossed his sister's body inside. Then he shut the door behind him and returned to stand by his father.

"What happened?" Hamish managed, his voice coming out far higher than he would have liked. Under the stern cold gazes from his brothers and his father, he made an effort to lower his voice. "Is she really dead?"

There was no need to answer that question. He'd seen dead bodies often enough.

All three fixed him with that stern stare. No one spoke. Finally, his father said, "Her name will never be mentioned again." With that, he walked to the women's quarters, pounded on the door, and told his mother and the cook to get his dinner. All voices behind the heavy door ceased. The two women came out, moving slowly, their faces averted from men. They slipped quietly into the back, ghosts—the way they should be.

Later that night, Hamish got part of the story from his other brother, who was only three years older. The twelve-year-old was clearly shaken by what he'd seen.

They had gone to the marketplace, to the alley where the younger sisters had last been. His sisters had been walking down the way when a group of soldiers had suddenly come upon them. They'd tried to get past, but had been grabbed, touched, their veils stripped away from their faces. The strangers, pale men with loud voices talking in an unknown language, ran their hands over the sisters, laughing and snarling at one another. The girls instantly froze.

Mistaking lack of resistance for some sort of acquiescence, the soldiers had dragged them up a flight of stairs and into a dirty room with a few blankets strewn across the floor. There, the girls had finally started to fight back, screaming in protest. The bruise and the split lip were the results.

His older sister fought the hardest, and it had taken two men to hold her while a third ripped off her clothes. Grabbing the opportunity, his younger sisters had fled. The men, occupied with his oldest sister, had not followed. The younger sisters had made their way home, shamed for all the neighbors to see by their condition, running as fast as they could to get off the dark streets. It was a miracle they had not been picked up by a patrol.

"My sister—why did they kill her?" Hamish asked, his voice agonized. At nine, he was just barely beginning to glimpse the possibilities inherent in the difference in the sexes.

His brother turned away, his face an immature imitation of his father's. Hamish felt tears well up again and panicked. It would not do to let them see that, no. Never.

He concentrated on his father's face, letting it replace his sister's in his memory. The high, hard cheekbones, the strong nose and full beard. He felt comforted by the strength he saw there, by the absolute surety. Around his father, there could be no weakness. No doubts. And especially, no crying. That was one reason the women had their separate quarters, wasn't it? Because they were given to those displays of emotion that distracted men from the important things in life.

With his brother, he returned to the main area of the house where his father and brother were. Hammish approached, cleared his throat, and said, "I sent the women to their quarters," his voice more unsteady than he would have liked initially, but firming it as he spoke. "They were too loud."

A faint trace of amusement flashed across his father's face, followed by an approving nod. "You did well." He turned to his brothers, and said, "Wash. We will pray."

So whatever those men had done to his sisters was too despicable to be discussed. Hamish decided that was it, and turned to follow his brothers to wash.

Three years later, he realized how wrong he had been. Their neighbor had come running over, asking for help. He had no sons of his own, only three daughters. The oldest one was gone, last seen in the company of a foreigner. He thought he knew where they were.

Without discussion, his father had summoned Hamish and his two brothers to join him. They proceeded to a poor outlying neighborhood, one where the houses were crowded close together, the rooms often rented to strangers. The smells were unfamiliar, the looks of the women far too bold. Hamish felt himself growing angry as they stared at him.

Without knocking, the men opened the door to a house and proceeded upstairs. Hamish brought up the rear. As the rear guard, Hamish was unable to see what initially happened. All he heard was a high, thin scream, followed by his neighbor's voice shouting. His brothers crowded into the room, his father lingering in the doorway to watch for anyone who followed. He summoned Hamish to him with a slight flick of his finger, then shoved him into the room.

His older brother had already grabbed the foreigner and jerked his head back, but the stranger was muscular and was fighting. His younger brother clung to one arm, trying to pull it back, and Hamish grabbed the other one. His neighbor crowded in, then suddenly drew his knife and slashed the foreign man's throat. Then he plunged the dagger into the man's heart. His brothers let the body drop to the floor.

Hamish stared, dumbstruck. Blood, so much blood. The body on the floor twitched, and air bubbled out of the ruined throat, forming a froth. There was a sudden stench, as the man's bladder and bowels let go. There was one final convulsion, and then all the joints relaxed into unnatural angles.

Then his brothers and his neighbor turned to the daughter. She was much easier to hold than the man had been, although fear and certain knowledge gave her strength and she fought them. Years of tradition fell away in the face of imminent death, and she screamed, kicked, and fought back, scratching at their eyes with her fingers.

Her struggles seemed to merely give the men strength, exciting them in some way that Hamish only felt an echo of. His father shouted encouragement from the doorway.

After a brief struggle, they held her spread-eagled on the bed. The father withdrew the bloody knife from the man's heart and advanced on her, rage consuming his face. He touched the knife to her throat, holding it there. She froze, a small animal caught in headlights. He spoke quietly, his voice dripping venom. The words were seared into Hamish's memory.

"You are dishonored. You are no longer of my house. You are no longer of my blood. By your actions, you are consigned to burn in everlasting hell. Let your fate serve as an example to others." With that, the father pressed the blade home slowly, puncturing skin. Blood welled, cascading down her throat and to the bed as he bore down. She jerked, trying to escape the sharp metal blade separating her flesh, but it was no use. All she did was twist the knife, making the cut wider.

Her father stared into her eyes, vengeance in his face as he watched her panic. An ugly smile curved his lips. She groaned, air rushing out of the ruined throat, trying to speak or scream or pray—Hamish would never know.

With one final movement, the man pressed the dagger up. It rammed through her throat and under her chin, reaching up higher behind her face to the brain. He saw her open her mouth to scream, and caught a flash of the blade deep in her throat. Her father gave the knife one final twist, then jerked it out of her throat.

Her body spasmed, the death throes giving her strength to toss his brothers away. She convulsed again, then rolled over on her side, her fingers slightly curled in protectively toward her palms. Her nails were red where she'd made contact with his brothers' faces, and one brother sported long, bloody welts.

Hamish's father picked up the stranger, staggering under the burden. Hamish's older brother took the girl, slinging her over his shoulder as he had their sister. The lines of her body against his and the unnatural way her arms tangled, her head lolled, it all brought it back to Hamish. Once again he was seeing his brother carrying his sister across the room and tossing her dead body into the women's quarters. And in that moment, Hamish knew.

It had not been strangers who had killed his sister. It had been his father.

Later, after they returned home, with the keening echo of

what he remembered from his own house in his mind, Hamish tried to pray. The horror was so fresh, but he mustn't think of that. It was the right thing, the only thing—his father would not be mistaken about something like that, would he? No, it was not possible. Therefore, it was Hamish who was the weak one, the unworthy one.

Back at their own house, as though sensing his thoughts, his father turned to him. "It is our law," he said, answering the unspoken question. "Women are weak, foolish things. This is an example to them all of what will happen when they violate Allah's natural order. It is the only thing that will stop them."

Hamish clung to the explanation, forcing it to make sense. There had to be some meaning behind what his father was saying.

Hamish was not a stupid boy, and he was still young enough to think for himself. The questions that arose in his mind could not be ignored.

How had his sister dishonored herself? In a way, he could understand the neighbor's situation. The daughter had left willingly, had known what she was doing and what the consequences were. But, from every account, his sister had not. She been forced and then abandoned. The disgrace was not of her own making, not unless you counted her failure to choose a path wisely as a mortal sin. So, were the two situations different? Didn't Allah emphasize an individual's responsibility for his own actions?

And if women could only be controlled by showing them consequences of their actions, then why hadn't had that worked in his neighbor's case? They had lived next door for years and all knew what had happened to Hamish's sister. Why had that not served as a sufficient example to the other daughter? Surely she had known what would happen if—when—she was caught.

And yet she had gone anyway. She had risked everything, her life, her family's honor, everything, to leave with that man. Why?

In time, the complexities of daily life drew Hamish away

from thinking of the two incidents. Life returned to normal, and he never asked his father those questions that bothered him, knowing immediately that it would be dangerous to do so. Yet, in odd moments when he was alone and caught the glimpse of a woman moving a certain way, one with particularly translucent skin, he thought again of his sister and her death.

Two years later, the call came to join the militia. Hamish, convinced now by the passage of time and the daily influence of their way of life, no longer wondered about his sister and her neighbor. Instead, like every other male over the age of fourteen, he obeyed the mullah's call and went to war.

Wild Weasel 601
0145 local (GMT +3)

Barry Hart glanced up and to his right and left, confirming that the Tomcat escorts were in place. There was something about being armed with only HARM missiles that made any jet pilot feel oddly vulnerable. Having to depend on someone else for defense against enemy air was no picnic, either. In his heart, every pilot was convinced that he could do the job better, harder, and faster than any other jet jock. It was that self-confidence that kept them alive, that gave them the ability to climb into the cockpit each day. Because the day you quit being invulnerable, the day you quit believing you were, and started believing that things could go wrong for you, too, was the day you got dangerous in the air, not only to yourself but to your squadron.

Still, there wasn't much help at this time. There were enough of those nasty little bastard SAM sites along the coast that he had a full load-out of HARMs and no room on the wings for antiair missiles. The Tomcats, he reflected, probably weren't too damned thrilled about it, either, riding herd on him and his load of weapons instead of flying high and tight looking for other fighters.

"Forty-five seconds," his RIO said, updating the information on his HUD. "I got nibbles but no bites yet."

On his HUD, Berry could see the arcs of yellow and green radiating out from the suspected shore stations, updated with the latest satellite imagery, calculated to a fine degree, and absolutely worthless until they had a hard hit. It was one thing to run the numbers for the atmospheric propagation and figure out how far out the radar site could detect you, then target you, and then reach out and touch you. Twenty minutes of computer crunching couldn't hold a candle to two seconds of tickle, or the first-rate indications that his RIO was reading on his own sensors.

"They'll get their chance," Barry said, letting his fingers run lightly up the stick, feeling the familiar shapes below them, his fingers automatically curling around to stroke the weapons-release button and weapons-selector switch. So familiar, as familiar as the smooth round curves of his wife's body, the delicate bones of her ribs, and the sweeping curves of her body below that. And so it should be—his fingers had known the stick a lot longer than he'd known his wife.

"They'll get a chance," his RIO answered. And that, Barry hoped, was the God's absolute truth. Because all they need was a solid tickle, a good, hard hit from a radar looking for them, and then the fat lady sang.

The antiradiation missiles slung beneath his wings were the latest in technology. They were fire-and-forget weapons with some features that would've astounded pilots of only a few years back. They had their own sensors that were wired into the aircraft's avionics, working as independent receivers. In addition to the data that they generated on the ground, the small electronic brains received a continuous stream of data from the aircraft's threat-detection system, which itself was continuously updated by the carrier, the Hawkeye, and the intel weenies as new intelligence became available.

At the moment of release, two things happened. First, the seeker head locked on to the designated signal, memorizing the location in relation to where it was and heading directly for it. Second, it began exchanging data over the airwaves with the carrier itself, slipping into the LINK just as though it were an independent aircraft. While in flight, it could be retargeted by either the watch officer on the carrier or by Barry.

Once it was clear of the Tomcat, the missile would make certain of its bearings, then descend rapidly to a preprogrammed altitude above ground—or sea, in this case. From there, it would home in on the site, hopefully sliding under the radar envelope and using terrain to hide itself. The altitude could be preset or altered from the cockpit, allowing for maximum flexibility in cases of high sea states. The lowest possible setting was nearly five feet, and any sea state at all could easily result in waves knocking it out of the air.

"Got it," his RIO snapped. The new target appeared on Barry's HUD. "Just where she's supposed to be."

"Range?" Barry asked.

"Release in three seconds," his RIO answered. "Two, one—release!"

Barry toggled the weapon off, feeling the aircraft jolt slightly as it left the wing. It shot out in front of them, then arced away, a slender white streak against the dark blue sea.

"Fox One, Fox One," Barry snapped over tactical.

"Looks good," the E-2 Hawkeye commented from overhead, overseeing the engagements a safe distance away from the shore stations.

"Damned right it does," Barry muttered. Nothing worse than having a critique offered by somebody who was well out of harm's way.

"Come left ten degrees," his RIO suggested. "I think I've got another—yes, there it is." He toggled another target onto the HUD, adding, "Your dot."

"Like shooting fish in a barrel," Barry said. "With the other fishermen standing on the bank afraid to get their feet wet."

There was a moment of puzzled silence from the backseat. Barry's fondness for homespun metaphors was exceeded only by his willingness to combine them in new and interesting ways, often to the confusion of his listener.

"Well, their bank is going to get a little crowded after

we're through," his RIO said finally, having deciphered the mixed metaphor and simply trying to go with it.

"That's right," Barry said. "Bank walkers, all of them." Leaving his RIO to puzzle that one out, he toggled off another weapon.

Viking
0150 local (GMT −7)

"Torpedo in the water, torpedo in the water!" Greenberg said, drowning them out. "Two torpedoes—no, three! Probable targets, carrier and cruiser." Even as he spoke, the tactical circuit was springing to life as the symbols he entered on a screen classifying the new contacts as torpedoes were immediately transmitted to everyone in the data link. The cruiser began a series of sharp evasive maneuvers, intending to throw the torpedo off track. The carrier began its own long, slow turn, popping out noisemakers and decoys in the water like confetti.

"Targeting solution—now," Greenberg snapped, sending the data to the TACCO, who promptly entered the point and sent it to Rabies.

"One fish away—two," Rabies reported, toggling off two torpedoes. "Greedy little shit, isn't she?"

"For now," Greenberg said, his voice grim. "But the carrier's blasting out so much noise off the water from her propellers and her noisemakers that I'm having a hard time holding contact on passive sonar. Recommend we go active immediately."

"Concur," his TACCO said crisply. They activated the dual-purpose sonobuoys, the ones capable of both passive detection and active ranging. Each one had a small sonar transmitter in it as well as a receiver—the transducer. They started pinging, and immediately acquired contact on their target.

"I got her!" Greenberg reported. "She's heading for the drilling rig, sir. The torpedoes are in active mode, search pattern now—man, she's putting out some noise! No way our fish will miss her!"

Rabies chewed his lip thoughtfully. Once the torpedoes acquired the contact, they would head for it at speeds in excess of forty knots. Minisubs themselves were not capable of much over ten knots, if that. Still, the torpedoes were mighty close to the drilling rig, and there was always a chance that they would nail one of the supports to the rig rather than the submarine.

"You keep an eye on them," he ordered, aware that it was unnecessary, but feeling he had to do something. "They head under the drilling rig, you pull the fish off. You got it?"

"Yes, sir. I got it." Greenberg's answer was almost off-hand, as he was already working the intercept solution himself.

Iranian shore station
0155 local (GMT +3)

Two hours into his watch, Hamish was already exhausted. The constant stress, the midnight alerts, and the imminent prospects of being attacked, coupled with little food and less water, were enough to do anyone in. The Stinger missile on his shoulder, the business end resting on the sandbag wall behind him, was increasingly heavy. It had not seemed to weigh that much when he'd first hefted it onto his shoulder, but over the hours, its weight had increased geometrically.

He patted the canteen at his side, and thought longingly about taking another sip of the water. But the thirst would be worse later on, and he'd better save it for then. Besides, the temperature of the water was near one hundred degrees now, and it would be better to wait until he went below and it had cooled off a bit. No point in wasting it.

Not that it was that much cooler below. The hasty construction of the series of antiaircraft posts along the coast had left little time or resources for creature comforts such as air-conditioning. The emplacement was little more than an antiaircraft battery position, surrounded by sandbags, with a control station hastily installed in a concrete-walled dugout below. In theory, the control station below was sufficiently fortified and reinforced to withstand most attacks, but nobody really believed it. Placing it all in the dugout did keep the computers somewhat cooler, and provided a little shelter from the sun for the crew.

For not the first time, Hamish wondered exactly why he was standing this watch at all. With the radar in operation, surely the detection would come first from that, not from the naked eye, wouldn't it? He had started to ask the question, but in his top sergeant's expression saw his father's face. Hard, cold, tolerating no disagreement or questions. It was, Hamish thought, what he hoped he would look like to his own sons one day.

Again he patted the canteen, reassured by its weight that it was almost full, and wondered if somewhere down the coast one of his brothers was at that moment doing the same thing. He thought longingly of his younger brother, younger by only fourteen months, who was still at home.

It is an honor. An honor and your duty to serve. Hamish tried to make himself believe that.

Sweat was gathering in his eyebrows, trickling down his forehead, and stopping there, waiting until it gathered sufficient mass to break the surface tension. Every five minutes, he was rewarded with a deluge of hot, salty water in his eyes. He ran a hasty, damp hand across them, feeling absurdly like a windshield wiper. It didn't seem right that his own sweat would sting him that much.

Suddenly, a horn sounded. He heard an excited jumble of voices rise up from the bunker below him before the trapdoor leading down to it slammed shut. What was it—what had they seen? He scanned the sky frantically, searching for a target, hoping against hope that the antimissile missiles in the battery would do what they were supposed to.

Then he saw it, lower on the horizon that he would have thought. Had his eyes not been staring at exactly the right position, he would have missed it. If it had been anywhere else, it would have taken longer to find. He raised the binoculars to his eyes, searching the sky for it, dropped them long enough to find that it had moved significantly, then refocused.

There was a small puff of smoke and a sliver separated itself from the wing. A contrail tumbled behind it, stark and startling against the clear night sky, illuminated by the full moon.

They've launched. They launched a missile at us! His mouth went dry and he felt his fingertips tingle. He raised the Stinger to his shoulder, focusing the eyepiece first on the missile, then on the aircraft.

They had been hastily drilled in the basic operations, but the Stingers were too scarce to be used for practice. Hamish had never actually fired one.

One hundred yards away, the radar dish came to life, rotating back and forth as it searched for its target. From the little he had picked up from listening to the radar technicians, he knew that it was now locked on the other aircraft, working out a targeting solution.

Get it! You have to! And when the aircraft is overhead—

Suddenly it occurred to him that his instructors had been oddly vague on this particular point. The Stinger, he knew, was on its own once it left the launch tube. Nothing he could say or do would influence its track. Even if he were to drop dead the moment after he fired it, it would still continue on.

And so what if they hit the aircraft? The missile is still heading here.

All this sprang through his mind in a matter of seconds, and it went against every bit of training he'd been given. It should have been so obvious—just as the knowledge of how his sister had died should have been, had he bothered to look at the facts and to ask the right questions.

The battery of missiles beside him erupted into flames and fire, and two missiles shoved themselves out of the launch tubes on a piston of compressed air, their tail ends a mass of smoke and fire. They seemed to hang in the air for a microsecond, and then picked up speed so rapidly they almost vanished before his eyes. He held his fire, waiting— was it possible his Stinger could hit one of their own missiles and undo the very thing they were trying to accomplish? Another question that had not occurred to him before this moment.

Unfortunately, Hamish had no more time to worry about unanswered questions. Perhaps it was a blessing that the radar and the missile launch distracted him from what was about to come, sparing him those moments of certain knowledge that he would die.

When he finally turned back to face the missile, it was to find that it was only a few hundred yards away, a distance it covered in less than a second. Its hungry seeker head slammed into the antenna, detonating with a shock that radiated into the ground. The impact was physical as well as aural, shock waves radiating out from it, smashing into his eardrums with a pressure gradient that popped them like a balloon. The pressure slammed Hamish into the sandbag side of his post with sufficient force to dislodge three rows of sandbags. He lay on his back sprawled across the coarsely woven sandbag fabric, and instinctively tried to pull himself into a sitting position. But just as he did, the wave of the blast reached him, carrying with it shards of metal and cinder block, a deadly hail. The shrapnel drove through the sandbags, knocking off more of them, and sending them tumbling down to the desert below and returning the sand to its natural environment. The shrapnel passed even more easily through Hamish's body, the first fragment slicing the edge of his neck, the next five penetrating his chest and exiting through the back. Hamish sucked in air, his mind still processing the sight of the missile just a few hundred yards away, still wondering whether or not he would live. The answer was, unfortunately for him, no.

He lay sprawled on the pale sand, the blood from his wounds no longer flowing vigorously since his heart stopped. Although the first piece of shrapnel had not entirely severed his head, his subsequent trip through the air had enlarged the jagged gash, virtually decapitating him. Had Hamish been in a position to observe himself, he would have noticed that he looked peculiarly like his sister the night his father had brought her home for the last time.

TWENTY-FOUR

"Evasive maneuvers! Countermeasures!" Coyote banged on the plotting table with his fist, glaring at Bethlehem. "Damn it, woman, don't you know what you're supposed to do?"

A shocked, horrified silence filled the bridge for just a moment, and then the watch team resumed the terse patter that always characterizes dire emergencies. Captain Bethlehem, for her part, stared at Coyote, her face impassive. Time seemed to stop, although in reality it could have been no more than a few seconds. Finally, she spoke. "Officer of the deck—hard right rudder. Starboard engines back, port engines ahead full."

She listened as the officer of the deck repeated back her orders, her gaze never leaving Coyote's face. He stared back in stone silence, then howled, "No! You're taking her right back toward the torpedo!"

"On the bridge wing, Admiral. Now." Without waiting to see if he followed, Captain Bethlehem stepped away from the table and walked the long distance to the port bridge wing, her footsteps soft but steady on the linoleum. "Officer of the deck—you have your orders." She swung the catch open and stepped out, finally turning to see if Coyote was following.

Swearing softly, Coyote ran across the bridge and stepped out. "Do you realize what you're doing? How in God's name you ever managed to get command of the ship I'll never know, but you're the one who's going to have to live with what you've done."

"I'll say this once, Admiral. Right now, I don't have time to pamper your ego." Bethlehem's face was molten steel. "This is my ship—it has been since the moment I read my orders to these people. It's not yours anymore. I will explain myself this once—no questions, no explanations. The turning radius of the ship is such that if I followed your suggestion, the torpedo would hit the ship in the port quarter. It would no doubt do serious damage to engineering. We would lose at least the port shafts, maybe one of the starboard. There is no way—no way—that we would avoid the torpedo. None. And you know it. What I have done is to turn the ship so that the torpedo will hit in the fourth section. If you were paying attention, I ordered that section of the ship evacuated. There may be casualties—yes. But the ship will be able to continue fighting and to launch aircraft. Now, by your leave, I'm a little busy right now." Without waiting for an answer, she turned abruptly and went back into the ship.

Coyote was enraged. He started after her, intending to throttle her with his bare hands. Then, as he looked at the pale, horrified faces of the men and women on the bridge, he stopped. Captain Bethlehem stood among them, and it was clear from the way they closed ranks around her that they were prepared to protect her. That they were her crew, not his.

She's right. You know she is. You just don't want to admit that there's no way out of this.

"All hands brace for shock," Bethlehem said, her voice calm and collected. The boatswains echoed her orders over the 1MC.

Coyote grabbed the left side of the plotting table and braced himself against it, leaning toward the port side.

Viking 701
0156 local (GMT +3)

Rabies put the S-3 into a hard dive, then pulled her up abruptly into level flight. "Where is she?"

"Headed for the oil rig," his TECO said.

"Viking 701, you are weapons-free on hostile submarine contact," a voice said over tactical.

"Too late," Rabies shouted, frustrated beyond reason. "Damn it, *Jefferson*, we could have had her!"

"701, be advised that you are weapons-free on this contact regardless of location," the voice said firmly. "We see where she is—the admiral says go ahead anyway."

"Our probability of kill isn't good," his TECO said.

"It's zero if we don't take a shot," Rabies answered. "If nothing else, maybe that damned oil rig will fall on her and crush her. Fire one."

There was a click as the torpedo was released from the wing, and a slight jolt as the S-3 was suddenly light on that side. Rabies corrected automatically for the shift in the center of gravity.

"Splash," his enlisted technician said. "Torpedo is hot and sweet—gaining contact—he has her." The crew compartment echoed with the sounds of the torpedo seeker head, the sonar pings coming closer together, the torpedo hungry for its contact. "Ten seconds," his technician said. "Nine, eight, seven . . ."

If it hits the oil rig, there's going to be hell to pay. It will rupture fuel lines and spew all that crap into the sea. Worst of all, the submarine may get away anyway.

"Six, five, four . . ."

She won't, though. She thinks she's safe under there. She'll sneak in behind one of the supports, thinking we won't dare take a shot at her there. There were times when we wouldn't. But that was then and this is now.

"Three, two, one . . ."

The survivors. How big is the crew on the oil rig? We

didn't even have a chance to warn them. There will have to be a search-and-rescue mission and, oh, God, there better not be any kids involved.

"Got her! Sir, I hear underwater explosions—secondaries now," the technician added, as the explosions from cold seawater hitting hot metal and machinery aboard the submarine followed the initial explosions.

"That's it, then!" his TACCO crowed. "We did it!"

"Not exactly," Rabies said. "There's still a torpedo in the water. And it's still headed straight for *Jefferson.*"

USS Jefferson
0157 local (GMT +3)

The carrier was turning, but slowly, oh, so slowly. As he watched the overhead radar repeater, it seemed to Coyote that there was no way they would ever get the stern out of the way of the torpedo. And just how maneuverable was this one, anyway? Was it a wake-homer?

As *Jefferson*'s massive rudders bit hard into the water, she started to increase her rate of turn. He could feel the vibrations under his feet changing as the two steam turbines that supplied the starboard shafts picked up speed, adding their counter-rotation force to the action of the rudders and steepening the turn. The deck took on a slight angle. Pencils rolled across the plotting table, and more than one face turned pale at the unexpectedly severe motion of the carrier.

"Four seconds," a voice announced over the 1MC. "Three, two, one."

The impact, when it came, was felt more than heard. There was a sharp change in the vibrations under his feet, echoing up through the steel plates and strakes. A microsecond later, *Jefferson* lurched hard to the left, then equally violently back to the right. The smoothly increasing angle on her deck changed abruptly, and the vibrations through the deck felt horribly, horribly wrong. It was the same massive jolt and sound you heard from immediately below the flight deck when recovering a heavy aircraft such as a Tomcat, but coming from an entirely wrong direction.

The chaos started immediately. Controlled chaos, but chaos nonetheless, as damage-control teams raced forward to assess the extent of the damage, to check watertight doors and compartments, and guide corpsmen to anyone injured in the impact. Damage-control actions were coordinated by Damage Control Central, or DCC, but Bethlehem was monitoring every step. She slipped on a set of sound-powered bones and put the jack into the damage-control circuit. For the moment, Coyote was tempted to tell her not to micromanage it, to let the men and women below do their jobs.

It wasn't necessary—Bethlehem was simply listening, nodding her head in approval or frowning and snapping out a short order, her expression clearing as the DCC team revised its plans.

The angle on the deck grew steeper as seawater poured into shattered compartments. They were nowhere near a dangerous angle, but it was still distinctly ominous to feel the carrier that barely ever moved heel to the right.

An hour later, the verdict was in. The torpedo had smashed into the hull two decks below the waterline, destroying an auxiliary machinery compartment and flooding part of the anchor deck. The watertight doors had held, preventing the flooding from spreading, and the electrical connections and waterlines affected had already been rerouted. One sailor had been killed, smashed by a watertight door that had not been properly secured, and fourteen others were injured in the impact. After a final refueling, the strike aircraft were quickly recovered.

"Captain," Coyote said when Bethlehem finally had a lull in the constant stream of reports and assessments flooding in. "A moment."

Bethlehem put down her clipboard and followed him out onto the bridge wing, casting a glance back at the bridge as though seeing it for the last time. "Yes, Admiral?"

"Good job," he said abruptly. "I won't apologize—

admirals never do. You'll need to know that soon enough, I suspect."

The faintest trace of relief spread across her face, and it wasn't until that moment that Coyote realized just how much of her ass she'd put on the line standing up to him. His admiration for her grew. "Thank you, sir."

"But if I were going to apologize, I'd probably start by telling you that when I was *Jeff*'s CO, the admiral I worked for had also been her skipper. I swore then I would not repeat his mistakes, that I'd let my captains run their ships their way. And, still without admitting that I was out of line, I'd ask you to remember that when you get back here as battle group commander. You'll make enough of your own mistakes—trust me on that—but see if you can avoid repeating mine."

"Captain, Fifth Fleet wants you," the officer of the deck said as he stuck his head out and interrupted them with an apologetic look.

"I'll be right there," Bethlehem said without looking at him.

"Go," Coyote ordered.

"Yes, Admiral." She turned and walked back to the hatch. She paused for a moment, then turned back to him. "Next time we're in port, have dinner with me." It wasn't exactly a request.

Coyote pulled back, startled. He started to voice a number of objections, then said, "Okay. I'd like that."

"Good." Bethlehem gazed at him for a moment longer, then said, "You're a good man, Coyote. And a good officer. Never forget that." She pulled the hatch open and stepped out of view.

Now what in the holy hells brought that on? he wondered. *And more importantly—just what am I going to do about it?*

EPILOGUE

Herbert Hoover leaned back in the deeply padded leather chair and blandly surveyed the three men sitting in front of his desk. There was no doubting their eagerness, their commitment to the cause. Passion burned in their eyes, spoke in every line of their bodies as they leaned forward on their chairs, eagerly awaiting his decision. Yes, they were truly committed patriots. There was no doubt about that.

And they were doomed to fail. They had no grasp of the larger consequences of what was going on, no appreciation for the subtleties of political maneuvering. Had they had their way, the war would have turned violent from the very first moment.

He shifted his bulk on the chair, trying to find a comfortable position. Old injuries ran deep in his bones and scarred his soul even more than his body. For just a split second, he wondered if there was more to his discomfort than his physical problems.

"I say we take them on," one man said. Jack Sauers, a gaunt, hard man, face and hands darkened by the sun, his body underneath his clothes pale. Like Hoover, Sauers had been a Marine, on the ground and in the front lines in Vietnam. The years had not been kind to him, nor had the government. He had every reason to want revenge.

"Everything is in place," the second man pointed out. There was a dry, precise tone to his voice that Hoover always found irritating. "The weapons and supplies have been checked and are quite safe. They will be disbursed in about"—he glanced at his watch—"four and a half hours, depending on the road conditions."

The third man laughed. "And the way you run things, the paperwork will take another six hours on top of that." He held up one hand to forestall protest. "Excuse me, five hours and twenty-seven minutes."

Frank Woods, a machinist, younger than the other two. His military service had begun and ended with Desert Storm and Desert Shield. The others knew that he had a slightly unrealistic viewpoint of warfare based on those experiences. Desert Storm had been a cakewalk, nothing like the assorted affairs the other men had been involved with around the world. He was bright, capable, and a good addition to the team, but he lacked tempering. Sensing his own inadequacies, Frank often found relief in tormenting the slightly built accountant responsible for all supplies and logistics.

And who would have thought we needed accountants? Hoover shook his head slightly, as though in disbelief. But we did in Vietnam, didn't we? They were the ones who kept the supplies and the ammo coming to the front lines. Not particularly glamorous, but a necessary part of any operation.

In the last three months, these three men had emerged as a group he had come to trust. Yes, they lacked his abilities to bring it all together, but each one brought something to the table that he could use.

"Ah, come on, sir," the first man protested. He had taken Hoover's involuntary shake of his head as a sign of disapproval. "This is just what we've been waiting for, isn't it?"

"It is, and it isn't," Hoover replied, picking his words carefully. It wasn't enough that he must discern the proper course of action. He also had to translate it into terms that men such as these could latch on to. "Yes, it's an opportunity—but there's also some danger." He considered a moment explaining to them that the Chinese symbol for *crisis* combined the symbols for *opportunity* and *danger*, but dismissed the idea. A good point, but they probably wouldn't appreciate the value of the insight.

"We can't let them get away with it," Frank said, outrage evident in his voice.

"He wasn't one of ours," the accountant pointed out.

"That doesn't matter."

"Perhaps it should. After all, our resources are limited. We can't take on every opportunity that presents itself. We have to wait for the right time." The accountant's voice held a note of finality, as though that settled the matter.

"In a way, it's even better that he's not one of ours," Hoover said, deepening his voice slightly. He saw the unconscious response in the others' body language, and sent a silent prayer up to the Marine Corps drill instructor who taught him about tone of voice and command. "There's no sense in what happened to them, not in the minds of the average Joe Citizen. These weren't dangerous radicals. Although," he conceded, "in time, they might have come over to our way of thinking. They were headed that way. But for now, there's a good case to be made that Kyle Smart was just Mr. Joe Average Citizen. A farmer, facing all of the problems that farmers everywhere know about. Weather, banks, the feds—there's a lot to identify with.

"But we've got to handle it the right way." He fixed Frank with a hard look. "No violence. No guns. Nothing like that. Not at first." He saw the grudging look of acquiescence in Frank's eyes and continued. "We are patriots. We are concerned citizens who love our country and don't want to see power-mad politicians murdering innocent citizens."

"That's not going to work in the long run, you know," the

accountant replied mildly. "No permanent change comes without bloodshed."

"I know that." They had the Marine Corps background in common, although they'd never known each other while in the Crotch. Still, service laid down some core fundamentals, particularly service in the Marine Corps. So there was that bond—and yet it was also a difference. Because the other man understood violence just as well as Hoover did, understood it and was willing to use it. Hoover had gone beyond that, looking for more effective ways. The danger was each knew the other so well that they could anticipate each other's objections. If there were ever a serious challenge to his leadership, it would not come from one of the younger hotheads. No, it would come from this man.

"But we need an icon, not a martyr," Hoover said slowly, still thinking it through. There was a difference—an icon was a symbol to rally around. A martyr, when you wanted revenge. If this was handled right, Kyle Smart and his doomed family would be a rallying point for everyone who knew—or even felt at some level—there was something wrong with the country.

Hoover took a picture out of his file and studied it again. The Smarts were a good-looking family, lean and hardworking. No softness to any of them—they lived a hard life and it showed. He was willing to bet that displaced auto workers in Detroit, dirt-poor farmers in the South, and even unemployed computer workers in California would find something in those faces to identify with. And parents, God, parents—no parent among them could look at the pictures of the murdered children without shuddering.

Hoover reached his decision. There were too many young Turks snapping at his heels, too many men eager to take his place. It was time for success, the kind of success that only he could pull off. And Kyle Smart and his family were going to insure that success.

Herbert Hoover believed no less fiercely than Abraham Carter in their cause. But while this intellectual commitment to patriotism and freedom matched the elder Carter's, he had more in common with Carter's son in terms of practicality. And, unlike the Carters, there was a degree of dark loathing and self-destruction that permeated Hoover's being.

Not that anyone would ever suspect such dark recesses in the man. On the surface, all they saw was a large, jovial fellow, one with an endearing, guileless sincerity in his blue eyes. Few people noticed that the eyes were often unblinking, staring a little longer than was polite, that his teeth were often bared what he smiled. His demeanor was as smooth and polished as a televangelist's, and he gave off the same dramatic sense of life-and-death that many of them did. A smaller man could not have pulled it off, but weighing in just short of 280 pounds, Hoover was built for dramatics.

Hoover's disillusionment with the United States had begun during Vietnam. Raised on a small North Dakota farm, the then-lean and hungry Hoover had fervently believed that what he and his high school classmates were doing was laying their bodies in front of the line of advancing Communism. Dramatic self-sacrifice appeal to him, and the idea that he personally could die seemed very remote. He had enlisted in the Marine Corps even before the lottery numbers were picked.

In boot camp, he found himself surrounded by similarly minded young men, with the occasional recruit simply trying to dodge service in the Army. Their drill instructors had encouraged them to believe in the rightness of their cause as they broke down the would-be Marines' characters and personalities and rebuilt them from the ground up.

It wasn't until later—within a week of arriving at his first assignment in Vietnam—that the illusion began to crumble. There, at the base camp, death became a reality. It was no longer self-sacrifice, but mutilation of dying flesh, death approaching screaming. There was nothing noble, he saw, about dying for your country. General Patton's words came back to him—better to make the other son of a bitch die for *his*. And the pain, dear God, the pain. Returning from patrol mangled, screaming, parts of bodies missing or protruding through the skin.

Sure, there was the camaraderie he'd expected, but all tainted and perverted. It was, he began to realize, the fault of the United States. They had taken brave men, men willing to risk their lives for what was right, and perverted their dedication. They had wasted their favorite sons.

And for what? Nothing, as far as Hoover could see.

After he returned to the United States, Hoover's disillusionment was completed. Besieged by rising gas prices and inflation, his parents had been unable to make the mortgage payments on their farm. It had been sold at auction and fallen into the possession of their family's arch-nemesis. In the airport, he was spat upon, jostled, and called a baby-killer. His experience was all too typical for men returning from Vietnam, but Hoover's anger took a different path. He blamed the government, not the hippies and the yippies and the protesters. At some level, he sympathized with them, because he knew firsthand just how misguided the war really was. He had been an intelligence specialist, and his quick mind had seen readily that America was not fighting to win. America was fighting to look good.

A knock sounded at the door. "Come in," Hoover said, standing up. He walked around the desk to greet the thin, disheveled man warmly, throwing his arms around him and then shepherding him to the desk with an arm slung over the man's shoulders. "You made it. Good, good. Let me introduce you to some new friends."

Hoover turned the man around to face the others. "Gentlemen, I'd like you to welcome Jackson Carter. He's got a little problem I think we can help him with."

GLOSSARY

0-3 LEVEL: The third deck above the main deck. Designations for decks above the main deck (also known as the damage-control deck) begin with zero, e.g. 0-3. The zero is pronounced as "oh" in conversation. Decks below the main deck do not have the initial zero, and are numbered down from the main deck; e.g. Deck 11 is below Deck 3. Deck 0-7 is above 0-3.

1MC: The general announcing system on a ship or submarine. Every ship has many different interior communications systems, most of them linking parts of the ship for a specific purpose. Most operate off sound-powered phones. The circuit designators consist of a number followed by two letters that indicate the specific purpose of the circuit. 2AS, for instance, might be an antisubmarine-warfare circuit that connects the sonar supervisor, the USW watch officer, and the sailor at the torpedo launcher.

C-2 GREYHOUND: Also known as the COD, Carrier On-board Delivery. The COD carries cargo and passengers from shore to ship. It is capable of carrier landings. Sometimes assigned directly to the air wing, it also operates in coordination with CVBGs from a shore squadron.

AIR BOSS: A senior commander or captain assigned to the aircraft carrier, in charge of flight operations. The "Boss" is assisted by the Mini-Boss in Pri-Fly, located in the tower on board the carrier. The Air Boss is always in the tower during flight operations, overseeing the launch and recovery cycles, declaring a green deck, and monitoring the safe approach of aircraft to the carrier.

AIR WING: Composed of the aircraft squadrons assigned to the battle group. The individual squadron commanding officers report to the Air Wing Commander, who reports to the admiral.

AIRDALE: slang for an officer or enlisted person in the aviation fields. Includes pilots, NFOs, aviation intelligence officers and maintenance officers, and the enlisted technicians who support aviation. The antithesis of an airdale is a "shoe."

AKULA: late-model Russian-built nuclear attack submarine, an SSN. Fast, deadly, and deep-diving.

ALR-67: detects, analyzes, and evaluates electro-magnetic signals, emits a warning signal if the parameters are compatible with an immediate threat to the aircraft, e.g. seeker head on an antiair missile. Can also detect enemy radar in either a search or a targeting mode.

ALTITUDE: is safety. With enough airspace under the wings, a pilot can solve any problem.

AMRAAM: Advanced Medium Range AntiAir Missile.

ANGELS: Thousands of feet over ground. Angels twenty is 20,000 feet. Cherubs indicate hundreds of feet, e.g. cherubs five = five hundred feet.

ASW: AntiSubmarine Warfare, recently renamed Undersea Warfare. For some reason.

AVIONICS: black boxes and systems that comprise an aircraft's combat systems.

AW: aviation antisubmarine warfare technician, the enlisted specialist flying in an S-3, P-3, or helo ASW aircraft. As this book goes to press, there is discussion of renaming the specialty.

AWACS: an aircraft entirely too good for the Air Force, the Advanced Warning Aviation Control System. Long-range command and control and electronic-intercept bird with superb capabilities.

AWG-9: pronounced "awg nine," the primary search-and-fire control radar on a Tomcat.

BACKSEATER: also known as the GIB, the guy in back. Non-pilot aviator available in several flavors: BN (bombardier/navigator), RIO (radar intercept operator), and TACCO (Tactical Control Officer) among others. Usually wears, glasses and is smart.

BEAR: Russian maritime patrol aircraft, the equivalent in rough terms of a U.S. P-3. Variants have primary missions in command and control, submarine hunting, and electronic intercepts. Big, slow, good targets.

BITCH BOX: one interior communications system on a ship. So named because it's normally used to bitch at another watch station.

BLUE ON BLUE: fratricide. U.S. forces are normally indicated in blue on tactical displays, and this term refers to an attack on a friendly by another friendly.

BLUE WATER NAVY: outside the unrefueled range of the air wing. When a carrier enters blue-water ops, aircraft must get on board, e.g. land, and cannot divert to land if the pilot gets the shakes.

BOOMER: slang for a ballistic-missile submarine.

BOQ: Bachelor Officer Quarters—a Motel Six for single officers or those traveling without family. The Air Force also has VOQ, Visiting Officer Quarters.

BUSTER: as fast as you can, i.e. bust yer ass getting here.

CAG: Carrier Air Group commander, normally a senior Navy captain aviator. Technically, an obsolete term, since an air wing rather than an air group is now deployed on the carrier. However, everyone thought CAW sounded stupid, so CAG was retained as slang for the Carrier Air Wing commander.

CAP: Combat Air Patrol, a mission executed by fighters to protect the carrier and battle group from enemy air and missiles.

CARRIER BATTLE GROUP: a combination of ships, air wing, and submarines assigned under the command of a one-star admiral.

CARRIER BATTLE GROUP 14: the battle group normally embarked on *Jefferson*.

CBG: *see* Carrier Battle Group.

CDC: Combat Direction Center—now has replaced CIC, or Combat Information Center, as the heart of a ship. All sensor information is fed into CDC and the battle is coordinated by a Tactical Action Officer on watch there.

CG: abbreviation for a cruiser.

CHIEF: the backbone of the Navy. E-7, 8, and 9 enlisted pay grades, known as chief, senior chief, and master chief. The transition from petty officer ranks to the chiefs' mess is a major event in a sailor's career. On board ship, the chiefs have separate eating and berthing facilities. Chiefs wear khakis, as opposed to dungarees for the less-senior enlisted ratings.

CHIEF OF STAFF: not to be confused with a chief, the COS in a battle group staff is normally a senior Navy captain who acts as the admiral's XO and deputy.

CIA: Christians in Action. The civilian agency charged with intelligence operations outside the continental United States.

CIWS: Close-In Weapons System, pronounced "see-whiz." Gatling gun with built-in radar that tracks and fires on inbound missiles. If you have to use it, you're dead.

COD: *see* C-2 Greyhound.

COLLAR COUNT: traditional method of determining the winner of a disagreement. A survey is taken of the opponents' collar devices. The senior person wins. Always.

COMMODORE: formerly the junior-most admiral rank, now used to designate a senior Navy captain in charge of a bunch of like units. A destroyer commodore commands several destroyers, a sea-control commodore the S-3 squadrons on that coast. Contrast with CAG, who owns a number of dissimilar units, e.g. a couple of Tomcat squadrons, some Hornets, and some E-2s and helos.

COMPARTMENT: Navy talk for a room on a ship.

CONDITION TWO: one step down from General Quarters, which is Condition One. Condition Five is tied up at the pier in a friendly country.

CRYPTO: short for some variation of cryptological, the magic set of codes that makes a circuit impossible for anyone else to understand.

CV, CVN: abbreviations for an aircraft carrier, conventional and nuclear.

CVIC: Carrier Intelligence Center. Located down the passageway (the hall) from the flag spaces.

DATA LINK, THE LINK: the secure circuit that links all units in a battle group or in an area. Targets and contacts are transmitted over the LINK to all ships. The data is processed by the ship designated as Net Control, and common contacts are correlated. The system also transmits data from each ship and aircraft's weapons systems, e.g. a missile firing. All services use the LINK.

DESK JOCKEY: nonflyer, one who drives a computer instead of an aircraft.

DESRON: Destroyer Commander.

DICASS: an active sonobuoy.

DICK-STEPPING: something to be avoided. While anatomically impossible in today's gender-integrated services, in an amazing display of good sense, it has been decided that women do this as well.

DDG: guided-missile destroyer

DOPPLER: acoustic phenomena caused by relative motion between a sound source and a receiver that results in an apparent change in frequency of the sound. The classic example is a train going by and the decrease in pitch of its whistle. When a submarine changes its course or speed in relation to a sonobuoy, the event shows up as a change in the frequency of the sound source.

DOUBLE NUTS: zero-zero on the tail of an aircraft.

E-2 HAWKEYE: command, control, and surveillance aircraft. Turboprop rather than jet, and unarmed. Smaller version of an AWACS, in practical terms, but carrier-based.

ELF: Extremely Low Frequency, a method of communicating with submarines at sea. Signals are transmitted via a miles-long antenna and are the only way of reaching a deeply submerged submarine.

ENVELOPE: what you're supposed to fly inside of if you want to take all the fun out of Naval aviation.

EWS: Electronic Warfare technicians, the enlisted sailors that man the gear that detects, analyzes, and displays electromagnetic signals. Highly classified stuff.

F/A-18 HORNETS: the inadequate, fuel-hungry intended replacement for the aging but still kick-your-ass-potent Tomcat. Flown by Marines and Navy.

FAMILYGRAM: short messages from submarine sailors' families to their deployed sailors. Often the only contact with the outside world that a submarine sailor on deployment has.

FF/FFG: abbreviation for a fast frigate (no, there aren't slow frigates) and a guided-missile fast frigate.

FLAG OFFICER: in the Navy and Coast Guard, an admiral. In the other services, a general.

FLAG PASSAGEWAY: The portion of the aircraft carrier that houses the admiral's staff working spaces. Includes the flag mess and the admiral's cabin. Normally separated from the rest of the ship by heavy plastic curtains, and designated by blue tile on the deck instead of white.

FLIGHT QUARTERS: a condition set on board a ship preparing to launch or recover aircraft. All unnecessary person are required to stay inside the skin of the ship and remain clear of the flight deck area.

FLIGHT SUIT: the highest form of Navy couture. The perfect choice of apparel for any occasion—indeed, the only uniform an aviator ought to be required to own.

FOD: stands for Foreign Object Damage, but the term is used to indicate any loose gear that could cause damage to an aircraft. During flight operations, aircraft generate a tremendous amount of air flowing across the deck. Loose objects—including people and nuts and bolts—can be sucked into the intake and discharged through the outlet from the jet engine. FOD damages the jet's impellers, and doesn't do much for the people sucked in, either. FOD walk-down is conducted at least once a day on board an aircraft carrier. Everyone not otherwise engaged stands shoulder-to-shoulder on the flight deck and slowly walks from one end of the flight deck to the other, searching for FOD.

FOX: tactical shorthand for a missile firing. Fox One indicates a heat-seeking missile, Fox Two an infrared missile, and Fox Three a radar-guided missile.

GCI: Ground Control Intercept, a procedure used in the Soviet air forces. Primary control for vectoring the aircraft in one enemy targets and other fighters is vested in a guy on the ground, rather than in the cockpit, where it belongs.

GIB: *see* backseater.

GMT: Greenwich Mean Time.

GREEN SHIRTS: *see* shirts.

HANDLER: officer located on the flight-deck level responsible for ensuring that aircraft are correctly positioned (spotted,) on the flight deck. Coordinates the movements of aircraft with yellow gear (small tractors that tow aircraft and other related gear) from maintenance areas to catapults and from the flight deck to the hangar bay via the elevators. Speaks frequently with the Air Boss. *See also* bitch box.

HARMS: antiradiation missiles that home in on radar sites.

HOME PLATE: tactical call sign for *Jefferson.*

HOT: in reference to a sonobuoy, holding enemy contact.

HUFFER: yellow gear located on the flight deck that generates compressed air to start jet engines. Most Navy aircraft do not need a huffer to start engines, but it can be used in emergencies or for maintenance.

HUNTER: call sign for the S-3 squadron embarked on *Jefferson.*

ICS: Interior Communications System. The private link between a pilot and an RIO, or the telephone system internal to a ship.

INCHOPPED: Navy talk for a ship entering a defined area of water, e.g. inchopped the Med.

IR: infrared, a method of missile homing.

ISOTHERMAL: a layer of water that has a constant temperature with increasing depth. Located below the thermocline, where increase in depth correlates to decrease in temperature. In the isothermal layer, the primary factor affecting the speed of sound in water is the increase in pressure with depth.

JBD: Jet Blast Deflector. Panels that pop up from the flight deck to block the exhaust emitted by aircraft.

USS JEFFERSON: the star nuclear carrier in the U.S. Navy.

LEADING PETTY OFFICER: the senior petty officer in a work center, division, or department, responsible to the leading chief petty officer for the performance of the rest of the group.

LINK: *see* data link.

LOFARGRAM: Low Frequency Analyzing And Recording display. Consists of lines arrayed by frequency on the horizontal axis and time on the vertical axis. Displays sound signals in the water in a graphic fashion for analysis by ASW technicians.

LONG GREEN TABLE: a formal inquiry board. It's better to be judged by six than carried by six.

MACHINIST'S MATE: enlisted technician that runs and repairs most engineering equipment on board a ship. Abbreviated as "MM," e.g. MM1 Sailor is a Petty Officer First Class Machinist's Mate.

MDI: Mess Decks Intelligence. The heartbeat of the rumor mill on board a ship and the definitive source for all information.

MEZ: Missile Engagement Zone. Any hostile contacts that make it into the MEZ are engaged only with missiles. Friendly aircraft must stay clear in order to avoid a blue-on-blue engagement, i.e. fratricide.

MIG: a production line of aircraft manufactured by Mikoyan in Russia. MiG fighters are owned by many nations around the world.

MURPHY'S LAW. The factor most often not considered sufficiently in military planning. If something can go wrong, it will. Naval corollary: Shit happens.

NATIONAL ASSETS: surveillance and reconnaissance resources of the most sensitive nature, e.g. satellites.

NATOPS: the bible for operating a particular aircraft. *See* envelope.

NFO: Naval Flight Officer.

NOBRAINER: Contrary to what copy editors believe, this is one word. Used to signify an evolution or decision that should require absolutely no significant intellectual capabilities beyond that of a paramecium.

NOMEX: Fire-resistant fabric used to make "shirts." *See* shirts.

NSA: National Security Agency. Primarily responsible for evaluating electronic intercepts and sensitive intelligence.

OOD: Officer of the Day, in charge of the safe handling and maneuvering of the ship. Supervises the conning officer and other underway watchstanders. Ashore, the OOD may be responsible for a shore station after normal working hours.

OPERATIONS SPECIALIST: Formerly radar operators, back in the old days. Enlisted technicians who operate combat detection, tracking, and engagement systems, except for sonar. Abbreviated OS.

OTH: Over The Horizon, usually used to refer to shooting something you can't see.

P-3's: shore-based antisubmarine-warfare and surface-surveillance long-range aircraft. The closest you can get to being in the Air Force while still being in the Navy.

PHOENIX: long-range antiair missile carried by U.S. fighters.

PIPELINE: Navy term used to describe a series of training commands, schools, or necessary education for a particular specialty. The fighter pipeline, for example, includes Basic Flight, then fighter training at the RAG (Replacement Air Group), a training squadron.

PUNCHING OUT: Ejecting from an aircraft

PURPLE SHIRTS: *see* shirts.

PXO: Prospective Executive Officer—the officer ordered into a command as the relief for the current XO. In most squadrons, the XO eventually "fleets up" to become the commanding officer of the squadron, an excellent system that maintains continuity within an operational command— and a system the surface Navy does not use.

RACK: a bed. A rack-monster is a sailor who sports pillow burns and spends entirely too much time asleep while his or her shipmates are working.

RED SHIRTS: *see* shirts.

RHIP: Rank Hath Its Privileges. *see* collar count.

RIO: Radar Intercept Officer. *See* NFO.

RTB: Return To Base.

S-3: command and control aircraft sold to the Navy as an antisubmarine aircraft. Good at that, too. Within the last several years, redesignated as "sea control" aircraft, with individual squadrons referred to as torpedo-bombers. Ah, the search for a mission goes on. But still a damned fine aircraft.

SAM: Surface to Air Missile, e.g. the standard missile fired by most cruisers. Also indicates a land-based site.

SAR: Sea-Air Rescue.

SCIF: Specially Compartmented Information. On board a carrier, used to designated the highly classified compartment immediately next to TFCC.

SEAWOLF: newest version of Navy fast-attack submarine.

SERE: Survival, Evasion, Rescue, Escape; required school in pipeline for aviators.

SHIRTS: color-coded Nomex pullovers use by flight-deck and aviation personnel for rapid identification of a sailor's job. Green: maintenance technicians. Brown: plane captains. White: safety and medical. Red: ordnance. Purple: fuel. Yellow: flight-deck supervisors and handlers.

SHOE: a black shoe, slang for a surface sailor or officer. Now, however, brown shoes have been authorized for wear by black shoes. No one knows why. Wing envy is the best guess.

SIDEWINDER: antiair missile carried by U.S. fighters.

SIERRA: a subsurface contact.

SONOBUOYS: acoustic listening devices dropped in the water by ASW or USW aircraft.

SPARROW: antiair missile carried by U.S. fighters.

SPETZNAZ: the Russian version of SEALS, although the term encompasses a number of different specialties.

SPOOKS: slang for intelligence officers and enlisted sailors working in highly classified areas.

SUBLANT: administrative command of all Atlantic submarine forces. On the West Coast, SUBPAC.

SWEET: when used in reference to a sonobuoy, indicates that the buoy is functioning properly, although not necessarily holding any contacts.

TACCO: Tactical Control Officer: the NFO in an S-3.

TACTICAL CIRCUIT: a term used in these books that encompasses a wide range of actual circuits used on board a carrier. There are a variety of C&R circuits (coordination and reporting), and occasionally for simplicity sake and to avoid classified material, I just use the world tactical.

TANKED, TANKER: Navy aircraft have the ability to refuel from a tanker, either Air Force or Navy, while airborne. One of the most terrifying routine evolutions a pilot performs.

TFCC: Tactical Flag Command Center. A compartment in flag spaces from which the CVBG admiral controls the battle. Located immediately forward of the carrier's CDC.

TOMBSTONE: nickname given to Magruder.

TOP GUN: advanced fighter training command.

UNDERSEA WARFARE COMMANDER: in a CVBG, normally the DESRON embarked on the carrier. Formerly called the ASW commander.

VDL: Video DownLink. Transmission of targeting data from an aircraft to a submarine with OTH capabilities.

VF-95: fighter squadron assigned to Air Wing 14, normally embarked on USS *Jefferson*. The first two letters of a squadron designation reflect the type of aircraft flown. VF = fighters. VFA = Hornets. VS = S-3, etc.

VICTOR: aging Russian fast-attack submarines, still a potent threat.

VS-29: S-3 squadron assigned to Air Wing 14, embarked on USS *Jefferson*.

VX-1: test pilot squadron that develops envelopes after Pax River evaluates aerodynamic characteristics of new aircraft. *See* envelope.

WHITE SHIRT: *see* shirts.

WILCO: short for Will Comply. Used only by the aviator in command of the mission.

WINCHESTER: In aviation, it means out of weapons. A Winchester aircraft must normally RTB.

XO: executive officer, the second in command.

YELLOW SHIRT: *see* shirts.

"Fasten your seat belt! *Carrier* is a stimulating, fast-paced novel brimming with action and high drama." —Joe Weber

CARRIER

Keith Douglass

U.S. MARINES. PILOTS. NAVY SEALS.
THE ULTIMATE MILITARY POWER PLAY.

In the bestselling tradition of Tom Clancy, Larry Bond, and Charles D. Taylor, these electrifying novels capture the vivid reality of international combat. The Carrier Battle Group Fourteen—a force including a supercarrier, amphibious unit, guided missile cruiser, and destroyer—is brought to life with stunning authenticity and action in high-tech thrillers as explosive as today's headlines.

AVAILABLE WHEREVER BOOKS ARE SOLD OR
TO ORDER CALL 1-800-788-6262